TYPE X

TYPE X
PROJECT W. A. R. PART TWO

M. A. PHIPPS

SEVEN SISTERS
PUBLISHING

Type X
Project W. A. R. Trilogy Book Two

E-Book ISBN: 978-1-64204-437-9
Print ISBN: 978-1-64204-438-6

7 Sisters Publishing
P.O. Box 993
Jupiter, Florida 33458

www.maphipps.com
www.7sisterspublishing.com

Cover Design by Nathalia Suellen

For the readers who have taken this journey with me

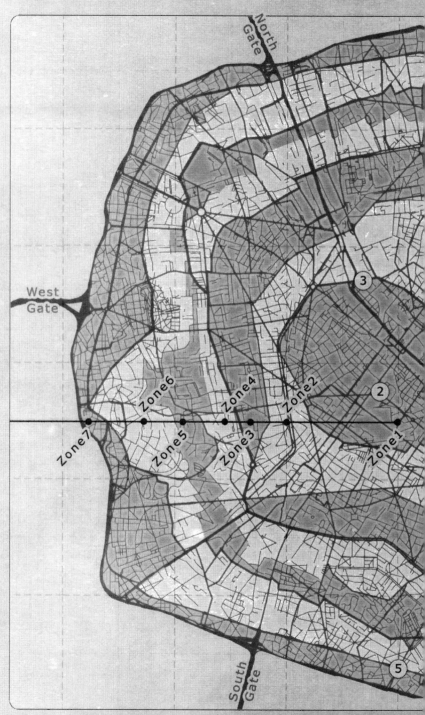

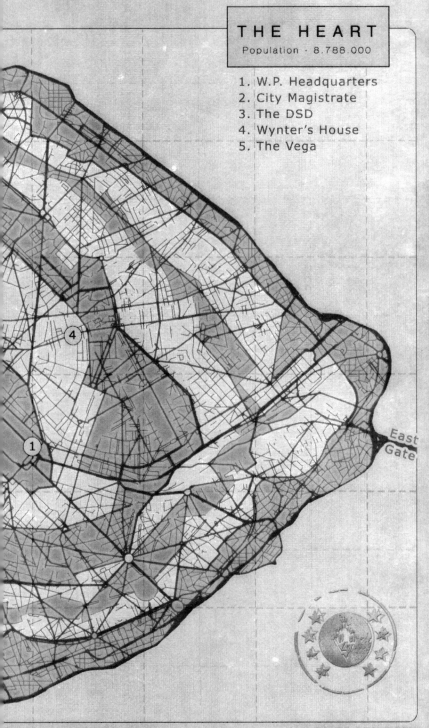

THE HEART
Population · 8.788.000

1. W.P. Headquarters
2. City Magistrate
3. The DSD
4. Wynter's House
5. The Vega

East Gate

STATE PROPERTY

When humanity dies, the world dies with it.

ONE

A HEAVY WIND SLAMS INTO the side of the helicopter, shifting the metal carcass with rough, repetitive jolts. The Enforcers around me don't take much notice, no doubt focused on our impending mission instead.

Leaning my head back against the wall, I listen to the roaring drone of the rotors. In a way, it's therapeutic. An escape from the reality I always find myself drowning in.

My eyes close as I take a deep breath. The steady beating of my heart is calming and allows me to distance myself from the very near and inevitable future. More than anything, I wish I could remain in this state of in-between forever, but I know better than to hope for the impossible.

A budding exasperation clenches in my chest, and I exhale through my nose in a bid to ignore it. Even without looking, I'm aware of someone watching me. It's a familiar enough sensation by now—the inescapable curiosity that goes hand in hand with what I am. After this long, I've grown to expect it.

Lifting my gaze, I lock eyes with the Enforcer sitting across from me. To his credit, he doesn't turn away, but what surprises me even more is how young he appears to be. In fact, I'd be willing to venture a guess and say he's barely older than I am. Although, unlike me, it's clear that he's afraid.

My brow furrows as I peer at him, curious what he must be thinking. A sheen of sweat coats his forehead, and he blinks in rapid succession before his eyes flick with a nervous glance to my throat. Sucking in a sharp breath, my nostrils flare as I straighten up in my seat, making the metal ring around my neck shift against my skin.

I drop my eyes, grasping what it is the Enforcer is truly afraid of.

It's ironic. The battle awaiting us poses far more danger to these people than I do, and yet, *I'm* the one he's second-guessing. Or, maybe, he's doubting the effectiveness of my collar.

I breathe in, holding back a mocking laugh.

Don't worry, I'm tempted to say to him. *You aren't the ones who have to be afraid of me.*

Another bout of turbulence jerks the transport helicopter. The straps holding me in place strain against my torso, digging into my shoulders. With the sudden dip in altitude, my stomach turns on itself, but I'm used to it.

I'm used to all of this.

A crackling sound assaults my ears when the speaker system purrs to life. A moment later, a husky voice echoes through the metal interior.

"We will arrive at our target destination in T-minus two minutes. Make your final preparations and ready yourselves for landing."

Out of the corner of my eye, I observe a wave of movement as my comrades-in-arms begin to busy themselves. A few individuals load ammunition into their guns while others reposition their gear. Pointless checks that do nothing more than prepare them for a battle they'll never actually see. After all, the Enforcers are only a last resort.

The State has other means to get the job done.

I remain still, passing the seconds until landing in silence. The noise surrounding the helicopter only gets louder as we descend, and the faint rumble of explosions rattle in the distance. The occasional shockwave rocks the cargo hold, reminding us what we're walking into.

Glancing up, I observe the young Enforcer across from me. Beads of sweat dot his upper lip, and his fingers fidget in his lap as he wrings his hands. His obvious agitation leads me to wonder if this is his first time in the field. If it is, then he should be glad it's with me.

Seeming to sense that I'm watching him, his eyes dart to mine before his entire face disappears beneath the barrier of his helmet. I purse my lips in response, curious if he even realizes that the very person he's afraid of will be the reason he stays alive.

The reason everyone here stays alive.

The aircraft trembles as we approach the ground, and a loud humming rings through the hold as the rotors begin to slow, creating a strange vortex where other sounds cease to exist. The engines shudder to a stop when we touch down, and the Enforcers unfasten their safety belts once the pilot gives us the all clear. In one cohesive unit, they rise to their feet— falling into formation as the loading ramp screams to life and drops with a heavy thud into the sand of the overpopulated beach waiting below.

Metal clashes against metal as the soldiers move in a controlled herd. I linger behind, refusing to lift a single muscle until I'm alone—just like every other mission I've been on. I'm not sure why I do this. Maybe it's my own form of silent protest, or maybe it's the only way I feel in control.

Savoring my fleeting solitude, I shift my fingers onto the harness, and as they loosen it, my hands are steady. I've done this so many times now that the thought of what's about to happen doesn't even faze me.

Breathing in, I push myself up. My eyes lock on the loading ramp, and although I'm well aware of what awaits me at the bottom, my pace is composed and confident.

The metallic soles of my boots reflect off the floor, despite how lightly I tread across it. The sound is deafening, even with the battle raging nearby.

As I descend the ramp, my gaze fixes ahead in an attempt to shut out the sea of faces beneath me. It's harder to ignore them than I thought it would be—a lesson I never learn, no matter how many times I'm forced to go through this. Before I can stop myself, my eyes lock on the crowd.

Heads turn when they notice my approach, and bodies move aside to make room for me to pass. All the while, I sense what the crowd is thinking. Their every thought radiates over the beach in a mental wave, seeping into my pores like a contagious sickness.

Astonishment.

Fear.

It's difficult to tell which emotion is stronger.

I advance through the parted crowd, avoiding the

hundreds of stares chipping away at my vacant shell. My expression remains drawn as my eyes go in and out of focus. After a few steps, I turn toward the solid mass standing in the distance, welcoming the distraction of the skyline up ahead. As the space between us shrinks, I register the militarized units converging on the outskirts of the city. To my annoyance, every member of the patrol stops what they're doing the instant they notice me.

I press on. The sand merges with an expanse of tiny rocks, which covers the length of the beach right up to the road leading to the city. The gravel crunches beneath my feet, and the sound is almost soothing considering the circumstances—not that unlike the rotors from earlier.

However, just like before, I know this moment of tranquility won't last for long.

I freeze in place when a quiet beeping drums in my ear. Lifting my hand, I press the tip of my finger against the button on my communicator.

My lips part to speak, but I remain silent. Instead, I wait for the familiar voice I know is present on the other side.

"Can you hear me?" Richter asks.

His words resound through my head, triggering that familiar unease and loathing. I take a deep breath before answering. "I can hear you."

"Good," he says after a brief delay. *"The target is 1.6 kilometers to the north of your location. A convoy is ready to accompany you—"*

"That won't be necessary," I interrupt.

At first, he doesn't respond. Yet, in spite of his silence, I can tell that he's pleased with me. When he eventually comes back over the signal, the tone of his voice makes it too easy to visualize his smug smile. *"It finally seems like we're on the same page. Good luck."*

His last words are a sinister purr in my ear, mocking me. A shudder runs up my spine as I press the button to disconnect the call.

When I look up, an eerie timelessness engulfs the beach as every eye within a hundred yards fixates on me. The Enforcers in the vicinity remain frozen in place, their faces contorted into a shared mask of respect and alarm.

I exhale and trudge forward. The crowd once again separates, allowing me to proceed unhindered toward the perimeter of the city. The blasts grow louder, and everyone here is aware that anyone who steps within range of the explosions will die. However, even knowing that, no one tries to stop me.

After all, this is what I'm here for.

The beach gives way to a paved road. The tarmac is worn in places and dented with potholes in others, but regardless of its flaws, the city the path leads through would be considered beautiful—or so I've heard. I'm sure I would agree if I still retained the ability to appreciate such things.

After the State launched the first dozen or so invasions, the places I saw became muddled in my brain until I could no longer differentiate between them. Or maybe I just didn't care to. Maybe they all look the same to me—much like this city looks to me now—because I'm too detached from everything to care. Maybe by refusing to acknowledge my surroundings, I can somehow escape the guilt of what I've done.

I thought I could fight it. I thought I could resist the numbness that has coursed through me since the moment this war began, but I can't. Not now. Not anymore. Not with everything I've seen.

Not with everything I've done.

I can't even recall why I agreed to this, or why I'm still doing it. It's possible Dr. Richter altered my memory as a way of getting me to comply with his orders, but I'm afraid it might be something far more ominous than that. My brain . . .

I don't think it wants me to remember.

For two years now, I've been the State's puppet and Richter's prize science experiment. Or for lack of a better word, their slave. A large portion of that time has been devoted to brutal tests, all conducted in the name of science. The rest has been spent invading foreign lands.

In the space of six months, the State has overtaken almost everything.

I know my experiences have warped me. Nothing feels real anymore. Nothing except pain. Even my memories feel distorted and surreal, often making me wonder if I'm able to trust what's in my head. I remember my life back before the DSD and this disease. I can even remember my initial time with Dr. Richter, although the events that led to it are now a mystery to me, almost as if the recollections have dissolved into thin air—with the exception, of course, of the experimentation and torture.

That I can remember far too clearly.

Adding further to my uncertainty, hiding behind the trauma of the past few years, there's a brief period I can't make sense of. The memory of it niggles at the back of my brain, letting me know it's there—probably living with the small piece of me that still feels human underneath this abomination I've become. It's growing weaker, though. Each day, another piece of my humanity is eaten away, taking whoever I was before with it. Gradually, I'm becoming less of what I was and more of what the State has always wanted me to be.

A weapon.

In spite of my increasing weakness, a large part of me clings to whatever my mind refuses to remember. I'm not sure why, but something tells me that my reason for doing this lies in those lost memories, making me suspect that I'm trying to protect something or someone. The recollections of my past are hidden behind a veil of confusion and corrupted by the repetitive nightmares about everything I've been subjected to. Still, I can feel their presence in the back of my brain, waiting for me to find them.

My feet slow to a halt, disrupting my thoughts as I feel the enemy's presence like a fog clouding my head. They're close. Only a little farther.

Then this can all be over.

The curve of the road takes me through an abandoned residential area. I cast an occasional glance at the darkened windows, but there's no visible movement inside. The small part of me that's still human feels thankful for that.

After another few hundred yards, the layout of the neighborhood begins to change, extending out like arms opening to welcome me home. My feet never falter as I push forward into the city center.

A vast plaza stands in front of me, and although it was likely once used for something less sinister than battle, the erect barricades and soldiers littering the ground make it completely unrecognizable. A handful of tanks are positioned along the outer confines of the square—no doubt a last-ditch attempt to save their home from our assault.

My eyes scan the area. I gather that this battalion is all that's left of their defenses—a pitiful contingent that the State could've eradicated in a single blow, just like they've done to the rest of this city.

Of course, I know why they didn't.

A surge of anger rushes through my body, and I can almost hear Dr. Richter's taunting laughter in my head. Why do something themselves when they have me to do it for them? After all, the State is seeking to oppress, not annihilate. Destroy just enough to make the rest of the world fear them. Kill just enough to make them surrender.

I blink in response to the abrupt sound of shouting. A male voice pierces through the tense silence of the plaza, high-pitched like the yowl of a dying cat. I glance up to see the remaining soldiers look in my direction. Similar to the Enforcers, they all wear the same apprehensive expression.

My steps slow to a standstill as I stare back at the army with indifference. The voice rings through the air once again, drawing my attention to the officer it belongs to.

Our eyes meet, and a small sigh escapes my lips when he yells out to me again. No matter how many times he repeats himself, I won't be able to understand the unfamiliar words passing between us. After a few more wasted breaths, he finally seems to grasp this.

Skin glowing red with frustration, he turns his attention to the soldier standing beside him. The other man's face goes ashen when a string of orders is barked in his ear. Eyes darting between us, he raises his rifle. His hands shake as he fires a single shot, the bullet hitting the ground mere inches from my feet.

I don't flinch. Remaining calm, I tilt my head and peer at the damaged stone in front of me before lifting my gaze to the soldier's face.

The moment our eyes connect, I feel an overwhelming pressure take hold, suppressing the one part of me that might have the power to stop this from happening. A heated anger flushes my body, coursing through my veins as it coaxes me into action.

Chaos erupts throughout the plaza. Shouts of warning carry through the crowd, and I hear the click of metal as their guns lock into place to shoot me down where I stand. Within seconds, the officer shrieks an order, giving them permission to do so.

My march forward is effortless as my mind redirects the rain of bullets. I am a rock, and their attempts are like water, forced to go around me when they fail to penetrate my body. Still, they keep firing.

The enemy's terror becomes more visible as the distance between us lessens. Determined to make him my starting point, my eyes remain fixed on the soldier who first shot at me.

They will see what I'm capable of.

They will know who they're dealing with.

Seeming to sense my intentions, he lifts his gun one last time. I reach forward, wrapping my fingers around the end of the barrel as I yank it with a single rough thrust toward my hips. The jerking motion drags him to the ground, causing him to fall into a patch of dirt.

A quiet gasp bursts from his lips as he scrambles backward onto his knees. His labored breathing deteriorates to wheezes as if his lungs are beginning to fail, and his eyes turn upward, the emerging realization that he's going to die clouding their pale blue depths with fear.

All the while, I feel nothing.

His screams slice through the air like a knife as convulsions overtake him, limb by limb. Driven to the brink of insanity by the pain, he drags his nails across his face, creating lacerations that cover his cheeks. Specks of blood bubble up from the cuts and coat his skin in a glossy sheen.

I watch his crazed response with boredom, my mind collected and body still, despite the havoc I'm causing his. The half-formed pleas entering my ears do nothing to deter my purpose.

At last, the whites of his eyes turn red with a sickening pop, and his body crashes to the ground in a fleshy, disfigured heap.

The surrounding gunfire ceases at the same moment. I peer over my shoulder before crouching to retrieve the dead man's pistol, and when I straighten up, I notice the unit's commanding officer out of my peripheral vision. The trepidation in his gaze is genuine, and his mouth opens several times as he trips over words that refuse to exit his throat. In the heavy silence between us, the terror etched into his face seems to scream how much he fears me.

With every step I take forward, he takes a step back in response. Panic keeps him moving, but it also cripples his body, causing him to stumble over his feet and collide with the ground. I watch with a vague amusement as he struggles like prey caught in a trap it has no hope of escaping. Finally, as if realizing this battle is over, he submits to me.

His hands tighten into fists as a stuttering breath breaches his lips.

My eyes narrow as I raise the pistol and press the

front of the barrel against his temple. As my fingers dance along the trigger, I'm reminded of the army still standing around me. Their awed stares follow my every movement.

Inhaling a long, slow breath, I close my eyes and concentrate. Using my senses to feel out every weapon present in the plaza, I bend them to my will, manipulating their power and turning them back on their owners. The resulting screams are drowned out by the sound of gunfire and explosions. Round after round is fired as blood splatters the dirt and stone.

My tongue caresses my lower lip as I look down into the eyes of the cowering officer in front of me. Without remorse, my finger finds the trigger—the sound of the shot joining the chorus of death ringing like thunder through the city.

As I watch the steady stream of red seeping from his head, I'm able to decipher what he said in his final moments. What he whispered to me.

What he called me.

I hear it again now, his foreign language no longer hiding that one simple word.

"Monster."

TWO

I GLANCE AT THE ENFORCER next to me as he slides a keycard through the panel affixed to the wall beside the door. A small light at the top of the console turns green, and a second later, the lock turns with an audible click. The steel entrance slides open, allowing us to pass into the place that's become my home.

The DSD.

I follow the Enforcer as two more trail behind me. Their footsteps keep in perfect time with mine as if they're the physical embodiment of my shadow. It should unnerve me, but I've become accustomed to this procession. Richter says they're necessary, and as a result, I'm never alone. Not really. He even insists they're my personal bodyguards, but I know better than to believe his lies.

The truth is, I'm nothing more than a glorified prisoner.

We move along the familiar path through the brightly lit hallways. At one point, the fluorescent lights made me nauseous. Now, they're just another aspect of my life I've learned to embrace—a second skin I have to wear if I'm to survive this hellhole.

Our steps slow as we approach the security checkpoint that bars further entry into the building. A female guard controls the full-body scanner, and all staff members and personnel are required to pass through it. No exceptions, not even for me.

The DSD is the one place where special clearance doesn't exist. The work they do here is considered too valuable to risk, so precautions are taken to the utmost extreme. Although, I suppose these limitations are in place to protect me—their prized weapon.

Their project.

Without meeting my gaze, the guard indicates with a subtle nod for me to step into the machine, and the Enforcers stand back as I slip inside the cylinder. The tube is made of glass with steel bands lining each pane and stands flush with the nearest wall, extending from floor to ceiling. A large metal ring pulses along the exterior casing, casting my body in a silver-blue glow.

The scan only takes around thirty seconds. After which, I'm escorted to the other side of the station where my finger is pricked for blood, and my collar is checked for any abnormalities that could suggest a possible breach. It's examined multiple times a day, not only for my safety but for the safety of everyone here. My collar is the most cherished object in the entirety of the DSD, and ensuring it remains functional is top priority.

A part of me is curious how it works while another part of me doesn't really care. It keeps my powers in control, but aside from that, all I know is what Dr. Richter has said in his incomplete explanations. Something about magnetic signals—probably along the same lines as those lightning-like bolts he enjoys shooting into my head. It would make sense, considering I'm always in some degree of discomfort. Like a persistent headache that refuses to die away, the collar keeps me in check by any means necessary. In this case, through pain.

As Dr. Richter often reminds me, control comes at a cost.

"You're all clear," the guard informs me, interrupting my train of thought.

As soon as those words leave her lips, the Enforcers return to my side, ready to escort me along the remaining length of the long hallway. Their footsteps never fall too far behind mine, and each click of their heeled boots is like a beating drum in my head. The reminder of their constant presence is almost unbearable.

Our route takes us into the main area of the laboratory where I notice an older woman standing on the other side of the lobby. A white coat adorns her body, and her posture is upright and still—except for her fingers, which dance across the surface of a computerized tablet. Her gaze flits to mine as if sensing our arrival, and with a tiny gasp, she pushes herself forward. She waves her hand to get my attention before hurrying over to greet us.

"Hello, Wynter," she says through a smile.

I stare at her but say nothing. Focusing back on her tablet, she seems unfazed by my lack of response. I assume she's grown used to it by now.

This exchange is nothing more than a formality anyway—the caretaker playing her dutiful role. I never even bothered to learn her name, which just goes to show how little the people here mean to me.

After a short pause, she adds, "Dr. Richter is waiting for you in Exam Room B." Lifting her head, she jerks her chin toward the Enforcers, relieving them of their duty with a pointed look.

I hear their retreating footsteps as she smiles at me once again.

In a deceptively warm voice, she ushers me farther into the depths of the DSD. "Shall we?" she asks.

We traverse the corridors, retracing steps I've traveled so many times before. I could walk this path blind if I had to—a thought that leaves a sour taste in my mouth. Familiarity is something I neither want nor need here. Yet, it's something I can't avoid, even if I try to.

As if reading my thoughts, the woman beside me spews a heap of verbal filth in my direction.

"Dr. Richter is pleased with your performance. You should be proud of your progress."

Her pitiful attempt at friendly chatter only makes me dislike her more.

I can feel her eyes watching me, but I don't turn to face her. Instead, I keep my attention focused ahead until we reach the entrance to Exam Room B. Her fingers flash across the keypad, inputting the sequence of numbers to unlock the door. As it clicks open, she gestures with her hand for me to enter the room.

I brush past her, all too aware of the door closing between us.

I always hate this part.

The part where I'm left alone with *him*.

Taking a deep breath, I glance up to see Dr. Richter leaning against the examination unit with his arms crossed as he appraises me with those perceptive gray eyes. A cool, detached smile appears on his lips.

"Welcome back." He straightens up and indicates for me to take a seat on the table.

A discomforting chill runs along my skin when he pats the metal surface. Crossing the room and hoisting myself up onto the cold slab of steel, I do as I'm told without question, just like usual. Dr. Richter reaches over my shoulder, and I watch as he retrieves a small device off the shelf behind me. It takes everything I have to keep my face vacant of emotion and not recoil from his sudden and unwelcome proximity. When he leans back, his eyes dart to mine before settling on my throat.

My airways tighten in the same instant he brushes the scanner against my collar. The handheld device beeps, relaying information to the computer beside us. I swallow when he touches my neck, but his fingers slip away as he shifts his attention toward the monitor.

"Looks good." Reaching into the pocket of his white coat, he pulls out a flashlight and shines it into my eyes. "Follow the light," he instructs.

Once again, I do as I'm told, observing the blinding glare as it swings from side to side in front of me. I can almost feel my pupils dilating, and the burn of the light forms fuzzy black spots across my vision.

"Excellent." Clicking off the light, he stows it back inside his pocket.

My eyes blink a few times to ease the fiery ache, and as I struggle to regain my sight, I'm aware of Dr. Richter watching me. Peering up to meet his gaze, I find the same sense of approval I suspected from him before.

"The data from your collar has checked out perfectly," he informs me. "Your vitals are strong, your reactionary responses are superb, and your abilities are evolving at an extraordinary rate. If you maintain this level of progress, it won't be long until your power knows no limits at all."

My lips press together, locking away my voice. For a moment, I wonder if he expects me to respond, but then I notice the way he looks at me—the way he regards me as a prized object or maybe even a pet. An obedient *thing* rather than a living, breathing human.

His fingers skim along my arm, sending another shudder across my skin. "You've come a long way. When we first began these experiments, we weren't even sure you'd survive, and now look at you. The perfect specimen we've been dreaming of."

He leans forward until our faces are mere inches apart before lifting his hand and caressing my cheek. Staring at me with an unwanted fondness in his eyes, his next words are a soft purr of demented adoration.

"My own little angel of death."

My nostrils flare as I suck in a ragged breath. For a split second, I'm reminded of that foreign officer. I remember the way he looked at me and what he said in those final moments.

"Monster."

Dr. Richter lowers his hand, and a weight lifts off my shoulders as the physical contact between us dissipates. Ignoring my reaction, he focuses back on the computer.

"Are we done here?" I ask in a hollow voice. "I'd like to return to my quarters now."

His fingers tap a few times against the desktop, filling the room with a soft eerie echo. "Not just yet."

The intensity of his expression when he looks back at me is overwhelming, and I'm struck with an irrepressible urge to shrink away. I ignore the temptation, remaining as tall and as still as possible.

His eyes narrow as a rush of words parts his lips. "Who's next?"

My brow furrows, bowing under the confusion that sits at the forefront of my brain. I scramble to make sense of his question, but nothing adds up to anything resembling a coherent thought.

With an irritating smirk pulling at the corners of his lips, he raises his hand to adjust his glasses. Clearing his throat, he clarifies. "I wish to know what our next course of action should be in regards to the countries that still pose a threat."

I consider him for a moment before casting an uncertain glance around the room. Whenever I've been asked to use my power in this way, it's always involved hooking my body up to a variety of machines. The information I saw was fed to their computers, which allowed them to extract and verify the data for themselves. Usually, I'm nothing more than a sort of leech, sucking out and retrieving the desired information.

Nothing more.

Reaching forward, he grips my chin, and with a gentle tug, he tilts my face until I have no other option except to look up at him.

"This time, I want you to tell me yourself," he whispers.

It's as if he knows what I'm thinking, but I still can't comprehend why he'd choose to do things differently. Why ask me when he can just see it for himself? He knows what works, so why change the process?

Or is this just another one of his games meant to test me?

"Why?" I breathe.

He runs his free hand through my hair, twirling the strands around his fingers to hold me in place.

"I think we've come far enough. Wouldn't you agree? Besides, I trust you to be honest with me."

His eyes dart to my collar, and as they do, I see the threat in his gaze. He doesn't have to say anything more to make his warning apparent. My jaw clenches in an effort to hold my strangled emotions at bay. The thought of lying crosses my mind, but the outcome would be far worse than just telling him the truth.

Any suspicion concerning my answer would only lead him to conduct a test or two to confirm it. Then, of course, there would be the obligatory punishment for my dishonesty. On top of that, there's my reason for doing this in the first place. I might not remember why I'm here, but I'm fairly certain risking an attack will put whatever I'm trying to protect in jeopardy.

Taking a reluctant breath, I nod my head.

Doing what he asks has become easier with time. What used to cause me agony is now as natural as breathing. All I have to do is allow my thoughts to drift, and then I fall into a dreamlike daze where whatever I wish to see appears before me at will.

As my eyes close, I descend into a separate level of my mind. I've seen many places this way, a number of which I've had to travel to as a result of what I saw.

I try not to remember those places.

My eyebrows scrunch together as I concentrate on any activity that could indicate a potential mobilization against the State. Soon enough, images of a city flash through my thoughts. I see their military. I see the preparations they're making. I even see enough to gather when the attack will happen. Above all, I see who they are.

The air catches in my lungs as I'm brought back to the present. My eyes blink a few times, fluttering like the wings of a hummingbird. I exhale, allowing myself a moment before turning toward Dr. Richter. When I fail to speak, his impatience breaks the silence instead.

"Well?" he asks.

My right eye twitches in irritation. "An attack will happen in four days' time." The voice that rises from my throat is toneless.

The haunting reality of these moments always makes me feel sick. This new enemy is only attacking because they don't see any other option. In a desperate bid for domination, the State has launched an all-out assault against the rest of the world, and it's only a matter of time before we come for them as well. They know this and hope to catch us off guard by moving first, but they fail to realize that victory is an illusion.

So long as I exist, the State is unstoppable.

Without another word, he turns back toward the computer, and his fingers skip in a mechanical rhythm across the desktop. A bright blue light shines up from the glass, forming a large holographic image.

I stare at the round sphere, watching as it moves in sluggish rotations. My eyes graze over the tiny names that appear across its transparent surface, scanning them for the one that matches the location I saw in the vision.

My hand shoots out, pointing to a small speck of light on the globe. "There."

Dr. Richter presses a button, freezing the image in place. My heart falters as he leans in close to me, the tip of his nose tickling my arm as he follows my finger to the name positioned just beneath it. Standing up tall, he realigns his glasses before peering down at his computerized tablet.

As he does, I can't help noticing how familiar this feels. Staring at the luminescent blue sphere in front of me, I'm reminded of something.

But what?

A dull buzz resounds through the room when he shuts off the hologram, interrupting my moment of déjà vu. I clear my throat as he turns back to face me.

For an extended length of time, we stare at each other. His piercing eyes bore into mine as his hand sweeps along the curve of his chin, and the amusement twisting his lips only fuels my annoyance. I'm unnerved by his silence, but I get the distinct impression that he's once again pleased with me.

Releasing a soft breath, he looks down at the tablet and swipes his long finger across the top of the screen. "We're ready for you," he murmurs.

The woman from before re-enters the room, smiling when she sees me. Despite her façade of kindness, I know her expression is just as empty as everyone else's here.

"Take Wynter back to her quarters, please. We're finished for the day." Dr. Richter waves a hand, shooing me like I'm a dog.

I lower myself off the table without making further commentary or asking questions. After all, I'm used to the way things are done around here now.

My feet pad in quiet steps across the tiled floor. Focusing on the woman's back, I watch as she disappears over the threshold, determined to join her as I'm overcome by the desire to get as far away from *him* as possible. Bile shoots up my throat when the unexpected sound of his voice prevents that from happening. Reaching out, it drags me back with a tormenting hiss.

"Wynter," he calls.

I pause in the doorway, glancing over my shoulder. Out of the corner of my eye, I notice the woman waiting in the hallway. The obedient servant as submissive as ever.

His footsteps reverberate through the room as he closes the distance between us. "One more thing."

Taking hold of my arm, he turns it with a jerking twist to expose the crook of my elbow. Before I can react, he plunges a needle into the throbbing vein there—adding yet another puncture mark to my already riddled skin. I grimace as blood fills the vial attached to the syringe, and when it reaches its limit, he yanks it out with a sharp tug. A cruel smile curls his lips in response to my expression.

"Can't forget this." He shakes the container in front of my face, flaunting his power over me.

A profound hatred floods my body as I tear my arm from his grasp, and just like every other day, I want nothing more than to see him dead. Preferably, by my hands.

Thinking he'd ever neglect this part of our little meetings was foolish. Taking my blood has become a daily occurrence—one he derives pleasure from since it causes me distress. What he needs it for, I don't know, but I do know it's important. Known as Type X, it's a brand new blood type that he wishes to study.

One of a kind, just like me.

"Get some rest."

His voice penetrates my ears, startling me with his uncharacteristic choice of words.

Letting out a heavy sigh, he meets my gaze, but light from the ceiling reflects off his glasses, shielding his eyes. Through an irritable grunt, he says, "The attack is in four days. We leave in two." Then, he turns back to his work, dismissing me with his silence.

My fingers tremble as my hands ball into fists, and I nod my head once before exiting the room.

THREE

THE BLUE LIGHT OF THE hologram illuminates the exam room, engulfing me in its glow. My eyes follow the image, watching as a slew of names take shape across its transparent exterior. They rise up in random intervals as if the places they represent are only just now coming into existence.

A strange apprehension floods my body, and pins and needles attack my skin as I reach out to touch it. Like a moth drawn to a flame, my hand is lured in by the light.

I gasp and reel back when my fingertips press against a hard surface. Yellowed with age, the wooden globe positioned in front of me spins in slow turns on its tilted axis. As I watch the rotations, my brain struggles to make sense of it.

Seconds ago, it was nothing more than a projection of a world I have personally had a hand in destroying. Now, it's something different.

Something important, I tell myself.

I take an uncertain step backward, only just now

noticing the glass desk sitting beneath the rotating sphere. As my eyes trail along its edges, I become plagued with the nagging feeling that I've seen this before.

But where?

A dream?

A memory . . . ?

Curiosity guides my gaze, coaxing me to investigate my immediate surroundings. My heart thumps with wild, erratic pulses, leaping into my throat when I grasp the full extent of the changes. The exam room is gone, replaced by an unusual combination of glass and wood. Everything is hazy and out of focus. Everything except for the globe, which seems to stare back at me from its place on the desktop.

A fuzzy sensation clouds my brain, dimming the room until I'm drowning in darkness.

Only one thing manages to break through the fog.

"What's this?" a male voice calls out from the shadows.

My lungs spasm in response, drawing a sharp breath as my body turns toward the sound. As I glance around the room, an uneasy chill crosses my skin . . . but there's no one there. Same as before, I'm the only one here, accompanied by nothing but glass, wood, and silence.

Questioning my sanity, I focus on the desk again. The instant my eyes lock on it, a faint buzzing begins to emanate from its surface. The embedded computer screen flashes to life a moment later, the light refracting off its transparent casing.

Inching forward, I peer through the glare, and the gleam is blinding in comparison to the thick gloom around me. As my vision adjusts, the words on the screen become clear.

I can't explain why, but they resonate with the flicker of humanity that still exists somewhere within me. Or, perhaps, they're simply responding to the memories that refuse to surface.

Without even realizing it, the words spill from my lips. "Project W. A. R."

A burst of static skews the screen. The glow pulsates outward like a beating heart as a mess of letters and images race past in a blur, making me wonder if the system has lost control. I can't keep track of them, nor do I try to.

Convulsions of light splash across the walls, and I find myself shrinking back when they reach out to touch me. Suddenly, an unfamiliar voice joins the confusion. Its nonsensical ramblings only add to the chaos.

"... *Twenty-two* ..."

"... *refuses to eat* ..."

"... *intravenous measures* ..."

I turn in place, searching for the source of the whispers, but I see nothing.

"... *Thirty-eight* ..."

"... *withstanding* ..."

"... *more resilient* ..."

A crazed alarm overtakes me, reacting to every word. My fingers grab at my head as I cower to the floor, covering my ears in an effort to push the voice out.

The voice that is beginning to resemble my own.

"... *Fifty-six* ..."

"... *extracted information* ..."

"... *will continue testing* ..."

Without warning, the whispers cease. Unsteady

breaths permeate the air as my body quakes with a bizarre and unsolicited sense of dread. I refuse to give into it. In a cautious move, I lower my hands, readying myself.

Still quiet. The voice is gone.

Or is it?

Exhaling, I lift my head, and my throat tightens as a choked scream blocks my airways. My eyes widen, locking with those of the woman standing in front of me.

In an urgent whisper, she mutters, "They're initials."

Her different colored eyes pierce right through my soul.

"W . . . A . . . R . . . Wynter Arabelle Reeves."

The minimal light in the room is extinguished once those words fade into silence, leaving me trapped in a cage of shadows. With each passing minute, my breaths grow more frantic. A sudden anxiety is eating me alive as my suppressed fear claws its way out from the recesses of my brain.

My eyes narrow as I turn on my heel. Taking a deep, calming breath, I concentrate on finding clues that will explain what's going on here. The woman—who I now realize was my own distorted reflection—is gone, leaving me alone again.

The seconds tick by. As I examine the black room, I glimpse a peculiar break in the darkness that wasn't there before. It's small and inconspicuous, not that unlike a dying ember in a pit of ash. Exercising caution, I inch forward, but intrigue gets the best of me. My fingers twitch as I reach out to touch it.

What I find there is smooth like glass and glossy like liquid. A loud shriek breaks through my lips when I flatten my hand against the odd surface, causing a bright light to erupt in response, exploding in a great flash. My body flinches as a crashing sound thunders in my ears, the high frequency making my eyes water. I stop myself from blinking and watch in amazement as thousands of tiny mirrors cascade like rain to the floor.

The shards land at my feet, and when I look into them, I notice the same reflection repeated in each cracked piece. Face, after face, after face—all wearing an identical expression of horror.

I try to move, but I'm frozen. I try to think, but I can't make sense of what's happening. The only coherent element in the room is the male voice wrapping around me as my surroundings descend into blackness once again.

"Wynter . . . ."

My eyes shoot open.

"Wynter—"

I blink a few times, bringing the bleary figure above me into focus. The irritating woman from before leans over the bed, repeating my name.

Inhaling a deep breath, I force myself upright. A head-rush impairs my vision, blocking out everything until I can only see the fading images in my head. When the sensation passes, I lock eyes on the familiar setting of my quarters—reminding me where I am.

With a heavy sigh, it occurs to me that my vision must've been a dream. A part of me feels relieved since I honestly didn't think I was even capable of it anymore. Sleep is hard enough to come by, but dreaming? No. I can't remember the last time I was blessed with that sort of escape.

Still, there's another part of me that can't help feeling unnerved by what I saw. The blue light. The

29

globe. That familiar voice.

I brush my hand across my forehead, pushing back a few rogue strands of hair. My chest heaves with each breath passing through my lips—my lungs working in short bursts that coincide with the rapid, frantic beating of my heart.

For a moment, I find myself wondering if the woman is taking note of my agitated state, and if she'll mention it to Dr. Richter. This change in my behavior is sure to spark his interest, and that will only lead to more examinations and tests. I glance up at her, but I'm met with an innocent smile—its questionable authenticity sickly sweet.

If she *is* planning to tell him, she doesn't mention it.

"It's time."

I nod and swing my legs over the side of the bed. Although I keep my eyes on the floor, I'm aware of her retreating figure as she returns to the hallway.

"I'll be waiting outside," she says, pausing beside the door. "Let me know when you're ready."

The lock clicks back into place behind her, and after a moment, I rise to my feet. My usual gear is folded on the table at the foot of the bed, and taking another breath to prepare myself, I reach forward to grab it.

Hands clenched into fists around the black material, I thumb the leather and mesh paneling, feeling the rough texture beneath my touch as each passing minute only delays the inevitable. For a split second, I swear I can see blood still ingrained in the fabric.

With a grimace, I turn away. A bitter taste crosses my tongue, but as I make for the sink to wash it from my mouth, I'm caught off guard by my reflection in the mirror hanging above it. The sight stops me in my tracks.

The woman staring back at me is healthy and fit with hair that falls to the small of her back in a billowing curtain of brown silk. Everything about her oozes strength and control.

Even though we're the same person, I feel like I'm looking at a stranger.

Unable to bear her unwavering gaze any longer, I shift my attention to one corner of the mirror. The sharp edges remind me of the tiled glass in my dream. The memory shrouds my brain, cutting through my thoughts as if the recollection is something physical and real. I remember the way it fell around me and seemed to swallow me whole. For a quick second, I can even hear the deafening crash in my ears.

In the time it takes for me to blink, the terror of my dream pushes to the surface—bursting out of my subconscious in a violent wave. The hallucination settles over my eyes.

My feet stumble back when I glimpse the shards covering the floor, reducing the mirror to a mess of scattered pieces. Breaths leak in ragged gasps from my constricting lungs. Overwhelming panic cripples my body, and I squeeze my eyes shut in a desperate attempt to escape it. I whisper numbers to myself through trembling lips, counting down from ten—a coping mechanism for these rare moments when sanity eludes me. The instant I reach zero, my eyes reopen. As to be expected, the floor is bare.

I turn toward the bed, shaking my head in wild jerks as my fingers grip the black material in my hands even harder. Uncertain of how much time I've already wasted, I hurry to dress in the same ensemble I'm always given for these missions. The plain black bodysuit hugs my body and consists of leather panels mixed with softer sections of layered fabric for easy movement. Heavy duty combat boots lace up to just below my knees.

Remembering Richter's new nickname for me, I look at the clothes with distaste. He called me an angel of death, and a part of me wonders if this outfit is intended to make me look the part.

When the last zipper is in place, I reach over and rap my knuckles once against the door. A second later, the familiar beeps echo through the wall as the woman enters the unlocking code into the keypad. The door springs open to reveal her standing in the hallway, dark eyes appraising me as she displays her trademark smile.

"Are you ready?"

I push past her, refusing to answer.

We proceed through the long corridors in silence, only communicating when necessary to discuss my next mission. It's strange. We've gone through this routine several times before, however, I can never escape the feeling that always follows me.

The feeling that I'm heading to my own execution.

As we round a corner, Dr. Richter joins us. He does so with such stealth that I barely even register his presence at first. Or maybe I'm so accustomed to him that I just choose not to acknowledge it.

Without speaking a single word, he offers me a communicator. In begrudging acceptance, I swipe it from his hand and insert it in place.

"Have you been debriefed?" he asks.

"Yes," I mutter, keeping my expression drawn and my eyes trained ahead.

He responds in a low, guttural breath. "Good. I'll be here, just like usual."

Sensing him watching me, I glance up to meet his gaze. Smiling, he taps his finger twice against his ear.

No further words are exchanged between us until we reach the back exit of the building. A group of Enforcers is already there waiting for us, including those belonging to my so-called security detail.

We stop a few feet away from them when I feel the blood-curdling warmth of Dr. Richter's hands. They grip my shoulders, nails digging through the fabric to the point I can feel them chafing against my skin. He stares at me with that familiar sinister smile pulling at the corners of his mouth, and lifting his fingers to my face, he grazes my cheek as he brushes a strand of hair from my lips.

"You know what to do," he croons. "I'm sure you won't disappoint me."

Despite the false tenderness of his words, I can sense the menace hiding beneath them.

His eyes bore into mine as he takes a step back, and my heart plummets when he raises his arm in the air. He watches me, gauging my reaction to his mocking salute.

"For the State." His voice is solemn, and every syllable in his tone seems to dare me to disobey.

I clench my jaw, determined not to give him that satisfaction. "For the State," I repeat, regurgitating the words like an emotionless marionette.

His lips twitch into an even deeper smile.

Disgusted, I turn away and proceed into the midst of the awaiting Enforcers. They stand aside, allowing me to pass, and the door behind them beeps open as if it can sense my approach. Bodies surround me—a wall of black forming a perfect circular formation as each footstep keeps in time with mine. The sound reflects off the tarmac as we make our way toward the truck waiting less than a hundred yards away.

An ominous tension always surrounds these moments, making me feel like a convict being transported rather than a soldier heading to war. I suppose, in spite of my vital role in all of this, I am nothing more than that.

The doors to the armored truck bang open, and I clamber into the back, followed by three of the Enforcers. As soon as we're inside, the engine roars to life, ready to carry us off to yet another battle.

Another slaughter, I correct myself.

Vacant thoughts fill my brain during our journey, giving me a temporary reprieve from the real world. I only snap out of my inattention when the winds outside the truck grow louder, alerting me that we've reached the airfield.

The vehicle skids to a halt, and the doors spring open, giving us permission to unload. Following after the Enforcers, I look up as my feet touch down on the pavement. The transport helicopter is already prepped for take-off, the rotors whirring with a taunting purr.

My entourage hurries me along, and I'm herded into the cargo hold like a mindless sheep. Sinking into my usual seat, my hands tighten the straps and click the harness into place.

My eyes scan the metal interior, watching as the seats around me fill up, one by one. For some reason, I feel on edge. The only sensation I tend to experience in these moments is a detached sort of nausea, but right now, something doesn't seem right.

Straining my thoughts, I search for anything unusual or out of place. I focus on the immediate future, but I find nothing. Everything is as it should be.

Letting out a tired breath, I toss it up to being nothing more than residual uneasiness from the dream I had earlier. In an attempt to force it from my mind, I tilt my head back against the seat and close my eyes.

Here, in this helicopter and on my way to destroy another piece of my humanity, I realize just how exhausted I am. I try to fight against it, but the sound of the rotors lulls me to sleep. Finally, lacking any logical reason not to, I give into it.

The darkness quickly rises to wrap me in its embrace. As it does, a broken mirror is the last thing I see.

FOUR

"WE ARE APPROACHING OUR TARGET destination. Prepare for landing in T-minus five minutes."

My eyelids dart open, and a startled breath fills my chest as I jerk awake. The sound of the announcement bangs around me like a crude alarm, making my head hurt. I shift in my seat, elongating my spine as I glance around the metal interior. The Enforcers are all preoccupied in some way, readying themselves for the battle ahead.

Lifting my shoulders, I tilt my chin toward the ceiling to stretch out my stiff neck. A heavy sigh trickles through my lips, and as it does, I find myself thinking of the Enforcer from my last mission. I remember his nervousness and blatant fear of me more clearly than anything I've been forced to endure over the course of the past two years.

Peering up, my gaze lands on the seat positioned opposite mine. For half a second, I expect to see him sitting there, staring back at me with those same terror-stricken eyes. The face that awaits me is older and more seasoned. A man rather than a frightened boy.

For some reason, I'm interested to know what became of the young Enforcer. I don't see him here, so unless he was relocated, there's an infinitesimal chance he didn't survive the previous battle. I find that unlikely since their involvement has been limited. Still, a part of me is tempted to search for him—to find out if he's alive. Although I'd be lying if I said I cared one way or another. This is nothing more than a selfish curiosity. A desire to know if there's even an ounce of humanity left within me.

I don't bother to find out.

The roaring winds die away when the helicopter touches down on the ground. With a taunting whir, the rotors slow to a halt as the loading ramp lowers to welcome our invasion. Another place we'll soon desecrate, just like the others.

I wait until the cargo hold has emptied before unstrapping my harness. Rising to my feet, I concentrate my thoughts on a point in the back of my mind, going through the familiar routine of distancing myself from the world around me. It's the only way to do what has to be done. The only way to cope.

My footsteps echo off the metal flooring. An invisible weight presses down on my shoulders, the burden of it overtaking me as I descend the ramp and approach the unavoidable sea of faces. I keep my gaze locked ahead in a futile attempt to ignore them, shutting everything out as much as possible.

With each step I take, the uneasiness I felt before creeps back to the surface, weaving its way through every inch of my body. It poisons me with an apprehension that's incompatible with my unfeeling nature, and yet, its parasitic latch only strengthens its hold, drawing us together like a pair of magnets. My aversion brings me closer to the very thing I'm dreading.

I inhale multiple deep breaths as my feet carry me off the ramp. The air is charged with a strange tension—something I've never felt on any of my previous missions. Looking around, I try to find the source of it, but nothing appears to be out of place. At least, not that I notice.

All I can see is the endless blanket of faces.

A movement to my left alerts me to the senior Enforcer stepping out from the crowd. His voice distracts me, drawing my attention.

"Your transport is ready—"

I cut him off with a glowering look. "I'll walk."

His petrified hesitation casts a stone-like coating across his eyes, and he immediately shrinks back when he hears me speak. Perhaps because the Enforcers have become accustomed to only expecting my silence and submission.

Do they honestly think I'm incapable of something as normal as speaking? That I'm unable to stand up to them? It's as if they don't believe that I'm physically able to. *It's like they've forgotten I'm human,* I realize.

I brush past him, moving toward the sound of explosions in the distance where the State has already begun the preliminary attack. The weight on my shoulders continues to bear down on me, and a weird, anxious feeling burns in my chest like a budding fire. I can't make sense of either sensation.

Why is my body reacting this way when I've been through this exact ordeal so many times before? Why is this battle any different?

A soft beep in my right ear rips me away from my confused thoughts. A grunt of exasperation tears from my lungs as I lift my finger to the button on the communicator.

"The transport is there for a reason." There's an undertone of irritation in Dr. Richter's voice. The owner scolding his disobedient pet.

"You've never minded before," I answer.

The silence that settles between us is somewhat foreboding, but I lack the will to care. In fact, I'm far more interested in the sound of crunching gravel beneath my feet. I raise my hand to disconnect the call when his voice comes back over the signal.

"Remember why you're there." The threat behind his words is apparent in each pronounced syllable.

My jaw clenches, holding back the anger that sets on my tongue. In a fit of rage, I press the small button on the communicator and rip the device from my ear, gripping it between my fingers. Without a single damn in the world, I drop it to the ground.

A smile curls my lips when I hear the plastic hit the dirt. I form a mental image of the abandoned earpiece, and as I do, the idea of Dr. Richter's wrath doesn't even faze me. I'll be punished, no doubt. Horrifically, too. Still, when the thought crosses my mind, I feel nothing.

Not dread.

Not fear.

After everything I've seen and done, I don't think I even recognize those emotions anymore.

My ears prick up at the increasing sound of detonations, and my eyes lift to the sky when a drone flies overhead. It seems to coincide with the swelling disquiet sitting in my gut like a cancerous tumor.

Nevertheless, I keep walking.

Death hangs like a fog, its presence almost tangible in the molecules around me. In truth, I'm envious of its victims. Death would be an escape from this repetitive war and the nightmare that's become my every waking moment.

Death would allow me to escape Dr. Richter.

Too bad he would never allow it. Past attempts have made that clear. Knowing I have to obey him is even worse than knowing I can never get away from him. No matter what he asks, I'm forced to do as he commands—to kill people. To destroy whole cities and watch them crumble to the ground.

Raising my hand, I touch the collar around my neck.

If I don't do it, he'll make me.

The very notion consumes my mind to the point that I've walked right into the ongoing first wave of our invasion without registering the other drones or the deafening explosions. I fail to notice the rubble landing at my feet until I'm standing in the midst of it. Everything is muffled and distant as if I'm in a separate reality. As if I'm isolated.

Alone.

I walk in a daze, only vaguely aware of any passing movement. My eyes trail across the ground, taking in the sight of the blood-soaked dirt. The deep red glistens in the occasional streak of sunlight.

The abrupt sound of cracking glass tempts me out of my stupor. My body freezes, and looking to my feet, I glimpse the broken fragments strewn across the ground. In them, I see my distorted likeness. Face, after face, after face. The cracked surfaces form a web, but through it, I'm able to catch sight of the unusual darkness in my eyes.

A darkness I've never seen in them before this moment.

All at once, I'm assaulted by a barrage of images. They spring to life, dragging me into their depths as if I've been pulled under by a violent wave.

A vision.

Memories . . .

I'm unable to tell which of the two takes hold of me.

First, I'm back in my quarters at the DSD, staring into the mirror above the sink. When I look at my reflection, the mirror shatters.

Static distorts my surroundings, transporting me away from that tiny room. Suddenly, I'm standing in a shower cubicle. My fingers grip the wall. A grinding sound fills the air as the concrete and tiles rupture beneath my touch. The pipes hanging above me spew a rush of water onto my head.

Static again.

Finally, I find myself back in my dream—back amidst the blackness with the rain of mirrors falling around me.

The images dash past as the seconds tick by, except for the final moment that suspends me in a brief illusion of timelessness. The shards float through the air, cascading like feathers as if to allow me the chance to see my face in each separate piece.

Is this even me that I'm seeing? The woman staring back at me *looks* like me. Yet, at the same time, she's different.

Short mousy hair brushes the top of her shoulders. An obscene amount of blood stains the pale skin of her face. Above all, her eyes mark the greatest difference. Mine are green and blue while hers are opaque and black.

Soulless like the monster I fear I'm becoming.

Time speeds up, causing the fragments to fall to the ground in an ear-splitting heap. All but one lay motionless at my feet, and I fumble backward as it moves toward me. It rises into the air as if it's weightless, the surface expanding until I'm looking at myself in a full-length mirror.

My reflection and I stare at each other for what seems like an eternity until I find myself questioning which one of us is real. The madness I constantly feel myself slipping toward—one toe always dipped in its dark waters—calls out, beckoning to me through the hush. It takes on the voice of the man I heard before, haunting me with the familiarity the sound triggers within my heart.

"Wynter," it calls.

The soundproof bubble surrounding me bursts, forcing me back into the only reality I know.

My eyes scan the crowd of soldiers. The same expression covers each of their faces, and I realize they must know who I am. I suppose I expected it. With everything the State's done, with everything I've done, it should come as no surprise that my reputation precedes me.

They stand their ground with their weapons raised, ready to attempt what so many before them have failed to do.

I wait for it.

I hope for it.

The sound of gunfire explodes throughout the city. Dust clouds the air, and I hear the faint tinkling of bullet shells as they litter the ground.

I breathe in as the pressure rises up to take over.

My feet push me forward, and I feel the outpouring

of energy that acts as my barrier. Muffled cries of pain resonate behind the overpowering commotion. Bodies fall with a loud thud as they pile up before me.

It's over within seconds. Every part of me is still as I stare off into the nothingness, waiting for the murky air to clear. In the meantime, I consider what I've done, making sure to keep everything at a safe emotional and mental distance. I think about how fast it went, and how it was so easy.

How it's always so easy.

A surprised breath catches in my throat when I hear a faint whimper. My defensive reactions kick back to life, but as I turn, I'm held in place by the sight of the soldier kneeling in the dirt.

In many ways, he reminds me of that young Enforcer. Seizure-like tremors cross his hands, causing him to drop his weapon to the ground. His entire body shakes as he lifts his arms in surrender.

"Please . . ." he mutters.

A single tear slides along his dirtied cheek. As it does, the faint flicker of my humanity responds.

The vision hits me like a flash of lightning, placing me in a new scene of destruction. Everything is ruined. There are no people. No lights. There's only me.

Me . . . and him.

I scrutinize the man, trying to make sense of why he seems so familiar. I must know him. Otherwise, why would I be seeing this?

The stranger meets my gaze, and an emotion I can't comprehend in my inhuman state burns in his eyes. Something tells me I might not want to understand it.

A few stray tears rush down his cheeks, and a single utterance expels from his lips a moment later.

"I'm sorry, Wynter."

My heart clenches at the sound of his voice, but the scene around me reverts to the death-filled battleground before I have the chance to react. Blinking away the vision, I lock eyes with the soldier still cowering on the ground. His expression lights up with hope, but I can't give him what he's asking for. I can't give him anything except the one service I was created to provide.

"Please . . . ."

In spite of my desire to spare him, I only hear the voice from my vision when he speaks. It beats through my head like a raging drum, haunting me.

Taunting me.

A flush of anger shoots through my body, and my head shakes in wild jerks as my hands dart to my hair. My fingernails dig into my scalp as if I'll be able to make sense of my crumbling sanity by doing so. As if I'll be able to manage my thoughts and end this madness, once and for all.

Irregular, shallow breaths pour from my lungs as I peer into the eyes of the soldier at my feet. Except, it's not him I'm seeing. It's the man.

I see his face.

I hear his voice.

My fingers grip my skull even harder, and the pressure climbs up my throat like vomit. The anger follows behind it until I can no longer hold what I'm feeling at bay.

I stare at him, but there's nothing I can do to stop my emotions from taking over. As I focus on his face, seeing only the man from my dream, I allow them to destroy what little humanity I have left.

A strangled gasp parts my lips as I grit my teeth. "Get out of my head."

The soldier's eyes widen in the exact moment I snap his neck.

FIVE

THE DOOR TO MY QUARTERS slides open in a blur. I dart through the gap, flinching at the sound of the lock clicking back into place behind me.

My breathing is heavy.

Panicked.

I try to focus on the room, but I'm blinded by hysteria. Similar to a wildfire sweeping across arid terrain, every nerve ending in my body screams, protesting the foreign sensation. Sweat bubbles from my pores, sucking the black bodysuit to my skin. My hair frizzes from the sudden extreme heat overwhelming me, and my lungs constrict until I can barely breathe. My heart races, hammering against my ribcage. Convulsions roll through my limbs as the sensory overload becomes too much to bear.

It took everything I had to maintain composure on the journey back here, although, I doubt my performance was convincing in any way. Even Richter's assistant seemed to sense that something was off—I could tell that by her unusual silence and the hurried manner in which she left me here. Her avoidance was for the best. I was and still am like a ticking time bomb, ready to explode at any moment.

Now that I'm alone, I can no longer contain the crippling frenzy that overtakes me.

My hands press against my mouth, muffling my screams. Paranoia and frustration rip through every part of me as my mental faculties unhinge, piece by piece, threatening to abandon the humanity I'm always so close to losing.

Aware of my surroundings, I peek over my shoulder at the security camera in the corner. The red light on the side blinks every few seconds, watching me as usual.

A violent spasm runs through my hands, and as I look at my shaking fingers, it becomes clear that I won't be able to hide this. Dr. Richter will find out. He'll *know*.

He probably already knows.

Another flash of heat swallows my body, turning my stomach. Throwing myself forward, I clutch the sink and turn the tap until the welcome mist of water pummels my face. In spite of its cool touch, the heat remains—consuming me in the same way as the budding madness consumes my sanity.

What is this feeling? I wonder.

What's happening to me?

My eyes lift to the mirror, and for a fleeting moment, I'm surprised to see that the glass is still intact. Trailing my gaze along its unbroken edges, I come face-to-face with the woman in its reflection. That peculiar captivation I felt before now seems magnified, drawing us together.

Seconds turn into minutes, but no matter how long

I stare at her, I can't find the similarities between us. I only see a stranger. An imposter who wears the same face I do.

Her lips curl at the corners. An unexpected sense of alarm fights its way through my brain, coming to the forefront of my mind the instant her deranged expression fills my field of vision. My body leans toward the mirror as I examine her face, wondering what she could possibly know that I don't.

As if in response to my unspoken question, a familiar image flashes once through my thoughts. I see the man from my dream again. From my vision.

From what I'm beginning to suspect may actually be a memory.

It's the same as it was before—the two of us standing alone together amidst destruction and ruin as the world collapses into chaos. Tears coat his dirt-stained cheeks. His lips whisper my name.

"Wynter," he breathes.

Static. The picture contorts, springing back in front of me a few seconds later. Everything is the same, except the distance between us is smaller now.

Static again.

Closer.

Static again.

Closer.

"Wynter . . ."

I try to take a step back, but my body has gone rigid. A shiver crosses my skin as my heart pounds in double time, suffocating me with its merciless repetition.

My eyes fix on the man's face.

Who are you? I want to ask him. *Why do I keep seeing you?*

But no words escape my lips.

"Wynter."

Closer.

"Wynter."

Closer.

I squeeze my eyes shut. Pressing my hands over my ears, I shake my head in an effort to escape his voice.

A weak plea dribbles from my lips. "Get out . . . get out . . ."

"Wynter . . ." he breathes again.

"Get out!"

Somewhere in the very background of consciousness, I notice the door to my quarters fly open. The air catches in my lungs as the abrupt sound of it pulls me back to reality. Spasms rock my body despite my best attempts to keep still.

I can sense him before he even speaks, just as I can feel the surge of anger as it flows through his veins, exploding from his throat in a fiery eruption.

"What the hell happened?" Richter shouts at me.

I don't turn to face him. Instead, I reach out to the nearest wall for support, suddenly exhausted by the events of the past twenty-four hours.

My voice is flat when I finally answer him. "They're all dead, aren't they?"

His footsteps resound off the concrete floor— ominous stomps that carry the weight of my inevitable punishment along with them. His vile warmth presses up against my back, but I resist the urge to recoil from him.

"The enemy has indeed been eradicated." His words are an eerie purr in my ear, and the rage behind them grows more noticeable with every breath. "However, perhaps you could explain why you also slaughtered the Enforcers that were sent in after you."

Without thinking, I glance over my shoulder to face him. Disbelief takes hold of me, spreading through my entire being. The Enforcers are only sent in once I've done my job. They secure what I destroy—I never even cross paths with them except for our initial landing. So, surely I couldn't have done what he claims.

"I, personally, couldn't care less," he says. "But, you see . . . my superiors *do* care. They are not pleased with that little display of yours."

Peering down at my shaking hands, my eyes dart in a manic fit between them.

That's not possible. I'm in complete control. I couldn't of—

The memory of what I've done rushes through my body like a chill. I see it all. I see it again as if it's happening now.

Could I have killed those people without even knowing it?

Without realizing it?

Turning away from Dr. Richter, I work to suppress my confusion—unwilling to let him notice my lapse in control and afraid of what will happen if he does manage to see it.

The distance I've gained in the past few moments shrinks as he takes a frightening step forward. He puts himself in front of me—our bodies so close that goosebumps prickle my skin from a combination of disgust and panic. His fingers graze my chin, tilting my face until I'm forced to meet his awaiting gaze.

If there's one thing about him that I admire, it's his ability to read people.

Especially when they're hiding something.

"I'll ask you again," he growls in a low voice. "What happened back there?"

My thoughts surround the soldier before focusing on the man I keep seeing in my head. They both pleaded with me, although, I can't help feeling they had very different reasons for doing so.

Swallowing the growing lump in my throat, I choke out a raspy breath. "I just lost focus."

Dr. Richter drops his hand. He moves back to widen the berth between us as his eyes search my face for the obvious lie. I look away, hoping he won't see it.

"There's something you're not telling me."

I tighten my trembling hands into fists.

"There isn't—"

A high-pitched squeak escapes my lips when his hand wraps around my neck. He throws me back against the nearest wall, causing black spots to flicker across my vision the instant my head slams into the concrete. I try to breathe, but my lungs refuse to work.

The words spit through his clenched teeth as he snarls like a vicious animal. "Don't toy with me!" His fingers continue to crush my throat.

I gasp for air, helpless beneath his touch, despite the power raging inside of me. As he leans in close, I glimpse the sick pleasure in his hooded stare. There's no doubt that he's enjoying every second he gets to watch me squirm.

The breath from his next words touches my lips with the heat of fire.

"You are insignificant," he breathes, "and if you can't do the job, *I* will do it for you."

His eyes fix on the metal collar surrounding my neck. Another warning. One I'm willing to bet he's prepared to act on. The trouble is, I have no way of knowing if it's an empty threat or if what he's implying is actually possible. With the way the collar functions, it wouldn't surprise me if he programmed some sort of puppeteer feature into it. It would've been foolish of him not to. If you choose to create a monster, you need to have a way to maintain dominance over it, and such an attribute would give him that power.

Besides, Dr. Richter is the type to have a backup plan.

Still, regardless of how much I hate him—how much I despise his very existence—I don't want to find out if he'll live up to those threats. I'd prefer to do whatever the State tells me to do than deal with the alternative, which I'm guessing is why he hasn't already acted on his warnings. He enjoys asserting his dominance over me, and truthfully, I'd rather live with my actions than let him violate me any more than he already has. At least this way, even if I am a murderer, I'm also more than just a lifeless marionette being pulled by her strings.

My expression seems to be enough to convince him that we've reached an understanding. His grip on me loosens, and my body crumples to the floor as he takes a step back.

Clutching at my neck, wheezing breaths pass through my lips, pounding against the inside of my bruised throat. A grimace distorts my face, and looking up, I watch Dr. Richter as he straightens his glasses. His hands glide along the front of his coat, smoothing out any wrinkles, and his demeanor is calm as if the past few seconds never occurred.

In an impassive voice, he says, "See that it doesn't happen again." He then moves away from me, making for the door.

My fingers prod at my tender skin. My jaw locks, grinding my teeth together. A number of emotions overwhelm me in this moment, but the thought of how pleasurable it would be to kill him is what consumes me.

I think of him on his knees, begging me for mercy.

I think of myself, denying him that very kindness.

The deaths I've caused over the past few years are meaningless in comparison to what his would be. I was aware of what I was doing when I took those lives, and yet, I felt nothing. I simply did what I had to do.

Killing Richter would feel good, and that wouldn't be nothing to me. Plus, it would be so easy.

All I would have to do is snap his neck.

The door to the room opens, and I only have a fleeting instant to decide whether or not to act.

Kill him here.

Kill him now.

Forget everything else.

In the end, I do nothing. My eyes trail after his looming figure, watching with bitter disappointment as he retreats into the hallway. The door closes behind him, reminding me of my failure and leaving me alone.

A deflated feeling washes over my body as I tell myself why I haven't killed him a thousand times before, and why I never will.

The reality is, without Richter, there's no cure. Without Richter, there's no control. As much as I loathe him and the State, I fear the thought of what this disease can do to me even more.

My fingers move to touch the collar around my neck. A peculiar sensation flips my stomach, turning my attention to a lingering thought that's been bothering me for a while now.

I may do what Richter asks for the sake of control,

but I also know there's another reason for this. There's a reason that doing what he wants is important. There's a reason control is important.

Closing my eyes, I breathe in. The idea of it plagues me, scratching at the back of my brain.

For the first time in so long, it feels as if the memory of why I'm really here is trying to return to me. The problem is, at this moment, I can't remember what that reason is.

With a heavy sigh, I lean my head back against the wall. Annoyance tears through my body, forcing me to acknowledge the growing cause of my unease. Pushing aside the thought of control, and of whatever it is I'm trying to protect, I'm finally allowed to face the far more menacing reason for my submission. It's something I've refused to admit, mostly out of shame, but now that I've laid myself bare, there's no going back.

I have to accept the truth, regardless of what it is.

My lips tremble as I come to the daunting realization that I crave this power. Once I was weak, but now I'm strong and invincible. The knowledge of that is like a drug racing through my system, and it fills me with an aching need, even in spite of the horrific consequences of my every action. It's why I don't fight back against Dr. Richter. It's why I do his bidding, even if I don't agree with the outcome.

I don't enjoy killing. I don't enjoy being this abomination, and the truth remains that I'd rather die than be his puppet for another day. However, as long as I'm alive, the pull of this power is irresistible, tempting me in a way I can't ignore.

Inhuman.

Emotionless.

Powerful.

A monster.

They're all pieces of a jigsaw puzzle that make me what I am. I can't avoid the truth any longer. Besides, it's as Dr. Richter always says.

Control comes at a cost.

SIX

THE ARMORED TRUCK HURTLES FORWARD, bouncing over every possible bump in the road. My back collides with the metal interior more than once, making it difficult to focus on anything other than the roughness of our journey. The Enforcers accompanying me remain still in spite of our jarring transport, and their motionless stance makes them appear more like statues than living people. The only movement that gives away their unease is the occasional flick of their eyes—no doubt watching me for any sign that might indicate another meltdown.

At least, that's what the rumors are calling it.

I keep my gaze fixed ahead, staring at the wall across from me. My fingers graze the black leather and mesh panels covering my thighs, my nails tracing small, unconscious circles as they scratch against the fabric. The sound is hypnotic, lulling me into a calming state not all that different from sleep. My vision goes hazy as I lose myself to its depths, allowing my thoughts to wander.

Considering what happened the last time I was

sent out on a mission, I should be concentrating on the battle ahead. Instead, I find myself dwelling on the past. Particularly on the events that have transpired over the course of the previous month.

Following my accidental mass slaughtering, Dr. Richter pulled me from combat to run tests on my collar and ensure there weren't any faults that may lead to a more permanent loss of control. Control that we've both worked so hard not just to achieve but to maintain.

I was out of commission for five weeks in total—an inconvenient length of time to the State who, for once, have had to fight their own war instead of expecting me to do it for them. They still took the information they needed from me to pre-empt potential attacks, but in terms of my other abilities, I was sidelined. Of course, when Richter couldn't find any problems with the collar, he had to reinstate me. His superiors demanded that I return to active duty, and he had no plausible excuse not to comply.

This mission will be my first engagement since then.

I recall my brief exchange with him prior to leaving this morning—no more than an hour ago. As I approached the group of Enforcers waiting for me by the back entrance of the DSD, he pressed something small and hard against the palm of my hand. Looking down, I saw a communicator identical to the one I had discarded.

"Try not to lose this one," he said.

I could sense the irritation behind those words, but there was also a level of strain there as if he was concerned about the upcoming battle. As if he was concerned about me.

I'm well aware that wasn't the case. It was never me

he was worried about—it was his position within the hierarchy of the State. After what occurred on my last mission, it's not surprising he seemed nervous about the possibility that it may happen again. Then, of course, there's the other obvious consideration.

What it might mean for him if I don't come back.

"Make sure to take the offered transport this time." In a threatening voice, he added, "That's not a request."

I nodded in acknowledgement but remained silent. Our eyes locked, sending a shudder along my spine, and desperate to put distance between us, I turned to scurry away. However, before I could take a single step, his hand clutched my upper arm. With an aggressive jerk, he yanked me hard against his body—pulling me close until our faces were only an inch or so apart.

"Don't disappoint me," he hissed in my ear.

As I peered up at him, the tension hanging between us was almost tangible in its intensity. The sensation, which bordered the fine line between terrifying and unbearable, only subsided when he released his grip.

Moving out of his reach, I hurried toward the open doorway, for once finding the escape of war appealing. With every footfall, I could feel his eyes burning into my back—watching me right up to the moment the doors of the armored truck clanged shut behind me.

The hard metal siding smashes into my shoulder as the tires speed over another bump. The impact pulls me back to the present, redirecting my train of thought to the upcoming mission. In spite of my calm and collected exterior, I feel anxious. Or as close to that as I'm able to comprehend in my current state.

I try not to think about it, focusing instead on the varied noises around me. Straining my ears, I pick up on the hum of rubber finding traction against the tarmac, the roaring sound of the wind, and what sounds like shouting. The truck begins to slow, alerting me that we've once again arrived at the airfield.

The vehicle skids to a full stop, and within seconds, the doors swing open with a metallic screech. A beam of light assaults my vision, blinding me in the time it takes to raise my hand. Blinking away the glare, I watch the Enforcers' silhouetted bodies as they disembark, disappearing, one by one, as the heavy soles of their boots stampede across the ground. The sinister sound echoes through the interior of the truck, driving me out before it has the chance to consume me.

As I step down into the dirt, a profound revulsion tears through my body. My lips purse, forming a tight seal around the nausea that threatens to spew across the pavement. My heart rate increases in response to my sudden disgust.

Around two dozen Enforcers stand at attention beside the truck, spaced apart evenly in a set of straight lines. My eyes follow along their perfect formation until I spot the last of them at the base of the loading ramp. Facing each other, their raised arms meet in the middle, forming a path to the awaiting helicopter.

They never move or look up, but that isn't what disturbs me. Instead, I'm unnerved by the mocking salute—much like the one Dr. Richter gave me at the DSD all those weeks ago—that suggests we're on the same side.

As if I chose to be here.

Was this his idea? Another way to remind me that I'm property of the State and can never fight against him, no matter how much I might try to?

It takes every ounce of self-control I can muster to prevent myself from reacting to this degrading spectacle. That's what he wants, after all. What he thrives on. The pleasure of knowing he's won.

The thrill of finding yet another way to parade his power over me.

Swallowing my pride, I push forward. My feet never falter as I pass beneath the overhanging canopy of arms, and my expression is calm to show how little this insult affects me. Still, I breathe a sigh of relief once I emerge from the pathway.

For the first time since I became the State's puppet, I find myself feeling eager to board the helicopter. Sprinting up the loading ramp, my movements are rushed and agitated as I lower into my usual seat at the front of the cargo hold—just a few feet behind the cabin. My eyes drop to the floor when the Enforcers file onboard, filling the empty space.

The buzzing hiss of straps tightening and the soft click of belt clasps reverberate through the metal interior. Considering my proximity to the cockpit, I can also hear a muffled voice announcing that we've been cleared for departure. The deafening drone of the rotors drowns out all other sound.

Leaning back, my lungs expand as the ground beneath us disappears. My stomach flips on itself in response to the sudden weightlessness that surrounds me, although I wonder if there's something more to what I'm feeling.

Ever since my unconventional examination with Dr. Richter, things haven't felt quite right. The dreams, the hallucinations, and the visions have continued, leaving me with a nagging impression that I'm missing something important.

But what?

Without any idea what to look for, I'm once again

faced with that deflating uncertainty. The sensation is draining, and I shake my head in an effort to rid myself of it—determined to spend at least a short while in peace. My eyes glaze over as I stare at a nonexistent point in the air, trying hard not to think. Fatigue washes over me, encouraging my mind to empty itself of every thought, every memory, and every inclination to see the future.

Gradually, I feel the mental shift into a different level of consciousness—somewhere between sleep and awake where nothing and no one can touch me. I abandon the unusual distress I've felt over the last month as well as my anger and hatred toward Dr. Richter, even if only for just this moment.

I have no idea how much time passes as the serenity of this trancelike state relieves me of the demanding burden on my shoulders. I give into it, no longer aware of the Enforcers or even the sound of the thundering rotors as they carry us farther away from who I used to be and closer to who I was always destined to become.

"Project W. A. R.," I hear a familiar voice whisper to me.

My voice.

Lifting my eyes, I half expect to see my distorted reflection again, much like I did in that dream. Instead, I find myself back in the cargo hold amidst the noise and crowded bodies heading for war.

A tired breath expels from my lungs as the last of the fleeting daze leaves my body. Reality rushes back to me, bringing my discarded emotions and the awareness of my surroundings along with it.

A soft tickling draws my attention to the inside of my wrist. Following the sensation, I glimpse my fingertips brushing across the skin, tracing a pattern along a jagged protruding line in the flesh.

I never noticed the scar before. Raising my arm, I bring it closer to my face. However, the proximity does nothing to remind me how I got it.

In a hesitant movement, I elevate my other hand, and I'm surprised to see that it's trembling.

Steadying myself, I carefully drag my fingernail along the length of the damaged skin. Fragments of memories lying dormant in the depths of my mind explode to the surface in response to my touch, engulfing me in a single vision.

First, I see a large shard of broken mirror slicing into my naked and scarless wrist. Deep crimson-colored blood pools from the wound as my growing nausea grips every nerve ending in my body.

The vision then changes, transporting me to a dank and musty room where I can only just make out the bleary figures standing in front of me. I feel myself swaying. Looking to the floor, my eyes fix on the puddle of red drowning my feet.

A blinding light pulls me away. My body feels heavy, and I get the distinct impression that I'm asleep—or close to it. Someone is leaning over me, but the shape of their silhouette is all I can see.

A woman's voice calls my name.

A loud gasp flies from my lips. The straps of the harness tighten around my chest, holding me in place when I jerk forward. Labored breaths fill the air around me as my heart begins to race. Beads of sweat dot my forehead and upper lip.

Despite the unsettled bout of nerves wreaking havoc on my system, I'm aware of the concerned expressions hiding beneath the Enforcers' helmets. They exchange glances—clearly unsure what to make of my outburst.

Taking a deep breath, I cast my eyes around the cargo hold. Spotting movement, they land on one of the Enforcers. Specifically, on his gun, which has been repositioned to face me.

A lump blocks my throat as I blink in quick, nervous bursts. A voice in the back of my head is screaming for me to compose myself, but an unrelenting bewilderment suppresses it. What's even worse is the familiarity revolving around each cryptic image that lingers in my brain. It torments me, causing my distress to re-emerge.

Calm down, I tell myself. *You have to calm down.*

My lips suck in a sharp lungful of air, and yet, I feel breathless as if I've just been punched in the stomach. I try to move, but everything is still—slowed to the point where time appears to have frozen altogether. The sounds cease until even my breaths are nothing more than faint echoes lost in the background of consciousness. A sudden image in my head blinds me.

My heart clenches.

My eyes widen.

I watch in horror as the gloved hand slackens, dropping the iron-cased ball to our feet. The impact resounds in my ears as it bounces twice across the floor.

Clink.

Clink.

All at once, the universe reconfigures itself, and time shifts to double speed in a bid to return us to the present. My movements seem sluggish as my head turns toward the loading ramp. Panic rushes through my veins, but it hardens into ice, weighing me down into my seat. My fingers fumble with the straps of my harness, desperate to unfasten them in an attempt to prevent what's about to happen, but my body is leaden.

I reach out, even though there's nothing I can do to stop it. I saw it too late.

Now everyone here will die.

"Grenade!" I begin to scream.

The explosion tears through the back of the helicopter before my warning has the chance to prepare anyone for the outcome.

A loud ringing clouds my ears as the straps break apart. A cry of pain breaches my lips as my body slams hard into the metal wall opposite from where I was just sitting. Red emergency lights cast an eerie glow through the cargo hold.

My fingers grip the nearest seat, using what strength I still possess to keep myself from slipping. The air forms a sort of vacuum, making it difficult to breathe as it devours everything around me, sucking whatever it can grab hold of through the newly formed hole.

My eyes blur as my vision doubles, and vomit rises in my throat as the helicopter loses control. Loud sirens blare through the damaged interior as we descend in a fiery spiral toward the ground.

Unsure what else to do, I hoist my body into the seat and strap myself in, preparing for the inevitable likelihood that this won't end well. My fingers grip at the sides as I clamp my eyes shut.

A wave of panic tears through my brain because, for the first time in years, I don't know what to do. I should've seen this coming sooner. My job is to look out for attacks and prevent them, not sit back as they happen right in front of me. Above all, I feel confusion. How did this even happen? There's no way this was an accident—State-issued grenades are designed to avoid any chance of misfiring, so that leaves only one possible outcome.

One of the Enforcers set it off on purpose.

Instead of wasting my time trying to comprehend the motive behind this attack, I focus on how I can stop us from crashing. I've never had to use my powers for this sort of thing before. Can I even do it? Should I even attempt to? If I don't and we crash, if I don't and I die, the State will no longer have their weapon.

That alone is worth the cost of a few lives, isn't it? Then I would no longer have to be this monster. I wouldn't be forced to submit to Dr. Richter and help the State in this pointless war.

Then, I would finally be free.

My eyes remain closed as I submit to my chosen fate, willing it to happen quickly. The pressure increases as we spin out of control.

I do nothing to stop it.

The alarm continues to sound, and the red lighting that accompanies it shines through my eyelids, reminding me of the blood I saw in my head earlier. The thought of it throws me.

What about answers? Don't you want to know? I ask myself. *Don't you want your memory back?*

I consider these questions. Of course, I want them back, but I want something else even more.

Answers.

Memories.

They're a small price to pay for freedom.

Not like this, I answer.

Not like this.

A calming warmth envelops my body, making me feel at peace. My eyelids twitch as I sense the approaching moment zooming toward me. I shift forward, ready to embrace it. However, through the chaos, the blaring alarm, and the unavoidable death that awaits the others who have managed to survive the explosion—I hear the one thing I could've never anticipated.

"Wynter."

My eyes dart open when I hear my name, the sound of it clear despite the deafening funnel of air.

Squinting through my blinding shock, I peer up to see an Enforcer positioned in front of me. His face is hidden behind his helmet, but I'm able to recognize him as the soldier who turned his weapon on me before.

I stare at him, taken aback by the familiar tone of his voice and impossible ability to stand while the vortex rips at everything around us. Unaffected by the intense pressure, he takes a step toward me. I only vaguely register the magnetic clang of his boots.

My eyes examine his shadowed figure, locking on his left hand where the pin from the grenade hangs off his finger. The air fails to reach my lungs as my brain searches for a memory to help me make sense of this moment. Nothing reveals itself except further confusion, and I don't have time to use my power to find out his motives or who he is. My fate from this point on is unknown, and his every footstep is a countdown to an end I'm unprepared for.

My lips part to speak, but before I can utter a single word, he raises his gun and pulls the trigger.

SEVEN

A SHARP PAIN HAMMERS AGAINST the inside of my head as my body fights to regain consciousness. At first, the bright light is so intense that I shy away from its excruciating glare. Regardless of my resistance, it continues to reach for me, stroking the skin on my face until I have no choice but to give in.

Without hesitation, I open my eyes, but for a long while, my sight remains crippled. My vision is fuzzy as if everything is covered with an opaque film, and what I can make out looks strange and distorted. Still, in spite of my temporary impairment, I'm able to register the square box of a room that surrounds me. Concrete walls and a reinforced steel door cage me in while a surveillance camera watches me from the top left corner.

I breathe in, tasting the stale air as the smell of it hits my nostrils. It's not pleasant by any means, but it is familiar.

It takes less than a minute for me to realize I'm underground. The thought makes me feel somewhat claustrophobic, although I'm at a loss for why. I'm not even sure how I recognize this place. Perhaps it's just the heaviness of the stagnant air affecting me.

A constricting sensation tightens around my lungs, almost as if something large is sitting on my chest. I take another deep breath as I blink several times and wince as my brain pulses in savage thuds against my skull. My fingers twitch as my hand lifts, but when I try to move, nothing happens.

My eyes flick with a cautious glance toward my lap, and a knot twists my stomach when I see the thick metal shackles around my wrists and ankles—holding me to a chair in the middle of an otherwise empty room.

I pull against the restraints, but as to be expected, they don't budge.

An exasperated sigh trickles in a loud breath from my lips.

I don't have the energy for this.

My head snaps up when the steel door screeches open. A middle-aged man stands in the unobstructed entryway, gazing at me with a curious expression sprawled across his weathered face. It reminds me of how Dr. Richter once looked at me—back when I first arrived at the DSD.

I stare at him, searching for motives. For answers.

For anything that will explain where I am and what they want with me.

A subtle smile pulls at his lips. I should be alarmed by it. Instead, I find it calming as the expression reignites that vague feeling of familiarity.

Before I can comprehend the muddled thoughts clouding my brain, a younger man charges headfirst into the room. His feet plod in angry steps across the floor, closing the distance between us until he's standing in front of me. With a suspicious glance at his hands, I regard the chair and sizable gun in his grip. When I look up at his face, something inside of me responds—giving off a very clear impression of recognition.

He releases the chair, dropping it with an ear-splitting thud against the concrete. Taking a step back, he meets my gaze, and as our eyes connect, a single menacing look reveals his distrust. I can practically feel it like a fire against my skin.

Cocking an eyebrow, I redirect my attention to the middle-aged man. He approaches the empty chair now, seemingly unaware what I'm capable of. If he does know, he must have a death wish. Either that or he doesn't realize how easy it would be for me to kill him, with or without the restraints.

He dismisses his subordinate with a wave of his hand. I feel the younger man's disapproving stare but keep my eyes trained ahead, evading his heated gaze. The door closes behind him with a deafening clang.

A number of minutes pass in silence. The older man watches me, but I remain mute—determined not to make the first move.

Crossing one leg over the other and straightening in his seat, he finally breaks the hush. His gruff voice cuts through the silence like a knife.

"Hello, Wynter. My name is Rodrick Nolan."

A blank stare crosses my face. This is usually the part where I would be expected to introduce myself, but considering he already knows my name, I fail to see the point.

He clears his throat. "We've met before. Do you remember?"

I maintain a neutral expression, keeping my lips sealed together, even though I'm screaming on the inside. The feeling of madness that has threatened to consume me time and again rises up once more, wrapping around my throat to suffocate me.

My eyes trace over his features. There's a warmth to his tanned, wrinkled face and the wild facial hair covering his cheeks in pale blond, almost white, tufts. Still, I can't escape the fact that he reminds me of Dr. Richter.

I avoid his question, instead asking one of my own.

"Where am I?" I breathe.

"A safe place." His tone is non-threatening.

I tilt my head, narrowing my gaze as I try to determine the unspoken reason behind why he brought me here.

Wherever here is.

"You'll forgive me for feeling a bit shocked right now," I grumble, "but maybe you can tell me how I'm still alive."

I can sense his heart rate quicken as he leans forward in his seat. Resting his elbows on his knees, his hands clasp together in a firm, intertwined lock. His thin lips downturn as his expression becomes drawn.

"You've been extracted."

The words resound in my ears, and my eyes widen as a number of images explode inside my brain. I see the helicopter. The explosion. The red lights flashing around me, so reminiscent of blood.

It all happened so quickly that I couldn't do anything to stop it.

The man's voice prattles on, becoming nothing more than an indistinct sound in the backdrop of my thoughts.

Extracted . . .

What the hell does that even mean?

Shaking my head, I try to focus on what he's saying, but it takes a great deal of concentration to hear. I only manage to pick up on one piece of his rambling speech.

"We've been working for quite some time to get you away from the State, and the opportunity finally presented itself."

My eyes dart up. "And what opportunity was that?"

Reeling back in his seat, his expression suggests that he's surprised by my question. "To rescue you, of course."

A sarcastic huff erupts from my throat. "You call murdering at least two dozen Enforcers and nearly killing me in the process a *rescue*?"

"I understand our method might've been a bit extreme," he admits, "but please understand. Getting to you was a real challenge, considering your level of security."

I think of the Enforcers. Not only the ones who were taken away in the explosion but the ones who had more than likely met their demise in the crash.

How many people will continue to die because of me?

An involuntary sneer disfigures my lips, and I'm overcome with the urge to laugh. This man's planning. All those deaths. Doesn't he even realize how futile this is?

"If you know so much about my security level, then you must know the lengths the DSD will go to. You're foolish if you think rescuing me was a good idea," I murmur.

As he relaxes back into his seat, an amused smile

twists his face. "If you're referring to that little collar of yours, you can put your mind at ease. It's been taken care of."

A chill of dread crosses my skin.

"What do you mean, it's been *taken care of* . . . ?" I whisper.

The idea of strangers tampering with the device my powers have become reliant on frightens me so much I can't even put it into words. I react to his every breath, fearing his impending answer.

"I mean that we've dislocated the tracker," he says. "From what I can tell, they never put one back in your wrist. So, unless you have another chip implanted elsewhere, the State won't be able to find you."

A tremor rocks my body. "Do you have any idea what you could've done?"

He lets out a loud, somewhat agitated sigh. "Nearly twenty-four hours have passed without incident. I think we would know by now if control was an issue."

My eyes widen in response to his words. How much do these people know about me? Enough, obviously, to grasp the inner workings of my collar. Still, none of this makes sense.

A few moments pass without either of us speaking.

"Who's we?" I finally manage.

The man—Rodrick Nolan—looks back at me in confusion.

"You keep saying *we*," I clarify. "Who exactly are you referring to?"

A cracked fingernail scratches against the whiskers on his chin. "Well, I believe you're already acquainted with the man who got you out. An old friend of yours by the name of Jenner Rhodes."

My last moments of consciousness before waking

up here return to the forefront of my brain. I remember the Enforcer who stood in front of me. The one who said my name while chaos devoured everything else around us.

"You mean the one who shot me," I correct him.

A flash of hesitation ignites in his eyes. He nods his head, feigning embarrassment, although it's easy to see that the expression is forced.

"The bullets were replaced with tranquilizer darts." He falters, taking a deep breath. "Believe me when I say that we never intended to harm you."

The silence returns like a fog, crowding the empty room. Nolan's chest rises and falls, and my body is unmoving as I wonder what he must think of me. If the extraction was intended to be a rescue, he obviously isn't working with the DSD. And yet, one question remains.

Does he see me as a human being?

Or am I only here to be used just as I was by the State?

My eyes squeeze shut, and frustration courses in a venomous rush through my veins. I'm growing tired of my disjointed memories and being treated like nothing more than a pawn in some game. I'm so used to Dr. Richter at this point that I'm not even sure if I can believe what Nolan says. It may be a trick—a ploy intended to gain my trust.

I think back to those final few minutes in the helicopter. I imagine the Enforcer standing in front of me and the voice that spoke my name.

If my rescuer is an old friend . . . then why can't I remember?

Dropping my eyes, I stare at the floor, attempting to gather my conflicting thoughts. After a moment, I glance back up. My eyes fix on the man in front of me, searching his face for answers.

"You're not with the State."

"No," he agrees. "I'm not."

Suspicion arises within me. It's common knowledge that everyone is either with the State or they choose to support it out of fear. Those who don't fall into another group. If he's not with the State, then there's only one option left.

PHOENIX.

Our heads turn at the same moment when the sound of raised voices penetrates the door. I stare at the slab of steel, willing myself to make out the jumbled, overlapping words.

Less than ten seconds later, the door bangs open—revealing the commotion on the other side. All the air rushes from my lungs when I see the man standing in the doorway.

Blond hair.

Hazel eyes.

Disbelief grips my entire being as I'm brought face-to-face with the image in my head. I've been exposed to it so many times now that, for a moment, I doubt what I'm seeing.

The man, on the other hand, has gone ashen with shock. His eyes widen, and although he doesn't speak, I can tell from his expression what he must be feeling. The relief on his face is extreme and apparent, suggesting he's never been happier to see anyone in his life. At the same time, it's reserved—almost as if he's worried that none of this is real.

Nolan jumps to his feet, putting himself between us. "This isn't the time—"

The man ignores him and moves into the room,

taking a step forward without any noticeable concern for his own safety. I watch him, taken aback by the flustered emotion in his gaze. It latches onto my very soul, growing in intensity as he reaches out to touch me.

"Wynter," he breathes.

The confusion I've been feeling attacks me from all sides, hitting its peak and overtaking my every thought.

"Wynter."

I hear his voice in my head. I see his face. I see his tears. Memories, no doubt, attempting to resurface.

The recollections stampede in a circle through my mind, assaulting me but never taking hold long enough for me to remember a single thing of value. They simply dance along the outskirts of my memory, taunting me.

I only manage to grab hold of broken fragments.

I recall his hands against my skin in the dreamlike touch of a forbidden moment together. I see his lips pressing against mine as I hear his voice whisper my name.

"Wynter . . ."

It's too much. My body convulses in response to the buried memories as a terrible pressure builds up in my chest, growing to the point where I can no longer contain it. Until I can no longer prevent the madness that's been threatening to take over.

My mind channels that energy to the shackles holding me in place, and within the span of a second, they're clattering in a loud bang against the floor. In the next breath, I'm launching myself out of the chair and using all my mental strength to pin him to the wall. I throw my body forward before anyone can stop me, gripping my fingers in a tight lock around his throat.

My words cut through the air in a shrill scream. "Why do I keep seeing you?"

His eyes stare back into mine, but he doesn't appear to be afraid. I tighten my hold, determined to get an answer.

"Why?" I ask again.

Instead of speaking, his lips turn up in a smile. The blatant lack of self-preservation in his gaze is alarming. A single tear begins to trail along his cheek, confusing me even more.

My entire body goes still.

Why? I wonder. *Why does he affect me like this?*

I peer into his hazel eyes, searching their depths. At the same instant, I focus on my broken memories, desperate to understand the gaps in my life that are becoming more evident with each passing second.

Before I get the chance to discern anything helpful, a cruel darkness washes over me. Black spots dot my vision as something hard slams into my skull, and a searing pain spreads from the back of my head, dragging me to the floor.

As unconsciousness takes hold of me, my fingers slacken, releasing their grip on the man's neck.

EIGHT

SLOWLY, I COME TO, PULLED into waking by the distant sound of dripping water. The rhythmic tempo is like a metronome in my ear, repeating the same words over and over.

Wake up.

Wake up.

My eyes flutter open as the rest of my body curls inward, wincing in preparation for the onslaught of light. I relax when the blinding glow doesn't affect me.

Glancing up, I turn my gaze to the bulb hanging overhead. The glare burns into my retinas, but for some strange reason, I don't feel the need to look away. The touch of the light is warm. Yet, it never truly reaches me. It's as if I'm only half-present in this place—dangling in and out of existence.

I cock my head, wondering why that is. Everything here appears real enough, and to an extent, it even feels familiar. In many ways, it reminds me of that peculiar dream I experienced at the DSD. The globe. The computer. That familiar voice.

The memory of what happened since then surges

back into my brain. Above all, I remember the blond man from my dream and the face that now haunts my every waking moment.

My fingers tingle as I recall the feel of my hand around his throat.

Lifting my arm, I risk a gentle touch to the back of my head, applying pressure to the exact spot where the object that caused my unconsciousness came in contact with my skull. Although the pain is gone, the recollection of how I got here is crystal clear.

I take a deep breath as the pieces fall into place, allowing me to recognize what this is. What it has to be.

A dream.

The instant that single word enters my thoughts, the door in front of me unlocks with a grinding click. My eyes fix on the growing gap as the steel creaks across the floor, and my body tenses in anticipation as I wait to see someone peek through the opening. The seconds tick by, but no one comes.

I rub my fingers across my wrists where the shackles were bolted. I can still feel them there, holding me in place, even though they're now nowhere in sight. Taking a deep breath, I rise from the chair, being careful to remain as soundless as possible. I make my way toward the doorway, casting a quick, cautious glance into the corridor before pulling against the handle.

Despite the fact that I'm aware this is only a dream, I'm still somewhat astounded to find the hallway empty. As I look down the length of the passage on both sides of me, my eyes trail along the network of pipes connected to the ceiling. The muted but harsh lighting reflects off the walls where a faint sheen of moisture covers the concrete. My damp and musty surroundings fully convince me that I'm underground.

A rush of déjà vu washes over my body, making me dizzy with the weight it presses onto my brain. I shake my head to clear it, but I'm unable to make sense of the jumbled images flooding my thoughts.

All the while, I can hear that metronomic dripping. The sound is louder now that I'm out of the tiny room, but I have no way to tell which direction it's coming from. Straining my ears, I listen for its source—hoping I'll discover why I'm here if I locate it.

Instead, I pinpoint the faint whisper of a voice. A siren chanting my name, beckoning me to come find it.

A soft gasp escapes my lips as my heart begins to race. The familiarity of the voice is powerful—more so than anything I've ever felt before. Taking full command of my body, the sensation makes me a prisoner to its every whim.

Without question or hesitation, I follow the distant calls. The lights above me blink with a sinister gleam, and my breaths are deafening in the otherwise complete silence. Near the end of the corridor, multiple passages branch off from my current path. I linger in the crossroads, unsure which one to take.

The voice reappears to guide me through my confusion.

It croons, *"Wynter . . . ."*

My heart stutters, but I don't waver. Following the sound of my name, my steps are hurried as I move through the deserted hallways. The entire time, I'm steered by the voice as well as by the faint repetitive dripping.

"Wynter," it says again.

The voice's pull is so enticing. So warm. A desperation to find the person it belongs to overwhelms me, and without thinking, I pick up the pace. My feet stumble forward until I'm practically running.

It reaches for me once again as I pass a corridor on my right. Looking up in response to its summons, my gaze lands on a male figure standing at the distant end of the passageway. He's too far away for me to make out his face, but I know without a shred of doubt that he's the one who's been calling me.

As soon as I step toward him, he disappears around the corner.

"Wait," I breathe.

My feet carry me onward, and I never stop to consider what I'm doing or where I'm being led. I follow the silhouette through the underground maze without fail, only just catching a glimpse of him every time I turn into a new pathway. Regardless of the distance between us, he keeps urging me forward.

The voice grows louder with each step I take, and the recurring echoes of my name creep closer together until I'm swallowed by endless whispers—consumed by the deluge of sound entering my ears. Keeping my eyes set ahead, I cling to the illusion that I'm on the verge of catching him.

"*Wynter,*" he beckons.

His voice leads me around a corner, but I stop short almost at once. Every inch of my body freezes. Breathing in, my eyes lock on the large metal door in front of me.

As I take a step toward it, a small puddle of water pooling on the floor distracts me. The familiar dripping returns, drawing my attention to a crack in the pipes hanging overhead. I watch the drops as they fall, one after another, hearing the cryptic sound of their reunion.

Everything about it reminds me of blood.

My eyes spring up when the door squeals open. Propelled forward by the still unclear reason behind why I'm here, I place my palm against the steel and give it a firm push. My fingers tremble as the apprehension and anticipation of the moment collide. Although I don't feel fear, what I do experience isn't that far off.

My knees buckle, and my ears ring as I walk over the threshold into the room. As soon as I step inside, my eyes land on the figure closest to me.

Rodrick Nolan.

He sits behind a metal desk with his arms crossed over his chest. The gesture matches the sullen expression etched into his face, and his forehead creases when his lips twist into a disturbed sort of grimace.

Following his gaze, I'm unsurprised to see the blond man is here as well. It dawns on me that he was the figure guiding me through the halls, calling my name, and leading me to this room.

They take no notice of me, but that's to be expected.

After all, I'm not really here.

"This was a mistake." Nolan's knuckles turn white as his hands ball into fists. "You saw it for yourself. She's dangerous."

The younger man glares back at him, anger brimming on the surface of his eyes like tears. "She's not dangerous. She's confused."

Confused?

Nolan releases a tired sigh. A sympathetic expression contorts his face, and when he speaks, his voice is soft and paternal. "She's not the same person anymore, Ezra."

My heart seizes in response to that name, cutting off the blood supply to the rest of my body. A swelling lump in my throat blocks my airways, and for many long moments, I feel as if I can't breathe—as if I'm drowning in a wave of unrelenting uncertainty.

The man—Ezra—shakes his head in furious denial. "I refuse to believe that."

My brow furrows as I scrutinize his face. Why is he so adamant about this? Why does it matter to him or to anyone else here? I'm nothing to these people.

Nothing except maybe a threat.

A pounding ache drills through my head as my brain tries and fails to make sense of what I'm hearing. It ties itself into knots, eager to piece together the fragments that have been gradually forcing their way to the surface.

Together, the visions, dreams, and hallucinations have formed a path of breadcrumbs, leading me to this moment.

So, what have my scattered memories been trying to tell me? Taking a step forward, I lean in close, hoping the two men might provide the answer.

"I'm not sure if she's even human anymore, and I don't think you should be so quick to assume she is," Nolan drawls in a reprimanding voice. "I don't think I need to remind you what she's capable of."

My lips purse, forming a tight seal.

What does *he* know about what I'm capable of? What does *he* know about my powers, about what I've been through, or about what made me become this way?

A darkness flashes across Ezra's eyes. "I know I can bring her back."

"No," Nolan growls. "She's too unpredictable. It's not a good idea to keep her here."

I flinch when Ezra slams his fist on the table. My gaze trails along the curve of his jawline, noting the visible tension behind his every strained word.

"That wasn't part of the deal!"

Nolan's chair groans with relief as he rises to his feet. Pressing his fingers against the steel surface of the table, he shifts forward, looming over the younger man. The movement seems to cast a shadow across the room.

"The deal was that we'd get her back. I never promised to let her live."

"She's one of us," Ezra says, standing his ground.

Nolan's expression changes when he hears those words. It's as if the compassion he displayed before was only for show, and he's now peeled away the mask, revealing the true nature hiding underneath.

"She was with us for less than a month," he scoffs. "She doesn't owe us any loyalty, nor do we owe it to her. Besides, you know the other Heads only agreed to her extraction because of who she is." He pauses for a moment, taking a deep breath. The sentiment that breaches his lips is a mere whisper. "I know that's not what you want to hear, and I'm sorry about that. But you're a smart kid. You know this is much bigger than us."

"She just needs time," Ezra pleads. "Think of what she's been through. She'll come around, I know it."

Nolan lets out an exasperated sigh. Straightening up, he scratches his chin before pointing an accusatory finger in the air between them. A physical warning to coincide with his verbal one. "You have one week to prove that to me. If I'm not convinced of it by that time, or if she loses control again, I'll shoot her myself. I'll do what has to be done . . . even if she is Freston Reeves' daughter."

My eyes widen at the mention of my father.

The one constant in my life.

The one memory I refuse to let slip away.

A shudder passes through my body as I release a choked breath. The room around me fades into the background, replaced by the sudden visual torment of my past. It displays in front of me like some sick re-enactment.

I see the blood.

My father's face.

"I'm sorry, Wynter."

Static overwhelms the picture, interrupting the memory when Ezra's voice enters my ears. The sound brings me back to the present, grounding me.

"Thank you," he whispers.

Without another word, he makes for the door as if taking Nolan's assent as a sign of his dismissal.

He closes the distance between us, and for a split second, I swear he can see me. Our eyes connect, and my heart falters as I await the moment when his future and my present will intersect.

Instead, he passes through me as if I don't even exist. The sensation leaves a foul heaviness in my gut, and the feeling only worsens when I hear Nolan's voice pulling us back into the room.

"Ezra."

Pausing in the open doorway, Ezra's hand grips the metal frame as he casts a surprised look back over his shoulder. His eyes are youthful. Naïve even. Nolan's, on the other hand, are the polar opposite. Aged, wise, but above all, dark.

"Don't make me regret this," he threatens.

NINE

MY EYES OPEN, REACTING AS if I've been awake this whole time. Cautiously conscious instead of asleep. Lost in a daydream rather than what it really was.

However, asleep or not, there's no mistaking what I saw. There's no mistaking that it was real—a moment in time outside of the present. Outside of myself.

A moment that I was allowed to look in on.

I remember everything I saw with an alarming clarity. The long hallways. Nolan. The man from my dream.

Ezra.

The desperation on his face. The anger in his voice as he tried to defend me. Although, for what reason, I'm still not sure.

Then, of course, there was the mention of my father—the most confusing aspect of everything I witnessed. How do they know him?

What does he have to do with this?

I try to swallow, but my mouth has gone dry. My entire body aches, and the agony in my head impairs any attempt at rational thought. The unavoidable pain I managed to escape in my unconsciousness now rushes back to me, reminding me that—in spite of my powers, and in spite of Nolan's remark suggesting otherwise—I'm still human. At least in the physical sense.

My eyes peer at the light above me, causing the brightness to stab like knives into my temples. The back of my skull throbs, and each pulse only contributes to the splitting headache crushing my brain.

I try to lift my hand, but the freedom I experienced in my dream is now lost to me. Glancing down, I expect to see myself shackled to the chair again. I am, but I can tell there's something else holding me in place. Something internal.

I try to wiggle my toes.

Nothing.

I try to shift my fingers.

Nothing.

I can't flex a single muscle in my body.

The people here must've had the foresight to prepare for the limitations of using restraints. I showed them how easily I could break them before, and now they've taken steps to ensure my captivity.

In a very Richter-like move, they must have injected me with a drug. That's the only explanation. A paralytic of sorts, I assume. Whatever would stop me from getting free, or as Nolan put it, losing control again.

I lift my gaze to the camera in the corner of the room. The red light on the side blinks every few seconds, similar to the one back in my quarters at the DSD. They're watching me, I know it.

Someone is *always* watching.

What do you want with me? I wonder.

I consider saying something—anything to distract me from the constant surveillance, or at the very least, get answers for it. Licking my lips, I ready myself.

The metal door squeaks open the instant the right words materialize in my throat, silencing me.

A male figure appears in the entryway, drawing my attention. His head of messy black hair peeks almost childlike around the steel, and his every movement as he lingers on the threshold is wary and unsure. Fixing his blue eyes on my face, he builds up the courage to speak.

"Wynter?" He whispers my name as if the word is fragile and likely to break.

Confusion overtakes me as I scrutinize his face. He seems unnerved by my expression.

My eyes fail to blink as I await his next move. For a brief instant, his feet stumble back, but he stops short, catching himself. Finding his resolve, he clears his throat and repositions his stance in the doorway. A moment later, he walks into the room with both hands raised in surrender.

"I just want to talk."

There's a trace of despair behind his tone, which is mirrored in his eyes. Like a wave of sadness, it floods his gaze, growing more prominent with each second he waits for me to answer. It's as if he's drowning. As if my voice is the only thing that can save him from the emotions threatening to suffocate us both.

The way he stares at me says so much more than words ever could.

Silence settles between us again, but the plea burns in his gaze like an open flame. His lips don't move. However, his soundless words beg me not to turn him away.

I consider him as my eyes trail over his features. His face is familiar to me, and just like with Ezra, I'm certain I recognize him.

But from where, I don't know.

Lowering my eyes, I nod my head. Or, at least, I try to. My neck is stiff from the paralytic weighing down my body, and it's difficult to breathe, let alone move. Wondering if he even noticed the gesture, I peek up at him. A smile twitches at the corners of his lips.

His body language gives off a certain eagerness as he approaches me, but at the same time, he appears to be restraining himself. Why, I can't be sure, but I have a feeling it has to do with the fact that we're no longer alone.

A sharp scraping sound cuts through the air as a second chair is dropped in front of me. My eyes lock with those of the figure standing beside it—the same man who accompanied Nolan before. He peers down at me, and his upper lip curls in disgust as his fingers tighten around his gun.

I stare at his hands, unfazed by his blatant and unexplained hostility toward me. My gaze follows the curve of his weapon where I glimpse a streak of red smeared across the metal.

Blood.

My blood.

Glaring at him, I tense my jaw. "So, I have *you* to thank for the headache then?"

The black-haired man ushers my assailant from the room before he can answer. Perhaps he pre-empted this confrontation or maybe he's afraid I'll have another outburst if he doesn't separate us. Regardless, the younger man relents. With a sneer, he storms out of the room without a backward glance.

The steel door closes, leaving us alone. Taking a deep breath, the black-haired man tugs on the chair, turning it around so he's straddling the seat. Resting his arms across the back of the frame, he lets out a sigh before plopping his chin on top of his overlapping hands.

An awkward hush fills the room as I wait for him to speak. I can feel him watching me, searching my face as if he's trying to figure out the answer to some unvoiced question. His eyes penetrate me on a level I'm not comfortable with, making me feel uneasy.

"It's good to see you," he finally says.

I resist the urge to tilt my head, aware how inhuman it makes me seem. Pressing my lips together, I listen to his voice play on repeat through my thoughts. My brain suddenly registers where I recognize it from.

"You're the one who shot me," I realize.

He winces as if my words are a physical slap. Running his hands through his mop of hair, he fixes his eyes on a random spot on the floor. He looks embarrassed, ashamed, or maybe even overwhelmed by the guilt of what he's done.

In a hurried breath, he splutters an apology. "I'm sorry, but it was the only way to get you out."

I remember what Nolan told me before. About the extraction.

About an old friend of mine being the one responsible for my rescue.

"How'd you do it?"

I don't expect him to answer, and from his expression, neither does he. Regardless, the words flow from his lips with ease.

"Inside help," he admits. "We have someone who was able to tell me how to infiltrate the airfield. Who knew how to pass me off as an Enforcer. There were only a limited number of people who even knew you were going to be there, so we couldn't just barge in. We needed the security clearance." He blinks a few times, clearly unsure how much to tell me. "Anyway, this person provided the gear I'd need to extract you, and we just customized it to suit the circumstances."

Thinking back, I remember finding it odd how balanced he was. Considering the unstable environment following the explosion, his body should've been tossed around like a leaf. In spite of that, he was in full command of his movements. Each step landed where he wanted it to, holding him to the floor as everyone else was pulled to their deaths.

I also remember the strange clang of his boots. The way they stuck to the metal.

Like magnets, I think.

"And after?" I press him.

He stares back at me but says nothing. His gaze reveals a conflicted confusion, and for a moment, I contemplate whether or not to push him. Ultimately, I decide that I need to know. I need to make sense of this. No matter what he says.

"I remember everything that happened before you shot me. There was no way we were getting out of there alive. So, how did we?"

My voice is soft, a mere whisper flowing around us like wind. The discomfort on his face is visible in the slight twinge of his cheeks, but in spite of that, he answers my question.

"The State's transport helicopters are equipped with ejector seats in the cockpit. I'm not proud of what I had to do to get us to them . . . but I couldn't turn back."

I'm tempted to ask him what he means by that.

Trouble is, I already know the answer. If he was willing to use a grenade in a fully occupied cargo hold, chances are, he was also willing to put down a pilot or two to get out of there.

The question is . . . why?

Why was extracting me so damn important?

"The entire operation was risky," he adds, "but it was the only way to get to you with how well-guarded you were."

I linger on those last words. He's right. I was well-guarded. So, how did they manage it? How was he able to get to me when the State took every effort to ensure I would never even be seen?

Curiosity gets the best of me, and I'm keen to know more. A jumble of questions rises in my throat, dancing across my tongue.

Before I manage to utter a single syllable, the man's voice breaks the hush once more.

"To be honest, I'm surprised it worked."

My eyebrows scrunch together as he hunches forward. His expression seems reluctant more than anything else—almost as if he doesn't know how to phrase his next words. As if he's nervous to ask me the one question we both know is impossible to avoid.

"I thought for sure you would've seen me coming," he murmurs, "and that the State would've known about our plan. That *you* would've known."

My eyes widen, but I suppress what I'm feeling by removing all trace of emotion from my face, so I appear as distant and uninterested as possible. A survival tactic I've mastered over the years I spent with Richter.

I huff out a short breath to steady myself.

"It doesn't work like that," I whisper.

Bewilderment skews his features. I waver, trying to

determine the best way to explain it. Or should I even explain it at all? Should I tell him? Should I reveal the deeper workings of my condition to these people?

His blue eyes glow with anticipation. I'm unsure why, but the sight of them unsettles me, causing that vague feeling of familiarity to resurface. By this point, déjà vu is my permanent mental state.

I drop my gaze to break the inexplicable connection between us, focusing on the floor.

"Sometimes these things come to me, but usually not until the last minute, and only if they're occurring in the immediate vicinity. If I want to know before that, I have to be on guard and at least somewhat aware of what I'm meant to be looking for. Otherwise, I'm as blind to it as anyone else." Pausing to shrug my shoulders, I sigh with exasperation when they still refuse to move.

"The price of full control." My words are nearly inaudible. "I should've been on the lookout, but I was . . . *distracted*. By the time I sensed what was going to happen, it was already too late."

Peeking up at him through the curtain of dark lashes lining my eyes, I'm taken aback by the intrusive way he looks at me. The expression on his face is indecipherable, but then again, maybe I'm not meant to understand it.

"I-I'm sorry," he stammers. "It's just . . . you're different than you were the last time I saw you. Before, you couldn't—"

"Control it?" I interrupt.

He nods his head but says nothing.

For a while, we don't speak. When he swallows, his throat shifts, and the sound is like a blaring drum in the tense silence. His eyes glaze over, assaulting me with the visible sadness hiding in their depths.

"What did they do to you?" The words part his lips in a shaking breath.

I can't handle the unbearable anguish in his gaze. The pity and remorse there are remnants of emotions I have no way to fully remember.

I turn away, desperate to escape them.

His eyes burn into my soul with the intensity of fire while piercing my heart with the rigidity of ice. The paralysis holds me in place, making me witness the full force of everything he's feeling, even though I want nothing more than to run away from it.

A shiver crosses my skin as the hush pulls me closer to the boundary of madness. Feeling the need to break it, I say the only thing I can think of.

"Why?"

His brow furrows as he straightens in his seat. Reeling back, he searches my face, but as the seconds pass, I realize that he doesn't grasp what I'm asking.

Over the course of the past few moments we've spent together, there's been one question on my mind that I've been unable to make sense of. It's plagued me since this conversation began, and now we're brought full circle—forcing me to finally reach out for an answer.

"If you were certain that I knew, that the State knew about your plan . . ." I hesitate, distracted by the dark desolation in his eyes. "Why did you risk your life to go through with it . . . ?"

His lips contort into an exaggerated grimace, and his body doubles over, cowering as if he's afraid. Or worse, as if he's in pain.

A far too familiar guilt bubbles up beneath my skin, but I push it back before it can break through the surface.

After a long moment, he sits up straight. Clearing his throat, he rises to his feet, and shoves back the chair, causing a faint scratching to echo around us. The sound is eerie, much like the friction hanging in the room.

He lingers for a few seconds, only meeting my gaze when he speaks. "Because you're my friend," he breathes.

My heart reacts to those words, creating an unsteady chorus of panicked palpitations.

My eyes follow his steps as he heads for the door. For some reason, I see myself reaching out to him. I can feel something deep inside of me grabbing hold and pulling him back—desperate to keep him here just a little bit longer.

"Jenner."

He pauses in the doorway. His movements are slow as he looks back over his shoulder, delayed by a peculiar combination of hope and fear.

Licking my lips, I whisper, "That *is* your name, isn't it?"

A veil of darkness crosses his gaze. Nodding his head, he proceeds over the threshold—keeping his eyes fixed on mine up until the last possible moment. The sound of metal resounds in my ears as he closes the door between us.

TEN

I SHIFT ON THE LEATHER sofa, twiddling my thumbs as my feet tap against the floor. Lengthening my neck, I lock my blank stare on the wall in front of me, trying to blink only when I absolutely have to. The whole time, all I can hear is my mother's voice ringing in my ears as a constant reminder.

"It's not polite to fidget."

Even at a young age, I knew she really meant, "Don't do anything to draw attention to yourself. Be still. Blend in."

Considering everything that's happened, I suppose I now find the subliminal warnings she ingrained in my childhood a bit odd. She went to the effort of teaching me how to survive in our twisted society, but at the slightest hint of trouble, she abandoned me to the very world she was meant to protect me from.

Father, on the other hand, was different. He never would've left me. He never would've given me up.

Not like she did.

I feel his warm hand brush a strand of hair behind

my ear, and with a single breath, his soothing voice melts away my hard exterior. The coldness of our world put it there. It turned me into just another mindless drone.

But where our world was ice, my father was fire.

I glance up at him. His lips twinge at the corners as if attempting to smile, although the expression doesn't reach his eyes. At the last instant, he suppresses it, and I watch as it dies away, fading into nonexistence like a smothered ember.

"You don't realize it," he says, "but your life has been robbed of many things, Wynter. Many wonderful things that you'll never have the opportunity to know or discover."

I stare at him in confusion, taken aback by the look of pity on his face.

"Like what?" I ask him. The voice that expels from my mouth is young and childish. Me, when I was no older than four years old.

He seems to consider me for a moment. In the silence, I observe how tired he looks as if he's been bearing a heavy weight on his shoulders. Making up his mind, he extends his hand toward me.

"Come. I want to show you something."

I place my tiny hand in his without hesitation. He pulls me to my feet, and I'm overcome with a strange burst of excitement—an emotion at complete odds with my otherwise reserved and monotonous life.

My eyes follow my father's every movement, more curious than ever to know what he plans to show me. However, just as I take a step, he extends an arm to hold me back. Turning around, he drops to his knees. His hands clasp around my shoulders, and I can feel the importance of his next words in the quivering of his fingers.

He leans forward so our eyes are level. "Now, Wynter, I need you to promise me that you won't mention this to anyone. Whatever I tell you or show you, no one can know. Not even your mother." He hesitates. "*Especially* not your mother."

His words should've alarmed me then, but they didn't. I trusted Father. He never needed to explain himself to me.

In my small, high-pitched voice, I express my dedication to him. "I promise."

Those words echo around me, warping into static that distorts the entire memory—replacing it with the one moment I can never escape.

I stand in the middle of the brightly lit hallway, staring at the puddle of blood where it seeps into the carpet. Lifting my eyes, I see a hand reaching out to me. The skin on the knuckles is torn and bruised with streaks of red crusting into the hair coating the adjoining arm. A lump swells in my throat, choking me until I'm forced to acknowledge the person the hand belongs to.

My father.

However, he's not reaching for me—not as I am now. He's reaching for her. My younger self. The six-year-old child who had no choice but to witness this. Who had to watch as her father was beaten to near death.

I can hear her screaming, just as I can see her visible distress as she tries to comprehend why any of this is happening. Her cries cut off, and suddenly, there's no one else here but me, facing this on my own.

Because, despite the passage of time, I still am that little girl.

Still alone.

Still helpless.

My eyes widen when my father meets my fear-filled gaze.

"I'm sorry, Wynter."

I watch him as my body freezes in place, reclaimed by the ice and coldness I was named for.

My lips begin to tremble. I want to intervene, but there's nothing I can do. I'm as powerless as I was then, and the awareness of it gnaws at me more than any of the atrocities I've committed since.

His hand stretches toward me one last time, his mouth shaping my name. The pained expression on his face reminds me of the words he spoke before. The promise he made me keep.

My eyes brim with tears. "I didn't tell," I try to say.

I repeat those words as I collapse to my knees. My heart caves in, dragging me to the floor, and the agony that's been tearing me apart from the inside now streams down my face in a wave of grief.

"I didn't tell . . ." My cry of denial saturates the air.

Lowering my gaze, I hide my face in my hands, unable to look at him any longer. My chest heaves as my lungs constrict, suffocating my very existence with the emotions I would rather forget.

A soft gasp rushes from my lips when a hand touches my shoulder. Glancing up, I prepare to see my father—hoping, deep down, that he's managed to escape his fate. Instead, I see the blond-haired man from before.

Ezra.

He takes a step toward me and brings his face close to mine. I can't move or think, too bewildered by his proximity. His unexpected, yet tender, movements only feed my confusion, and my heart races when he brushes his hand across my cheek. His thumb trails in a gentle curve along my lower lip, wiping away my tears.

"Please don't cry," he whispers.

My eyes shoot open, waking me from the dream. The bright light above impairs my vision, and when it clears, I'm startled to find that I'm not alone. Ezra kneels in front of me, the distance between us minimal, just like it was only seconds earlier.

"Come on," he says in a hushed voice. "Let's get you out of here."

I'm too stunned to speak. The last time I saw him in person, I had my hand around his throat, so why is he here now? Isn't he afraid I'll try to hurt him, or worse?

The conversation I saw between him and Nolan enters my thoughts. I remember what he said. How adamant he was about every word.

Perhaps it's for that reason, I don't fight against him.

A wary shudder runs through my body as he waves a small device across the arms and legs of the metal chair. The shackles pop open with a hollow-sounding snap, releasing me within seconds. Ezra leans forward, wrapping his hands around my waist to help me to my feet. Our eyes meet for the briefest of moments, but neither of us speak.

I'm surprised by the abrupt change in my response toward the man beside me. Before, I wanted to hurt him and get answers by any means necessary. Now, however, my dream has cast a cloud of doubt over this entire situation. I'm confused, just as he said.

My feet stumble forward. Despite the fact that the paralytic is no longer raging through my system, my body is still weak as a result of whatever these people injected me with. Although it makes me uncomfortable, and I'm not accustomed to such intimate behavior, I have to rely on Ezra to help me across the room. I lean against him as each awkward step takes us closer to the door.

When we make it there, I almost trip over an unconscious body in the hallway. Stepping around the figure's unmoving legs, I peer into the face of the young man I encountered earlier. His gun lay on the floor beside him, the blood from my head wound still visible on the metal.

I glance up at Ezra, but he doesn't look back at me.

Our pace through the corridors is quick and urgent, growing more hurried as my legs regain their strength. I never ask him where we're going. Maybe I don't want to think about the future for once, or maybe I don't really care. As I learned at the DSD, anything is better than being chained up like a dog.

After a few more twists and turns, we come to a flight of stairs in a decrepit part of what I'm now certain must be an underground compound. Ezra moves to pull me forward, but my body becomes leaden, holding me in place.

"Wait." I step away from him, shrinking back against the wall. "I'm not going any farther until you tell me what's going on."

His face is half-cast in shadows, but through them, I see the way he stares back at me. I swallow, waiting for him to speak until I realize that he's the one who's waiting. At first, I'm not sure what for, but it doesn't take long for me to grasp what he's after.

Biting my lower lip, I ask the one question standing between us. "Why do I keep seeing you?"

The moments spent waiting for him to answer are agonizing. He doesn't blink once, and goosebumps rise across my skin in response to his piercing gaze. It's as if he can see straight into my soul.

Assuming I have one.

The words rush from his lips in a steady breath. They pin me in place, knocking the air from my lungs.

"Because you love me."

A flush of heat tears across my skin in a violent wave. My heart pounds, feeling as if it's about to explode from my chest. Dropping my eyes, I run a hand across my forehead—desperate to understand this.

"Nothing makes sense," I mutter.

He shifts toward me, closing the already limited distance between us. "I know you're confused," he says in a gentle voice, "but I'll help you through it."

Peeking up at him, I focus on his face. The expression I find there is overwhelming but genuine.

Still, it seems like an impossible task—a secret my brain is intent on keeping locked away. Not only from me but from everyone else. I shake my head as confusion floods my body, overpowering me more than ever.

Out of the corner of my eye, I notice his hand reach out to me. At the last second, he pulls it back.

Instead, he whispers, "It's okay to be afraid."

"Afraid?" I scoff. "I don't even know what fear is anymore."

Everything I've seen.

Everything I've done.

I don't have the right to feel fear.

Ezra looks away, but he's unable to hide the pain casting a shadow across his face. It resonates with me in a way nothing else ever has. Or ever could.

"I do," he admits. His tone is soft, muted by the emotion building in his throat.

When he glances back up at me, the sadness I find in his eyes reminds me of my father.

"I've known nothing but fear since the day you left me."

His words frighten me, igniting a powerful urge to run away in the darkest depths of my heart. I try to take a step back, but the wall behind me prevents any hope of escape.

There's nowhere to go.

Shaking my head, I choke out a weak rejection. "I'm not who you think I am."

He smiles, and lifting his hand again, he plucks up the courage to place it against my cheek. The space between us is no longer existent, and my heart rate increases further from the unexpected contact.

"You are," he breathes. "You just need to be reminded of it."

The intensity of his stare sets every hair on my body on end, and for a split second, I wonder if he's going to kiss me. My emotions are uncertain. Less than forty-eight hours ago, I was ready to kill him. But now?

Now, I'm not so sure.

Clearing his throat, he takes an abrupt step away from me and lowers his hand so that we're no longer touching. I gape at him in bewilderment. His eyes avoid mine as he turns to face the door at the top of the stairs.

"I have something I want to show you. Will you come with me?" he asks.

He offers me his hand, and as I peer down at it, I take notice of the peculiar and sudden change in his body language. It's as if he's aware of me in a way he wasn't only seconds earlier. Shrugging it off, I accept his awaiting grasp.

Our footsteps echo off the concrete in dull thuds, although the sound seems much louder in the otherwise still silence. I follow him to the top of the stairway, curious as to where he's leading me. His fingers only release mine for the brief instant it takes to push open the door.

The metal screeches across the floor as light streams through the entryway. In a reflexive move, my hand darts to my eyes, but when I peek through my fingers, I find that the glare isn't as bright as I thought it would be.

Lowering my arm, my jaw drops as I take in the late afternoon sun. It dances across the room, seeping through the moth-eaten curtains in streaks. Everything the light touches is aged and wooden—remnants of the old world that I never thought I would see. Dust covers every surface and floats through the air like a thick, timeless fog, making this moment feel even more surreal than it already is.

The floor creaks when I take a step, and a breath catches in my lungs when I feel a body press up beside me. Peering over my shoulder, I see Ezra standing there. His eyes are turned toward the window, but something about his expression is distant.

"It's an old farmhouse," he explains, answering my unvoiced question. "It hasn't been used since the State erected the walls, so it's the perfect hiding place. They wouldn't think to look for anyone here."

I can feel his eyes watching me as I drag my hand across the top of a floral fabric sofa standing in the middle of the room. I rub the dust that comes off it between my fingertips.

"Where are we?" I ask him.

He moves toward a door positioned in the corner

of the far wall, just next to an adjoining hallway. The floor groans as he walks, and I find myself tensing, worrying that we'll be overheard. We're too exposed. Someone's bound to find us here.

The State will find us here.

Ezra doesn't seem to share these concerns. Placing his hand on the doorknob, he looks over his shoulder at me. Jerking his head, he beckons me to join him.

My eyes narrow. Everything about this puts me on edge, but as the distance between us shrinks, I can't escape the stronger emotion that eclipses my fleeting doubt.

A small voice scratches at the back of my brain, telling me to trust him.

Once I'm at his side, he pulls open the door, letting in a deluge of fresh light. As he does, he utters the one answer I wasn't expecting.

"Outside."

I stumble onto the large porch in shock. My eyes graze across the beams and panels hanging overhead, following the wood as it wraps around the house, embracing the foundation.

I can feel Ezra beside me, but I don't look up at him. Instead, I turn my gaze toward the overgrown fields. The land stretches on for miles, covered in wild plant life reclaiming the earth. The landscape of neglect is in tune with the abandoned house looming over us.

Lifting my hand, I shield my eyes from the sun. Its rays are beginning to set over the horizon, and standing just in front of it, I notice the outline of a city. But not just any city—the one where I grew up.

My home.

The Heart of the State.

"This isn't possible," I gasp.

"When you left, we were forced to relocate away from Zone 7 in case the Enforcers learned of the compound."

I blink, trying to remember the events from a life that doesn't even feel like my own.

"I know you wouldn't have told anyone," he adds, "but the others weren't as confident about that. We couldn't take the risk. So, we hooked up with another sect who helped move us out here."

His words swirl through my thoughts like an unsolvable puzzle. I can't make sense of them, no matter how hard I try to.

Shaking my head, I regurgitate my confusion. "How?" I stammer. "No one leaves . . ."

"The tunnels. There's an entire network that goes on for miles, even beyond the Heart's walls. It was already set up for us."

I swallow the lump growing in my throat, feeling the extreme toll this information is taking on my brain. Why won't it add up?

Why can't I comprehend what I'm hearing?

"I don't understand how they wouldn't know about it," I whisper. "Certainly, they would've figured it out."

A small laugh parts Ezra's lips, but the sound lacks humor. I peer up at him, surprised by the conflicted expression on his face.

"You probably don't remember this, but back before you left, my brother told us that PHOENIX was never a real threat. According to him, we had actually made ourselves *useful* to the State." He winces as if the words are painful to speak. "Looking at it now, I think he was telling the truth. I think the reason we're still alive . . . the reason they never checked the tunnels . . . I think

106

it's because they never felt the need to."

My eyes widen.

Brother . . . .

Richter's face darts like a bullet through my brain.

Taking a deep breath, I watch the sunset in an attempt to discard my overpowering confusion. When I first heard Ezra's voice in my dream all those weeks ago, I wasn't sure what to think. I thought I was going mad, and truth be told, I'm still not fully convinced that I'm not. The only thing I know for certain is that I need answers. The most logical solution would be to look back, but I don't want to *see* my memories.

I want to remember them.

Spinning on my heel, I turn to face him, meeting his hazel gaze head on.

"Why did I leave?"

He looks at me, and his eyes are warm but also full of an unmistakable remorse. "To protect us. You were afraid of what your power might do to us if you stayed."

Reaching up, I grab hold of my collar. My fingers glide across the metal surface.

My breath hitches as I turn away from him, and the familiar distance I've become so acquainted with rises up between us like air. The inhuman façade I've developed over the years returns, taking hold of me once again.

At least this much makes sense. If I really do love him like he claims, then, of course, I would want to leave him. No one is safe around someone like me, especially the people I care about.

Swallowing my discomfort, I mutter the only words I can think of. "You know what I can do."

He nods his head once but says nothing.

For some unexplained reason, I become angry with him. It seems like an odd reaction to have, but of all the things I've heard over the past two days, this one unspoken admission confounds me the most.

I grit my teeth together as my hands ball into fists. "Then why rescue me?" I ask in a strained voice. Turning the full force of my gaze on him, my expression demands the truth about why this is happening.

The reality is that I'm dangerous, and he knows it. So, why?

I don't understand.

"Why bring me back if you know what I'm capable of?" Tears linger behind my words.

In spite of my outburst, his expression is calm, and I swear I can see a hint of a smile on his lips. My own lips tremble with unfamiliar emotions. Or maybe they're so devastating because they *are* familiar, and I'm simply refusing to accept that fact.

He takes a step toward me, and the heat from his body rolls off him in a wave, making me aware of the proximity between us.

It's strange. Considering what I'm capable of, right now I feel powerless.

"For the same reason you keep seeing me in your head," he answers.

My mouth shapes a number of syllables but no sound exits my throat. I struggle to find the right words, but my brain can't comprehend what I want to say.

I stare at Ezra. A heavy weight sits in my stomach as my heart pounds in savage bursts. Goosebumps prickle my skin as a hard lump lodges in my throat, choking me into silence.

I jerk my head when he moves closer to me.

Closer.

"I don't remember—"

The feel of his hand against my cheek interrupts my weak objection.

"It's okay," he whispers.

The air flows from my lungs in short, shallow gasps, making me feel like I can't breathe. My eyes widen as mere inches separate our faces, and although I try to back away, an invisible force holds me in place.

His breath is warm against my lips as he croons, "I'll remember for both of us."

ELEVEN

THE EMOTIONS I'VE LOST OVER the past two years seem to resurface all at once. I can't explain it, and I certainly don't understand it, but I know one thing for sure.

It's happening because of Ezra.

Everything I've done. Every step that I've taken. It all keeps pointing me back in one single direction. Although my memories remain distorted, it's clear that whatever humanity I possessed prior to becoming this abomination revolved around my feelings for him.

His lips are warm as they press against mine, and a familiar saltiness lingers on his tongue, causing an unusual stirring in the pit of my stomach. I may not remember the events that led me here, but I can't ignore the tiny ember that sparks back to life in the depths of my soul. Perhaps it's the small degree of humanity that still exists beneath the monster.

All the same, I feel unsure about the foreign emotions flooding my body. A strange urge jolts through my veins like an electric current, but I can't tear myself away from the detached persona I've grown so used to wearing. It's been my shield—my way of dealing with what I've done.

In many ways, it's as much a part of me now as the lost memories were before.

Releasing a soft breath, I step back from Ezra. A pained expression crosses his face, but I try my best to ignore it.

His lips glisten as they whisper my name. "Wynter—"

I hold up my hand to interrupt him. His words cut off as mine take their place.

"You have to understand how confusing this is for me."

We've come a long way in a very short space of time. Only a few days ago, I was ready to kill him, and now we find ourselves on the opposite end of the spectrum. That progression was based on two factors. First, the uncertainty instilled within me because of my dream, and second, my decision to give him the benefit of the doubt.

Unfortunately, even combined, they aren't enough. There's so much to process, and I can't do that if he's pushing me. He needs to be patient. He needs to understand that this may not happen overnight because, no matter how much he reminisces or how much he says he'll remember for both of us, we're still talking about memories that once belonged to me too.

I deserve the opportunity to try to revive them for myself.

Shaking my head, I let out an exasperated breath. "People keep telling me all this stuff I'm supposed to remember . . ." I avoid his gaze, not quite sure I want to witness the disappointment I'm bound to find there. "But I just don't," I whimper.

He shifts his weight from one foot to the other, perhaps out of discomfort or maybe because he's trying to think of something to say. It's a long moment before he breaks the awkward silence between us.

"You know we're telling you the truth, though. That *I'm* telling you the truth."

A trace of reluctance behind his words makes it seem as if he's afraid of my answer. Still, I consider him for a moment, aware of the lack of a question in his voice.

In a careful tone, I ask, "What makes you say that?"

He raises an eyebrow at me. "Would you have let me get this close to you if you thought I was lying?" As if to prove his point, he grasps a lock of my hair. His hand trails along the length of the strands until the ends slip between his fingertips.

His knuckles graze against my hip bone when he drops his arm, sending a shudder up my spine and forcing me to realize how right he is. Of course, I know he's telling the truth. I would've never given him the chance to say otherwise if I didn't. The trouble is, I'm still not sure what that means to me.

Or for my situation.

Shaking my head, I lower my eyes to the ground. "No," I admit. "I don't suppose I would've."

Glancing up, I look out toward the horizon as my hands run across the wooden banister separating the porch from the earth below. The wind nips at my cheeks as I focus on the silhouette of the city in the distance. It's surreal to look at it now—to know I'm free of the State. Free from the DSD.

Free from Dr. Richter.

Perhaps it's because I feel even more trapped than I did before, despite my liberation. My inability to remember certain events of my life is part of the reason.

Then there's the other, larger facet of this feeling. The part that lies with the collar secured around my throat.

It presses against my skin when I swallow, making its presence known with even the slightest movement. Reaching up, my fingers touch the metal, dancing along its surface as they have so many times before. As they've done since the very moment Richter locked me in this permanent shackle.

No, I tell myself. *So long as I have this, I will never be free of him.*

Dropping my hand, I recall what Ezra said to me concerning why I left.

If I did so of my own volition, I must've had a good reason, and if what he says about our feelings for one another is true, then it's easy enough to guess the cause. Is that why I feel so uneasy about being here? Is it the subconscious fear that I'll hurt him?

Or is it something more?

A loud gasp bursts from my lips as a feeling of dread turns my stomach. A faint hum carries on the wind, reaching my ears at the same instant the image of its source explodes inside my brain.

Spinning around, I grab hold of Ezra's arm. "Get inside. *Now*," I hiss.

I force him back into the house with a violent thrust and quickly follow him over the threshold. In a panic, my hands slam the door shut behind us. Before he can take a step, I shove him to the floor. He looks up at me but says nothing as we huddle beneath the nearest window.

His ragged breaths beat against my neck, and the heat from his body grows more intense as the humming becomes louder. My arm shoots out when he tries to move, reaching across his chest to pin him in place. Casting a sharp look in his direction, I bring my forefinger to my lips.

Our breathing hitches when the sound hovers over us, loitering on the other side of the window. It lingers there for what seems like an unnatural length of time, and I feel my body tighten—my instincts taking over as I ready myself for the possible fight ahead.

Ezra's hand intertwines with mine, calming the sudden blood thirst twisting my gut. Exhaling through my nose, I press against the wall, trying my best to stay out of sight.

A few seconds later, a blue light seeps in through the moth-eaten curtains, coating every inch of the room in a blinding glow. It repeats this process multiple times, scanning the inside of the house for life forms.

For me.

Several moments pass before the light disappears, and gradually, the humming dies away. When the sound is out of earshot, we both turn onto our knees and risk a cautious glance through the dirtied glass panes. Through the tattered fabric of the curtains, I notice two black machines retreating toward the Heart.

"Surveillance drones," Ezra grunts under his breath.

My eyes never leave the receding black specks. I watch them until they disappear into the shadow of the city—its very existence imposing and threatening, even from this distance. The entire time, my thoughts dwell on what information they'll report to their owner and if Dr. Richter was the one who deployed them.

"They know I'm here," I whisper.

I notice Ezra shake his head, but I don't turn to look at him.

"We don't know that," he says.

I only meet his gaze when his hand touches my shoulder. Peering up, I'm taken aback by the concerned expression on his face—by the unspoken way his eyes ask me if he's wrong. If I know this or if I'm only guessing.

Gripping his arm, I pull him down with me as I slump to the floor. He blinks a few times as I wrap my finger around the collar and lean in close until our bodies are touching.

"They can track me." My voice is steady and clear, but I can feel my temper flaring. I'm unable to suppress it when my next words breach my lips. "Did you honestly think the State wouldn't keep tabs on their precious weapon?" The statement comes out far more aggressive than I intend, but it has to be said.

Ezra needs to understand the gravity of what I'm involved with.

He shakes his head once more. "We deactivated the tracking chip." As he says this, he casts an uncertain glance at my collar. His lips curl as if the very sight of it disgusts him.

I wish I could fake my emotions to appease him, but I can't. Not when I know the lengths the State is willing to go to—that Dr. Richter is willing to go to.

Lowering my eyes, I focus on the jagged protrusion on my wrist. My fingertips caress the skin, feeling along the bumpy and awkward tissue. Although I still have no idea how I got this scar, I do know what lies beneath it—or rather what *should* lie beneath it. After all, I now realize mine is no longer there, hence why the DSD installed a tracker in my collar.

"So Nolan claims," I grumble, "but this isn't like the chips they put in our wrists. If the State wants to find me, I'm not sure you can stop them."

Turning away from Ezra, I lean back against the wall and fix my eyes on the dusty interior of the room. He repositions himself next to me.

"We'll remove the collar. Nolan said they couldn't, but we'll find a way."

His words are soft—an arrow in the silence piercing straight into my heart.

My eyes widen as I gape at him. A powerful anger courses through my veins, traveling along every inch of my body on its way into my throat. It expels from my mouth before I'm able to stop it.

"Then you may as well kill me now," I snarl.

He reels back, his expression a combination of shock and bewilderment. My cheeks flush as I close my eyes, and counting backward from ten, I inhale a slow breath—filling my lungs with as much air as possible to calm myself down.

Running my hand across my forehead, I scoop back my hair.

I know I'm not being fair to him. He doesn't know what I know, so how can I expect him to understand? I can't. At least not without spelling it out for him in the most brutal way imaginable.

I peek over at him out of the corner of my eye.

He needs to hear this.

"Don't you find it odd that I'm so different from how I was before?" I ask. "So in control?"

His left eyebrow twitches. I can see the gears working in his brain, turning my words into information he can process. I know he's beginning to grasp what I'm saying because I notice the confusion transform into fear.

Although, what I fail to comprehend is why he

doesn't know when Nolan does. Why would Nolan keep such an important piece of information hidden from the one person most intent on helping me?

"Without the collar, the control ends," I murmur. When he doesn't respond, I press him further. "Do you understand what I'm telling you?"

Clearing his throat, he averts his eyes and nods his head.

For a long time, neither of us speak. I can feel the emotions rolling off him like heat, but I can't make sense of what he's actually feeling. Unable to bear the silence any longer, I put my hands on the floor and shift my body to stand up.

The abrupt sound of Ezra's voice holds me in place.

"Richter said there was a cure."

His tone is dejected, but when his eyes lift to mine, I can see the ray of hope shining behind them. He stares at me, waiting for me to tell him that everything will be all right.

Waiting to hear me say we'll figure this out together.

"Don't you get it?" I breathe.

A sudden guilt bears down on my chest, gripping my heart like a metal vise. As if Ezra can sense what I'm going through, as if he finally understands, a similar darkness flashes across his eyes—smoldering the faint light of hope.

The guilt grips tighter.

In a dejected voice, I whisper, "The collar *is* the cure."

TWELVE

EZRA HASN'T SPOKEN SINCE I told him the truth about my collar. The truth about the cure—or lack thereof. The hope in his eyes when he mentioned it was painful to witness, but the emotion that took over when I crushed that hope was truly unbearable.

From the instant the confession slipped from between my lips, I could tell it shattered something between us that I had no way of fixing. Nothing I say now can undo the damage I did.

So, I haven't tried to.

This revelation, just like everything I've endured over the last few years, arose because of Dr. Richter's lies. His relentless need to twist the truth for personal gain, regardless of what it does to anyone else. The promise of a cure was nothing more than another falsehood, and one that we all clearly fell for.

The metal noose around my neck is the only cure I'll ever see.

I follow Ezra back through the compound in silence. There was a desperate urgency to our steps when we last walked these corridors, but now that aura of importance is gone. Instead, all we're left with is a strange acceptance—an unwilling resignation of everything I've been through and the harsh reality that Ezra has, in turn, been forced to come to terms with. With each step, it feels less like we're former lovers and more like we're criminals on our way to death row, biding the time as we await our executions.

The air between us is charged with tension. Before, Ezra made any excuse to touch me, but now he seems determined to keep his distance. He won't even look at me.

His feet drag as he walks a few paces ahead of where I trail behind him. I'm not sure what to make of this entire situation. Is it fear causing this response in him? Confusion? Disbelief? Whatever it is, one thing is certain above all else.

He isn't taking it well.

My eyes dart to his waist when a soft beeping emerges from the depths of his left pocket. He stops short, and I pause just beside him, watching his face for any noticeable changes.

Clutching his communicator, he glances at it once before cursing under his breath.

"What's wrong?" I ask.

He looks over at me, then glances down the length of the corridor ahead of us. With a nervous glimpse back the way we came, he clears his throat but still doesn't speak. An unnerving expression crosses his face, making me wary of his impending answer.

"I wasn't supposed to let you out of that room," he admits.

He appears embarrassed, although his words come as no surprise to me. The unconscious guard was proof enough that he was breaking the rules.

In an awkward murmur, he adds, "Jenner's been keeping watch for us. We both knew it was the only way I could be alone with you." He stares at me as if gauging my reaction.

Taking a deep breath, I shift my weight, unsure of how to handle such an uncomfortable silence and even more unsure of how to break it. I don't know what to say to him. I can sympathize with how he must feel, but at the same time, what about how *I'm* feeling? What about how difficult this is for *me*?

I exhale, feeling more lost than ever.

"Let me guess. They found out what you did, and now everyone is panicking because I'm gone."

Ezra runs his hand along the back of his neck. He avoids my gaze, but I don't need to see his eyes to comprehend what he's thinking. The stress taking hold of him is visible in his rigid posture, boiling beneath his skin like lava waking a dormant volcano, ready to explode at any moment.

"More or less," he says.

Shaking my head, I ask, "What'd you do to him anyway?" When a dumbfounded expression crosses his face, I elaborate. "The guard outside my door."

"Oh, *him*."

Ezra's lips pull into a devious smile, and I take a step back when he lets out a hollow laugh.

"His name's Quinn Stohler. The guy used to be an Enforcer, if you can believe it." He pauses for a moment to let this information sink in.

I picture the man's face, remembering the hostile way he looked at me. The hatred there was unmistakable, although the basis for it remains a mystery, even now.

My eyes scan Ezra's face, narrowing as I penetrate

him with my judgmental gaze. He clears his throat, and all traces of humor vanish from his features.

His tone is indifferent as he shrugs his shoulders. "I may or may not have put him in a chokehold until he passed out."

A growing irritation swells inside my body, building up in my lungs as a strangled scream. It takes every ounce of willpower to reject the foreign emotions threatening to overtake me. Biting my lower lip, I glare at the floor.

"You're going to get yourself into trouble, and for what? It's not worth it."

I'm not worth it.

Shaking my head again, I begin to walk past him, ignoring the heat from his skin where my shoulder brushes against his arm. I can feel his eyes watching me, but I don't turn back.

Without warning, he grabs my wrist. Startled by the sudden movement, I glance back over my shoulder, but I'm silenced by the ominous way he looks at me.

The ferocity of his gaze carries over into his words as he growls, "That's where you're wrong."

For a moment, it feels as if I'm staring at the sun. He's too luminous—too intense for my eyes to handle. My heart beats in fitful pulses until I find myself turning away, unable to bear the overwhelming passion lighting up his face for a moment longer.

It feels like an eternity before he releases my arm.

"We should head back." His words are void of emotion, and he says nothing else as he trudges past me.

My eyes follow his every movement, but I don't respond. Instead, I shadow his steps as we retrace our path through the corridors. This time, the hush between us is different—full of the same confusion I always find myself drowning in. It builds until I can no longer take it.

I stop in my tracks, held back by the words that expel from my throat.

"Why wasn't it you?"

Ezra wavers. Turning in place, his brow furrows, but I cut him off before he can speak.

"On the helicopter." My hands clench into fists as I take a step forward.

His breathing accelerates as the distance between us closes.

"If what you said about us is true, then why wasn't it you?" I ask.

He drops his eyes and licks his trembling lips.

"I wanted to, believe me, but Nolan wouldn't allow it. He said I was too close to the situation emotionally. I think he felt there was a chance I'd screw it up once I saw you again, or maybe he thought you'd be more likely to know what was going on if it was me there instead of someone else." Releasing a sigh of frustration, he runs a hand through his blond hair, disheveling the strands. As he peeks back up at me, he whispers, "About Jenner . . . You don't remember it right now, but he means a lot to you."

His words rush through my head, but I don't know what to do with them. I never asked for PHOENIX to come to my rescue.

I never asked for any of this.

Silence overtakes us once more as we continue through the hallways in a sullen march. In spite of the unknown message Ezra received on his communicator, we don't come across any resistance on our way back to my prison cell. It's only when we round one of the final corners that we even see another human being at all. Unfortunately for us, the person standing at the opposite end of the corridor is the last person we could hope to encounter right now.

Heavy stomps echo off the concrete as Quinn storms down the long pathway.

Ezra and I both freeze in place.

"Well, he looks pissed off," I grumble.

A part of me is tempted to say, *I told you so*, but I resist that urge as I glance up at Ezra. He shifts his body, repositioning himself so he's standing between me and the oncoming wave of anger. Sensing my gaze, his eyes meet mine.

We stare at each other as the sound of Quinn's footsteps increases in volume, bringing him closer to us. My lips part to speak, but the feel of Ezra's fingers intertwining with mine causes a soft gasp to rush out of my mouth instead.

In spite of my conflicted emotions, I don't pull away.

My eyes lock on our conjoined hands, forcing me to embrace the familiarity of his touch. It's calming as if the mere sensation of physical contact with him can provide the answers to countless questions I never even knew I had.

His thumb moves across the side of my hand, caressing it and sending a seizure-like shudder throughout my body. A memory emerges from the back of my thoughts. The recollection overwhelms me, springing out of hiding after all this time.

I see a flash of what appears to be an intimate moment between us. Our faces are close together, and my hot breath kisses his skin as I whisper against his lips.

"I love you . . . ."

A warm blush reddens my face as the blood collects in my cheeks. My heart pounds in wild repetition, suffocating my every breath.

I try to make sense of the strange ache gripping my chest, but the sound of Quinn's voice distracts me from the sensation. Snapping out of the memory, I find myself back in the present. As the ex-Enforcer barrels toward us, his words are hazy in my ears, although I can tell from his tone that they aren't directed at me.

"What the hell were you thinking?"

Ezra squeezes my hand. "I just needed to talk to her alone, away from the cameras."

Quinn's footsteps cease a short distance away, leaving only a small berth to protect us from his wrath. His eyes narrow as they dart between us.

"All that just to have a little catch-up with your girlfriend?" He nods his head in my direction as his voice raises several decibels. "She's dangerous. That's why the limitations were put in place. *You* don't get to make those calls!"

Ezra's body tenses. For a split second, he seems to grow taller, blocking me from view.

"She isn't a threat," he bites back.

"You know what she's capable of," Quinn counters. "What she's done."

Ezra's composure is beginning to crumble, causing him to tighten his grip on my hand. The tempo of the rapid pulse beating beneath his skin increases, racing up his throat in an explosion of fury.

"She didn't do it by choice!" His voice thunders around us, carrying through the isolated passage.

My eyes shift between the two men as I take a step forward, inspecting their expressions and the aggressive way they lean in toward each other. They remind me of a pair of squabbling children.

Pulling my hand away from Ezra's, I utter the three words that will put this to rest. "Yes, I did."

Reeling back, he ignores Quinn as he stares at me with an incredulous grimace. "Wynter—"

"I did what I had to do to survive." My words cut him off, stunning him into silence. He doesn't need to know that only part of this statement is true, or that survival wasn't exactly my top priority at the time. Not mine, at least.

After a few seconds, his expression changes. "Stop it," he says. "I know what you're trying to do."

There's a warning behind his words. One that I choose to disregard as a stifling impatience rips away at my chest, burrowing into the core of my being.

Unable to contain my frustration any longer, the filter holding back my true opinion snaps.

"I'm trying to point out what you're either too biased or blind to notice!"

Regardless of our history—regardless of any feelings we might have once shared—he needs to embrace the reality of the situation. If he loves me as he says he does, then he needs to accept what I've done.

He needs to understand that I'm not the same person I was before.

Moving his body close to mine, he takes hold of my arm. His grip is uncomfortable, but I don't struggle against it.

"You're trying to push me away." His tone is biting and accusatory, but he's right.

I *am* trying to push him away.

I'm not good for him. So long as I still have this collar around my neck, the people nearest to me will always be at risk—which ultimately means I will be a danger to them forever. Without the collar, the control ends, and I can't allow that. With it, I'm a threat, and I can't allow that either.

I might not fully remember my life before I became this monster, but I don't need those memories to know that I want to keep Ezra safe. Try as I might to ignore it, the desire to protect him is programmed into me, running through every inch of my body like blood. I fought against it before, but I can't deny it any longer. Not when so much is at risk if I do.

"Enough!" Quinn shouts. In a swift movement, he pulls a handgun from his belt, and the slide clicks into place when he aims it at my face. "You're coming with me."

Ezra's arm stretches out in front of my chest. With a rough push, he forces me behind him, acting as my shield.

"Lower your weapon," he growls.

A rush of dread floods my body when Quinn pushes the barrel of the gun against his head.

Enough, I tell myself.

Lifting my hand, I pinch Ezra's shoulder. He looks back at me in shock, and his eyes widen when my lips form a consoling smile.

"It's all right," I whisper.

I step out from behind him. I can tell that he wants to fight me on this—that he doesn't agree with me— but for whatever reason, he decides not to argue.

For once, he's finally listening.

We tail Quinn through the compound, following like submissive prisoners—minus the restraints. Then again, I'm sure he knows how pointless they are by now.

Within minutes, we arrive back at my home for the

foreseeable future. Quinn pulls open the door to my cell, signaling for me to enter with a violent jerk of his head. Although he must be aware that these walls have no power to hold me, I take a step forward anyway, ready to comply. At the last second, something about him holds me back.

I scrutinize his face, feeling that distant sense of recognition again. More than ever before, I'm certain that I know him.

Clearing his throat, he raises his gun. I don't feel threatened by the weapon, but I make a show of pretending I am to make this easier on everyone involved.

I head back into the cell without complaint or delay.

"Wynter."

My body freezes at the sound of Ezra's voice. Peering back over my shoulder, I find him standing in the doorway. His expression is solemn, and his eyes are fixed on the floor as if he's trying to find the courage to look at me. To face me.

When he speaks, the words spill out in a stifled breath. "I wish things didn't have to be this way."

It occurs to me how inconsiderate I've been. How unfairly I've acted when I should've tried to understand what this must be like for him.

My fingers twitch as I lift my arm, but Quinn's glare stops me from moving any more than that. Pursing my lips, I try to ignore his presence for the moment.

Locking my eyes on Ezra, I coax him to look at me.

"The people here know what I am," I remind him. "I don't blame them for wanting to keep me locked up."

"But you're not a threat to them. We both know that."

I don't respond, mainly because I don't feel as

certain of that as he does. After all, I still remember what Dr. Richter said to me—back when I was still in the hands of the DSD.

"If you can't do the job, I will do it for you."

The threat behind his words torments me even now, reminding me of the very real vulnerability surrounding my condition. I may be in control, thanks to the metal shackle around my neck, but that doesn't mean I'm not dangerous—a hard truth, which Ezra is refusing to comprehend. He's blinded.

By love.

By denial.

Maybe by both.

"Nolan will be the one to decide that," Quinn says.

Ezra and I both look at him. I take the finality of the ex-Enforcer's tone to mean that visiting hours are over, but as I take a step back, Ezra reaches through the doorway. His hand takes hold of mine, and the warmth of his skin sends an electric current racing through my body.

"No matter what happens, I won't lose you again." His words are a promise—an oath reaffirmed by his determined gaze.

I press my fingers against his.

Deep down, I find myself hoping he doesn't have to.

Intruding on this moment, Quinn moves forward to separate us.

"Time's up."

My eyes never leave Ezra's even as our hands are forced apart. As the door closes between us, I never look away, even though I'm haunted by his expression. His countenance closely mimics the one materializing in my head, overtaking everything until I'm aware of little else.

I see his face.

I hear his voice.

"I'm sorry, Wynter."

As a tear trails down his cheek, the image crumbles, falling to my feet in a mess of disjointed memories. Breathing in, a sudden apprehension takes hold of me. Blinking it away, I meet Ezra's gaze, watching his eyes glisten and feeling the stab of every emotion crossing his face as the slab of steel moves to cut us off from each other.

We may stand on opposite sides of a doorway, but right now we may as well be standing on opposite ends of the world.

THIRTEEN

THE CONCRETE WALL IS COLD against my back. I hug my knees to my chest, keeping my eyes glued to the camera in the far corner of the room. The red light on its side blinks in timed repetition, flashing in short bursts that last a second or so each. It's a sign, I'm sure of it.

A reminder that the people here are watching my every move.

A number of scenarios ramble through my head as I try to determine the best course of action. It would be easy enough to break out of this room. The only threat beyond these walls are Nolan's men, and their little toy guns don't frighten me. Still, the thought of escape doesn't sit well in my gut. Getting free of the compound is one thing, but it's the *after* that concerns me. I have nowhere to go. Where else could I go?

Back to the DSD, a small voice mutters in the back of my brain.

I almost laugh at the thought.

Releasing a strained breath, I shake my head, focusing on the other issue.

Ezra.

There's still so much that I don't understand. So many questions that need answering. The bits and pieces resurfacing and reviving the remnants of the humanity I had thought were lost for good are enough to make me second guess any notion of leaving. I can't run away. Not yet.

Not without discovering the truth.

Shifting my body, I rise to my feet. My eyes remain fixed on the camera, never once looking away as I pad across the floor. My strut is confident and determined, even though my heart is racing.

Keeping my back tall, I stop just short of where the walls intersect in the corner. Every muscle in my body stiffens as a wave of doubt washes over me. For a long moment, I do nothing but stare up at that blinking light, considering every aspect of what I'm about to do.

Inhaling a deep breath, I announce my intentions in a loud, clear voice. "I want to speak to Rodrick Nolan."

A grim uncertainty sets in, but I keep my eyes locked in position while trying to remain as still and unthreatening as possible. After what feels like a lifetime of waiting, I hear the sound of muffled voices on the other side of the door. I spin on my heel when the steel screeches open.

Quinn enters the room first, bearing the same distrusting expression I've come to expect from him by now. He aims his gun at me in warning, but I refuse to give him the satisfaction of acknowledging it. Nolan crosses the threshold behind him, and I can tell he's taken aback by my request from the way he looks at me. He almost seems excited about the idea.

Another trait that reminds me far too much of Dr.

Richter.

After an aggressive charge forward, Quinn stops in front of me. His eyes connect with mine, and the hatred within them is as noticeable as ever. He nods his head toward the chair positioned in the center of the room.

"Sit down," he barks.

A large hand takes hold of his shoulder, silencing the animalistic growl building in his throat.

"That won't be necessary," Nolan counters.

His trusting sentiment disturbs me, reminding me of the faux niceties I was shown at the DSD. None of it was real, so why should this be any different? It's just another ruse to gain my trust, nothing more. But I won't fall for it.

Not this time.

Keeping my movements to a minimum, I choose to play nice and return to the chair, even going so far as to allow the ex-Enforcer to secure restraints around my wrists and ankles. As he kneels on the floor in front of me, I observe a hint of pleasure in his gaze. Strangely enough, I can also sense something else. Something that resembles fear.

I scrutinize his face. Once again, I'm unable to ignore the odd familiarity I find there. That I keep finding there. The recognition runs through me like a flush of heat, assuring me that I've seen him before.

However, the image of the individual I have in my head is far different from the man in front of me. He's distant and callous now, but in my memory, he's one thing and one thing only.

Afraid.

Registering the difference is all it takes, and like a light turning on in my head, I remember where I know him from.

"You," I whisper. "I know you."

His eyes dart to mine, and for a brief instant, I see the young Enforcer on the helicopter. The frightened way he looked at me. The terrified uncertainty when he glanced at my collar.

I remember it all so clearly.

His reluctance.

His apprehension.

Stumbling to his feet, he takes a cautious step back. His fingers tighten around the base of the gun, and as he stares at me, I wonder if he intends to use it this time.

We both jump when Nolan slams a second chair on the floor in front of me. Settling himself on the seat, he calls over his shoulder in a sharp, commanding voice. "Leave us."

Quinn casts a final heated glare in my direction. I have no clue what he's thinking, but the frustration he's feeling carries over into his distorted expression. The silent screams of anger I imagine running through his head reveal themselves in the twisted grimace warping his lips.

Regardless, he says nothing. Instead, he does as he's told without question, a trademark of the obedient soldier he used to be.

My eyes follow his retreating figure as the metal door slams shut between us.

I glance back at Nolan, who sighs as he stretches out his arms in front of his chest. A few of his joints readjust with a loud crack, and I hear another deep breath emerge from his lungs as the seconds tick by without either of us speaking.

As if able to read my thoughts, he addresses my

unspoken question. "The methods the State uses aren't to everyone's taste. As a result of that, many have defected quite recently."

Defected?

I don't know why I'm surprised. After all, Nolan himself has admitted to having a contact within the State. It just never occurred to me that such betrayal could be widespread—at least not to the extent he's implying. I learned growing up that people are either devoted to the State or they're against it, simple as that. It's black and white with no gray area or room for argument.

Suddenly, I find myself thinking of my mother and her loyalties.

There was definitely no gray area there.

I swallow. My words rush up my throat like regurgitated food.

"And what methods would you be referring to exactly?"

Nolan examines my face as he considers my question. The entire time, a smile plays at the corners of his lips, hinting that I might already know the answer.

Shrugging his shoulders, he says, "The way they conduct warfare, for one."

My eyes fix on the door as I wonder what horrors drove away the man on the other side. I remember him on the helicopter, just as I remember the agitation in his gaze. He was terrified, that much was clear. In spite of that, I had the distinct impression that he was loyal to the State. Potential recruits had to be to become an Enforcer. The preliminary checks before entry into the program made sure of that.

So, what could he have seen that was bad enough to make him leave? To make him turn his back on the very system he once fought for?

It doesn't take long for me to grasp the deeper meaning behind Nolan's words.

"You mean me."

He doesn't confirm my suspicions, but then again, he doesn't have to. The look in his eyes is more than enough to tell me I've hit the nail on the head.

Lifting his chin, he repositions himself on the seat, staring down his nose at me as he folds his hands in his lap.

"What is it you wished to talk about?" he asks, sidestepping my accusation.

Clenching my jaw, I inhale a steadying breath.

Straight to the point, I remind myself.

"I want you to tell me how you knew my father."

The smile on his face widens, revealing a perfect set of white teeth. "I should've known you'd be eavesdropping."

The way he says this makes it seem as if he's proud— the way a parent might commend a child if we lived in a different world.

When I don't say anything, he clears his throat. "Your father and I go way back," he answers.

"Specifically?" I press.

His fingers rub across the stubble on his cheeks, concealing the lower half of his face. Still, I'm able to see the hesitation behind them.

What isn't he telling me?

Leaning forward, the words tumble from his lips. "Freston and I were the founding members of PHOENIX. This organization only exists because of him."

My eyes widen. "T-That's not possible," I stammer, trying to make sense of the numbers flashing through my brain. "That would mean the State's—"

"Barely thirty years old, yes," he says, finishing my sentence.

The shock hits me hard, confusing my already jumbled memories. It's always been common knowledge that PHOENIX was born around the same time as the State. With one came the other—they went together like twins. The State was never shy about admitting that fact since it provided the basis for the fear that kept the populace under their thumb. Complete authority through the power of oppression.

But thirty years? That would mean there are plenty of people still alive today who not only witnessed the State's rise to power but who were also citizens of the old world. People who saw what society and life were like *before* the State took over.

How can that be? How is that even possible? How would the State have been able to suppress this information and keep the younger generations from knowing about it? What power did they use to erase history from the eyes that were there to see it?

My thoughts work in circles, trying to understand this notion, but only one of the explanations in my head finds form.

"Tunnels . . ." I whisper.

Of course. Why didn't I see it sooner?

My father hid his illegal possessions in the tunnels and underground compounds beneath the city. When I was a child, it never occurred to me to wonder how he was able to conceal something as conspicuous as a piano. Now that I know his origins—now that I know of his involvement with PHOENIX—I realize how much deeper his crimes really went.

I try to wrack my brain, but I can't visualize the

place he used to take me to. It was our special secret, but the setting never mattered to me. It was the bond of sharing something with him that was ours and ours alone that left its everlasting mark on my heart.

"Your father was a good man," Nolan reminisces, intruding on my reflection. "He might've cast aside our mission, but I still considered him my friend. I was sorry to hear about what happened to him."

The memory of my father's bloodied face threatens to invade my mind. I work to extinguish the images surfacing in my head, trying my best to focus on Nolan and everything he's said.

My father created PHOENIX. This entire rebellion was *his* idea, apparently. Yet, according to Nolan, something made him leave. What was it? What possible reason could he have had to abandon what others have died to protect?

Perhaps my father and I are more similar than I thought. We both turned our backs on the people who needed us most, and while I'm aware of my supposed motives for doing so, his aren't as clear to me. I wonder if it caused a panic when he left. Did PHOENIX have to relocate out of fear that he might report them to the State like Ezra said they felt they had to do because of me?

But he didn't. I know that. His heart was stuck in the old world, so he would've never betrayed something that was so deeply rooted in it. Why else would he have risked exposing me to everything he did? He never gave up hope that the world could change. After all, I saw it there, glistening behind the sadness. So, what changed?

Why did he stop fighting?

Nolan's gentle smile is consoling, but just like with

Dr. Richter, the expression seems forced.

"I understand this must be difficult to process, but I'd like to talk about you right now. If that's all right." He chooses his words carefully, turning the conversation in the direction he wants it to go with a mastered subtlety while making it seem as if he's doing me a favor.

"What about me?" I ask.

His eyes narrow, exposing the doubt behind his curiosity. "When you were with us before, what made you leave? What made you go back to the DSD?"

For a long while, I don't answer.

My teeth bite along the inside of my cheek as I deliberate over what to tell him. Nothing comes to me. Even when I contemplate offering the truth, the specific memories that coincide with it remain lost in the muddled depths of my subconscious, clinging to their stubbornness when I urge them to resurface. It's ironic, considering that period of my life is responsible for everything that's happened since.

Unfortunately, lying isn't an option either. Nolan will never respond to my questions if I'm not upfront with his. Plus, he seems too smart for that. He'll see through any attempt at deception.

I'm left with one choice.

"Ezra told me I did it to protect everyone." My voice sounds weak as the words pass through my lips.

"You don't remember?"

My entire body tenses in response to his baiting tone.

"I remember I had a good reason," I bite back. "Good enough to do what I've done."

All the battles. All the people I've killed. As I told Ezra, I did what I had to do. I've committed atrocities

I will never be able to forget, and I will live with those deaths for the rest of my life. However long that may be.

That's also why I became what I am now—what I *had* to be. I became inhuman so I could live with my crimes. So I could push away the guilt that would otherwise undo me.

"So, you admit to being dangerous."

Nolan's voice cuts through the darkness of my thoughts, reminding me of the conversation I witnessed between him and Ezra.

"I'll do what has to be done . . . even if she is Freston Reeves' daughter."

I remember the threat with perfect clarity.

"I never said that I wasn't," I mutter.

Silence rises between us, and as it does, I study his face. I find myself wondering if he's afraid of me— if he even has the capacity to feel fear and concern, or if he just fakes those emotions when the situation calls for it. A man who wears a mask and disguises his intentions well.

Just like Dr. Richter.

"You must understand, I'm responsible for the lives of many people. I need to be certain that you won't pose a risk to them." The mask remains in place.

His whole façade irritates me because I can sense the indirect warning behind it. I never sought their intervention. I never asked for them to extract me that day from the helicopter.

I never asked for any of this.

My anger boils up, spitting out through my teeth. "If I'm so dangerous, then why are you keeping me here?"

"When Ezra first brought you to us, we didn't fully

understand the true gravity of the situation. Or your importance," he adds after a short pause. "When you returned to the DSD, and we got word of what they were planning . . . Well, we knew it was paramount that we get you back."

"Why? With the State turning their attention elsewhere, your lives would've gotten easier."

A mischievous grin pulls at the corners of his lips. "You don't know, do you?"

My annoyance continues to grow, expanding beneath my skin until I can no longer take it.

"Know *what*?" I growl.

"What the DSD was really planning to do with you."

I reel back as his words seem to collide with my chest, knocking the air from my lungs in a strangled breath. "What the hell are you talking about?"

Nolan releases a taunting huff of laughter. "Do you think we would've waited two years to retrieve you if we gave a damn about their conquest for domination?"

My heart begins to race as his voice plays through my head on an endless loop. The madness I always feel myself slipping toward reaches out for the first time in days, grabbing hold of my brain and yanking me toward the edge of my own mental precipice.

What could the DSD possibly have planned for me that's any worse than what they were already doing? This is a lie, surely.

It has to be.

"This is much bigger than you," he continues. "Didn't you ever wonder why they kept harvesting your blood?"

My lips part as a small, inaudible gasp seeps from between them. Just how much does Nolan know about me—about my time at the DSD?

An uneasy shudder runs up my spine. "Richter wanted to study it," is all I can manage to say.

"Ah, yes. Austin Richter," he scoffs. "Not exactly known for his honesty, is he?"

My heart seizes as if a hand has just taken hold of it, squeezing my only lifeline into pulp. A scream of deranged lunacy rises in my throat. If I wasn't trying to maintain my composure, I'd break these shackles and start ripping out my hair.

In a trembling breath, I whisper, "What do you want with me?"

"Simple." His head tilts forward, casting a shadow over his eyes. "I desire your help."

All at once, I grasp why I'm really here. Like the last piece of a puzzle slotting into place, the ends in my mind connect, and I see the bigger picture.

I can't believe I didn't realize it sooner.

"You want to use me against the State."

A venomous smile forms along his lips, and for a moment, I witness the real face behind the mask.

"That's the beauty of it," he purrs. "We won't have to."

I'm taken aback by his words and the malicious tone lingering behind them. I never thought I would encounter anything worse than the DSD or Dr. Richter.

How quickly I'm beginning to suspect that I may be wrong.

"Ezra told me about your condition. Well, what little he knew of it at least. The rest we learned from what our informant was able to garner from the records he had access to."

"I'm assuming this is the same informant who helped you extract me."

Nolan's eyes glow with amusement.

Breaking my gaze, he rises from his seat. I watch his every movement with careful observation, and my stomach twists with apprehension when he retreats toward the door.

He places his hand against the metal before turning to look back at me.

His voice echoes in an eerie cloud through the room. "You say you have difficulty remembering what happened before you left us. Maybe meeting him will help those memories to resurface."

His fingers curl into a fist and bang twice against the steel. The sound reverberates around me as the door creaks open. Deep breaths fill my lungs as I brace myself.

However, nothing could've ever prepared me for this.

FOURTEEN

MY EYES WIDEN AS I register the face of the man standing in front of me. His broad frame fills the doorway, casting a shadow of intimidation across the room. The fluorescent light reflects off his hair, making the peppered gray strands stand out amidst the black. His forehead shines where the glare hits the skin just below his receding hairline.

"Wynter." Nolan's voice enters my ears. "This is—"

"Wren Bilken," I breathe.

I'm only vaguely aware of Nolan's response because I'm too consumed by the inexplicable memory exploding inside my brain.

A chain reaction follows. The whisper of his name sets the gears in motion, causing my thoughts to go into overdrive and bombard me with a number of images. They dart through my head in quick succession, forcing me to remember.

I see the compound Ezra spoke of as well as the tunnel system spanning beneath the Heart. Beams of light flash along rounded walls, and the sound of waterlogged steps bounce off every surface, echoing through the passage like torrential rain. The physical recollection takes hold of me, bringing me back to that moment.

I see Ezra and Jenner.

I even see myself.

As the images race past, I also see the Magistrate's Building, along with the string of events that transpired there that night. I remember all of it. Every detail. Every moment.

Above all, I remember Rai.

The memory weighs heavily on my heart, threatening to crush me. My lungs contract until it feels like I can't breathe, and my eyes begin to burn as if hot pokers are stabbing into them—a much deserved punishment for forgetting her.

I try to move.

I try to breathe.

I try to think.

But I can't.

All I can see is Rai, hovering over me like a ghost.

Throughout my descent into madness, Nolan prattles on in the background. His words are muffled—a mere fog of sound that I'm deaf to.

Once the memories cease their relentless re-enactment, I'm able to focus on my surroundings. Lifting my eyes, I fix my gaze on Bilken. His expression is drawn and void of emotion.

For that, I hate him even more.

"She's dead because of you." I spit out the words between clenched teeth, straining my jaw in an effort to maintain my composure.

My body trembles as the battle raging inside of me claws its way to the surface, struggling to break free with every racing beat of my heart. Loathing pumps through my veins, feeding the internal conflict.

Nolan's voice dissipates the instant I speak. Out of the corner of my eye, I notice his fingers splay out, and taking a hesitant step forward, he raises his hands. The gesture is slow and guarded as if he hopes it will calm me down.

It has the opposite effect.

"Wynter . . . ."

I ignore him, keeping my eyes locked on Bilken, who finally decides to enter the conversation. His words fully break my already damaged heart.

"I assume you're referring to Raina Dorne."

My hands grip the arms of the metal chair. "Don't you *dare* say her name." The animal locked within me thrashes in a wild fit, desperate to rip out this man's throat with her bare teeth.

Bilken steps into the room, but keeps his distance, leaving a wide berth between us. As I watch him, my rage builds until I can barely retain my hold on it. My control slackens further when I glimpse his face. Of all the expressions he could display at this moment, the one he chooses to wear is boredom.

"I believe your anger is misdirected," he drawls.

Everything I've been suppressing—not only my memories but the many emotions I've buried over the years—now comes to a head. Like stacking one object on top of another, the bottom of the pile can no longer bear the weight, causing everything to tumble down in a landslide of self-destruction.

I've subdued the anger, guilt, and regret for so long, and now they all rush out at once, hitting me full force.

"You were the one who set that trap for us!" I cry. "The trap that got her killed!"

The heat from my tears burns my cheeks like a

trail of fire. Bilken stares back at me, but his stony expression gives nothing away of his own feelings. Or his intentions.

Maybe because he doesn't have any. Maybe he's no different than Richter . . . or *me*. We're all just puppets who have been taken in and drained by the State— robbed of the very essence that makes us human until we're incapable of feeling anything that even resembles remorse.

This is what the State does to the people who are loyal to it.

"Yet, I wasn't the one who pulled the trigger," he counters.

My nostrils flare as my infuriation grows. "It doesn't matter."

"Doesn't it?" He looks at me with feigned surprise, and the distance between us shrinks as he takes another step forward. "I think the truth is that you're angry with yourself. After all, you've spent the last two years completely submissive to the one person actually responsible for your friend's death."

His callous statement pushes me over the edge. I no longer care about maintaining control or Nolan's unspoken threat about what will happen if I don't behave.

I only care about making Bilken pay for what he's done.

Narrowing my eyes, I concentrate on his throat and muse over how it would feel to snap his neck. However, at the same exact instant the thought crosses my mind, I hear Rai's voice. Speaking to me.

Reminding me.

"Everyone here has lost someone or something. That's why we fight. So our losses don't have to be for nothing."

Hesitation delays my wrath as every molecule in my body hones in on those words. Rai wouldn't want this. She wouldn't want me to become what they had all vowed to fight against.

The trouble is that it's too late for that. I'm already a monster. Already a murderer.

What would Rai think if she could see me now?

My indecision holds me back, but the emotions coursing through me are much harder to contain. A powerful pressure builds up in my chest, screaming to escape.

Bilken peers down at me as a smirk crosses his face. It seems as if he *wants* me to attack him—to show them what I can do. Despite what he said before, I know Nolan wants that too. Or, at the very least, he has a good reason for risking it.

Why else would he bring Bilken here?

Why else would he dangle this insult in front of me?

This is a test, I realize.

Well, I refuse to give into them. I refuse to be a pawn just like I was for Dr. Richter.

Making up my mind, I take the steps to suppress my anger, but with the emotions returning to the empty shell I used to be, it becomes clear even the collar can only do so much. This power wants to be seen, and I'm not sure there's a damn thing anyone can do to stop it. Myself included.

A small release of energy spills out of my body, trickling from my skin like sweat leaving my pores. Nolan's voice tears through the silence as the walls and ceiling begin to crack.

"Enough!" he shouts.

The air catches in my lungs, and the distraction of his intervention helps to contain the feelings overwhelming me. Closing my eyes, I spend the next several seconds focusing only on my breathing. I count backward from ten, just as I have so many times in the past.

"How odd," Bilken grunts. "All the reports were quite adamant that you could control it."

My eyes flash open, settling back on his face as a menacing smile pinches the corners of my lips. "Oh, I *am* controlling it." I lean forward in my seat until the shackles creak in protest. "Trust me, if I wasn't, you would already be dead."

Nolan steps between us. Raising his arms, he presses his palm against Bilken's chest. "That's enough for now," he warns. "You'd better step outside before things get out of hand."

With a condescending nod of his head, Bilken turns to leave without speaking a single word. He passes through the open doorway, and I watch his fingers grip the steel slab, pulling it closed behind him. Just before the metal locks back into place, he glances over his shoulder to meet my gaze.

That one look is almost enough to provoke me.

Swallowing my pride, I turn my attention toward Nolan as he returns to the seat in front of me. The rage detonates from my lungs before he even has the chance to sit.

"Why is he here?" I scream. "PHOENIX . . . you're supposed to be the good guys, aren't you? So, what are you doing joining up with someone like *him*?"

As those words leave my mouth, I hear a voice—somewhere in the recesses of my distorted memories—spewing a similar sentiment. I hear myself trying to convince someone that Bilken can't be trusted.

As the recollection finds form, I realize this happened

prior to the night Rai died.

A huff of exasperation spills from my lips. None of this makes sense. Why would Bilken turn against the State?

What could he possibly gain from such betrayal?

"I understand how confusing this must be for you," Nolan murmurs. "Not to mention distressing. If you must know, it was never Wren's intention for anyone to die that day. Rai was . . . an unfortunate casualty."

An unfortunate casualty?

I inhale a deep breath to stop myself from laughing. "So, what *were* his intentions?" I ask in a sour voice.

Nolan reclines in his chair. Tilting his chin, he stares at me for a long, drawn-out moment before answering.

"To leave a clue. Something that would express his wish to join PHOENIX. He couldn't contact us without being discovered, and my guess is that he knew he would only be desirable to our organization as an informant. He's a good ally to have, but even his usefulness has its limits."

A breath of bewilderment climbs up my throat.

Nolan crosses one leg over the other before continuing. "With that in mind, he proposed a plan to the State. He would act as the contact needed to set up a trap to lure in PHOENIX. And in turn, you. He knew Richter would never seek to harm his prized subject and figured, worst case scenario, you would just be taken back to the DSD if things went downhill, which turned out to be an inevitability anyway."

After everything that happened that night, he expects me to believe Bilken's offer for aid was genuine? I'm not sure I buy it, especially since we never found any evidence to suggest what he's saying is true.

"Did you know about this?" I whisper. "Or did you

think it was a trap?"

"I was acquainted with Wren back in the pre-State days. When the world changed, and I made the choice to move underground, I told him all he had to do was say so if he ever decided he wanted to help us." His eyes seem to glisten with the memory.

"The trouble was, he couldn't send us a direct message. If he tried, the transmission would've been tracked back to both of us, and I'm sure you know what the result of that would've been."

As he cocks an eyebrow at me, I grasp the implication behind his words.

"Execution," I breathe.

Clearing his throat, he carries on. "So, he put it out there in a place he thought PHOENIX might be watching. We keep a firm eye on Enforcer unit rotations to make our movements throughout the Heart easier. They don't tend to monitor the tunnel system, but better safe than sorry." Shaking his head, he lets out a quiet laugh. "He attached the message right in the middle of their weekly schedule. Kind of hard to miss, don't you think? Anyway, that was his way of telling me he was ready to do things my way. With his position in the State and the information he had access to, I wasn't willing to refuse that offer."

"So, you sent us there, knowing the risk."

A flash of anger burns in his eyes. "It was the only way to know for sure and to make the initial move to set up communication the State couldn't track." Taking a deep breath, he adds in a calmer voice, "Rai's death made that part harder but not impossible."

My body tenses at the mention of Rai. The sound of her name on his tongue is vile as if the mere whisper of it is taboo in some way. A shudder runs along my spine, but I try to ignore it, telling myself to concentrate on determining the truth.

"What was the clue?" I press.

"Your file," he answers. "Well, more specifically, the military order he included with it."

My file? What could *that* have possibly told them? I begin to protest, but Nolan cuts me off.

"State-issued computers are equipped with the highest form of security. Only someone truly gifted could hack their systems."

Someone like Rai, you mean, I'm tempted to say to him.

His voice resounds in my ears, bringing a rush of doubt with it.

"Didn't you find it odd that his computer wasn't at least password protected?"

I consider him for a moment. Truthfully, none of this had even occurred to me until now. Then again, I wasn't the one who accessed the computer that night. Ezra was.

Still, something doesn't add up.

"Richter knew that was there," I point out. "Besides, how would that have proven anything to PHOENIX?"

Nolan rolls his eyes.

"Richter overlooked one thing when he agreed to set that trap. Your doctor has an . . . *interesting* fascination with playing his best cards all at once. Because of that, he failed to see what Bilken hoped we would."

"Which was what exactly?"

One corner of his lips twitch, the gloating smile fighting to break through.

"The fact that one simple piece of information in that order showed us how we can defeat the State," he sneers.

I don't understand. I read that order. In fact, I

understood more of it than Ezra did. Everything the report detailed was about how I would be beneficial to the State—it made no mention of weaknesses. Even if it did, I doubt Dr. Richter would've missed something like that. He wouldn't allow such important intel to fall into the enemy's hands.

I shake my head in denial. "He's smarter than you think he is. If there was something like that in there, I can guarantee he knows about it."

"Maybe. Maybe not." His tone is indifferent. "Either way, he agreed to Wren's plan. As a result, he put the pieces in place that have allowed the tables to turn."

Everything he's said over the past few minutes coalesces in a jumbled knot in my head. It presses against the forefront of my brain, but no matter which way I view it, there's still too much that doesn't add up.

"I don't understand," I whisper. "How would he benefit from agreeing to that?"

Nolan shifts position, and for the first time, he looks at me with an expression of pity.

"It allowed him access to *you*, and gave him the opportunity to use the promise of a cure to lure you back. After all, that is why you left, isn't it?"

My eyes widen.

The promise of a cure.

A cure . . .

"A cure is the only hope I have to stop this and to keep you all alive."

I remember saying those words. I remember feeling them in the very core of my being and believing them to be true.

Suddenly, the one question that's been haunting me resolves itself in a single breath. The answer falls at my feet as if surrendering to me.

I left because Dr. Richter promised me a cure, and because I was afraid that, if I didn't, my condition would kill everyone I had come to care about.

Jenner.

Ezra.

My fingers flex, aching to touch my collar, but the shackles prevent me from moving. My entire body melts into the chair as a thick lump rises like bile in my throat. I can feel Richter's lie there, choking me a little bit more with each breath. Knowing this isn't even the first time I've learned this makes the sensation worse.

"You know," Nolan croons, interrupting my thoughts, "you actually did us a favor by returning to the DSD."

"What is *that* supposed to mean?" I snap.

His fingertips press together as he forms a pyramid with his hands in front of his chest. A taunting smile plays on his lips. "Without you, the State has no way of anticipating attacks. They've spent a lot of time and energy disconnecting themselves from the rest of the world and have made a fair number of enemies who may wish to use that knowledge to their advantage. Enemies they wouldn't have if it wasn't for you."

Everything he's been saying finally makes sense to me. Bilken's defection. My file. The military order.

My extraction.

Everything has finally fallen into place.

"You want them to be attacked," I realize. "That's why you relocated Outside." My jaw drops in horror as the words tear from my lungs.

I feel sick. The notion that I'm nothing more than a pawn—a playing piece being shuffled between two opposing sides—is enough to make me want to bury myself in a hole and never resurface. No matter what I do, no matter what steps I take to avoid it, I'm always playing right into somebody's hand.

Playing the role I was destined for.

Why did I have to develop this disease? Why did this have to happen to me? I played by the rules. I always did what I was told. Yet, here I am—caught in the middle of a war I never asked for.

A war that can only end one way.

"Fear can oppress a population, but it can also turn that same populace against the hand that feeds it." Nolan pauses for a moment, and as he does, his eyes darken. "The people will never answer to PHOENIX unless they see that the State can no longer protect them."

"And you can?" I ask.

"We can offer them an alternative, and negotiate peace terms with those who wish to see the State eradicated."

Peace? I wonder.

If only it was that easy.

"Is that PHOENIX's goal, then? To lead?" An unwilling huff of laughter accompanies my words.

His eyes narrow. "I can see the judgment in your gaze, but PHOENIX is not the first, and it won't be the last to seek power. We have ideals and hopes that we wish to see fulfilled, and we're convinced our ability to lead far surpasses the State's. Besides," he says, "if you rise up against something, you have to be prepared to take its place."

I admire his last sentiment. Or I would if I wasn't convinced that it's a front—another mask to conceal the reality I'm sure is far more menacing.

In a bid to see under that mask, I press him further.

"If you wanted power, why didn't you just take it? You have hundreds of sects in the Heart alone."

His hands squeeze into fists as a sudden anger reddens his face. "Because, believe it or not, I don't wish to lead through fear. If we seized control, we would be no better than the State. From what I know of history, regimes that oppress don't last in the long run. They are always overthrown." Suppressing his heated emotions, he adds, "This was the only way to get the people on our side."

For the first time, I feel like I'm beginning to understand the inner workings of what I'm involved with. When all is said and done, only one question remains.

"I understand why you extracted me. With me gone, the State is vulnerable. I *get* that," I breathe, staring back at him with every ounce of intimidation I can muster. "But why wait two years to put this plan in motion?"

A devilish smirk pulls at his lips. "I was wondering when you'd get around to asking me that."

I say nothing as I wait for an answer I might never receive. Nolan deliberates for a moment before ending my torment.

"Watching the State make enemies was one thing, but hearing of how they would completely destroy them was another." When he sees my blank expression, he says, "I don't need to tell you how special you are. I wonder if Dr. Richter ever told you *how* special."

"Stop being cryptic and cut to the chase," I growl.

"Very well." His smile broadens. "What do you know about your blood?"

My stomach twists as I'm brought back to my time at the DSD. I relive everything Dr. Richter ever said to me, especially concerning the unique blood pumping through my veins.

"It evolved," I murmur. "It's an entirely new blood type that Richter calls Type X. He said I'm the only person who has it and that it makes me one of a kind."

Nolan nods his head in feverish repetition. "What he said is true. For now, at least."

I reel back, bemused by his statement. He continues before I can press him about it.

"What would you say if I told you that your blood was being injected into other people with the same condition?"

The air rushes from my lungs in a crippling blow.

"What?" I gasp.

"They had already determined the genetic markers. Those lovely eyes of yours," he explains in response to my confusion, pointing at my face.

Unfolding his hands, he brushes his palms along his thighs and rises from his seat in a fluid bolt-like movement. His posture is tall and domineering as he paces back and forth in front of me.

"When they found a way to keep you alive, you officially became the first of your kind. Richter believes infusing your blood into other Ultraxenopia candidates may help speed the evolution process along. He's hoping it will bypass the incapacitating side-effects you experienced."

The words seem like the description of a horrible nightmare I'm having.

Is what Nolan's saying true? Is it even possible?

A part of me questions whether he's making it up while another part knows he wouldn't have knowledge of my blood at all—not unless it was true.

Here I thought this situation couldn't possibly get

any worse.

"Why would he do that?" I ask. It's all I can manage.

Nolan snickers under his breath. "Why do you think?"

When I meet his gaze, he utters the very answer I was beginning to fear I'd hear.

"To create an army."

"No," I grunt. "Even he wouldn't go that far."

Nolan's footsteps cease, and suddenly, I find him leaning over me. Placing his hands on the arms of my chair, he shifts forward until our faces are only a few inches apart.

"Wouldn't he?" His left eyebrow cocks in amused disbelief. "This is a man who killed the woman he once claimed to love. I don't think someone like that knows limits."

He's right. Richter doesn't have limits. I don't think that word even exists in his vocabulary.

Inhaling a slow, steadying breath, I try my best to remain calm. "So, you took me to stop that from happening?"

"Enforcers we can handle," he says as he straightens up. "A thousand of you . . . probably not."

The thought of others having this power unsettles me more than I care to admit. I've taken lives. While I'm not proud of that fact, as I told Ezra, it had to be done. Over the past two years, I've both loathed and embraced this disease, but I've found a way to live with the cards I've been dealt, and on some sick level, I've even enjoyed my invincibility. However, knowing I would be the cause of this curse in others is a terrible possibility I never prepared for. How will I ever live with myself if this becomes reality?

How could I doom others to this cruel existence?

"Did he succeed?" The words funnel into my ears as if they've been said by someone else.

"Not yet," Nolan answers, "but we both know how persistent he is."

He returns to his pacing while I try to organize the millions of questions rustling around in my skull. After a moment, I hear his voice break the agonizing silence, but the sound is clouded and somewhat distant. It takes an extreme amount of concentration to hear anything he says at all.

"You saw how unstoppable the State was with only one of you. Imagine the devastation if more were created." Freezing in place, he looks down at me once more. "We had to do this."

It took twenty-one years of my life to realize how abhorrent the State truly is. But PHOENIX?

It's only taken me two.

What Nolan's done—what PHOENIX has done—is nothing compared to what they intend to do. Even worse, what he's aiming for is far more gruesome than he's willing to accept.

"If you keep me here, the State *will* be attacked and many innocent people will die," I say slowly.

For the briefest of moments, I expect Nolan to prove me wrong—to show me that he's a decent, caring human who really is just hoping for a better world.

Until, I remember the mask. Until I remember the façade he's been putting on since the moment we met.

"You've killed many innocent people yourself, have you not?"

I swallow. The guilt attempts to strangle me, but I force it away, unwilling to let him make this about me. What I've done is in the past. What matters now is what awaits us in the future.

"You won't have a country to lead if everyone is dead. Mindless violence won't bring about change." The words escape my lips automatically, making me wonder if I've heard them somewhere before.

Nolan shakes his head in response. "I don't wish for it to come to that, but this is the reality of war. One of the many downsides, if you will. All we can hope is that peace will be restored before too many have to suffer."

Lowering my eyes, I allow silence to overtake me. I roll his statement over in my head, considering whether what he's trying to accomplish is the only way to make room for a better world.

No, I tell myself.

I refuse to believe that.

There's always a better option.

"And what if your plan fails?" I ask. "What if they don't want peace?"

I glance up, and for once, I'm surprised by the expression crossing his face. Whereas before there was a grim and determined acceptance, now there's only sadness.

He exhales a quavering breath before answering. "Then there's no hope for any of us."

FIFTEEN

MY FEET SHUFFLE ACROSS THE floor as my teeth click against the tip of my thumbnail. The mangled remnants of my shackles lay in pieces on the floor behind me. After everything with Bilken, the people here will never see me willingly restrained again. I plan to make sure of that. A part of me is ready to explode out of this room and bring justice to the traitor while another part is too confused to even know what I'm feeling. So, I pace back and forth, unaware of how much time passes.

Too lost in thought to care.

My mind is a jumbled and conflicted mess. It seems like, no matter how hard I focus and try to make sense of what I know, there's even more that I still don't understand. My conversation with Nolan brought many revelations. I won't deny that. Yet, I have a nagging feeling that I'm missing something important.

My stomach twists, causing a horrible nausea to rise in my throat. The way the State used me—that was to be expected. However, when I think of how PHOENIX has used me . . .

As much as I might wish to, I can't ignore the truth. Not anymore. When I consider the efforts the people in PHOENIX have gone to, as well as the reality behind my extraction and the fact that I'm here at all, I'm led to one foreboding conclusion.

Nolan wants to cause an even greater war.

He spoke of peace. Of change. But when it comes down to it, PHOENIX isn't any better than the State. They're simply two sides of the same coin.

Not all of them, a small voice whispers in my ear.

Without warning, Ezra's face comes to life in my thoughts.

I'm certain he couldn't fake what he's told me about us—despite what I've seen from people like Richter and Nolan.

His feelings back then.

His feelings now.

They're real. I know it.

Releasing a small sigh, I shake my head.

No, I tell myself. *He wouldn't have been involved with this.*

I remember the way he looked at me when I first arrived here. A combination of incredulity and intense relief lit up his face, hidden behind a veil of desperation. Only one emotion outshone the others.

Love.

If anything, that one emotion reassures me of his innocence.

I run my fingers through my hair before cupping them around my face. My feet stop moving, and the frustration coursing through my body seems determined to exhaust me. It feels like I could collapse at any moment. The confusion I've felt for months now also lingers in the back of my mind, exacerbating my muddled and fragmented memories.

"Why can't I remember?" I wonder.

A loud gasp bursts from my lungs as my eyes widen with realization.

The uncertainty.

The questions.

I've held the answer to all of it this entire time.

For so long, I've been forced to use this unwanted power. For strategic gain. To kill others. Yet, I never considered using it for myself. Or, maybe, I just didn't want to.

Using it for the sake of retrieving my memories isn't an option—not when I know that I would only be able to fully embrace them if they come back to me in a natural way.

But what about someone else's memories? Someone who could help me make sense of everything.

In eager anticipation, I ransack my brain. I'm curious to know more about the origin of the State, but I'm also aware how difficult that would be to accomplish. Without more information, I wouldn't even know where to begin.

The price of full control, I remind myself.

I roll my eyes in annoyance until another starting point occurs to me.

The one moment I want to see more than anything else.

The one *person* I want to see more than anyone else.

Exhaling a slow breath, I close my eyes, centralizing my thoughts on my father—trying to send my mind back to a time when he was still alive. To a time when I didn't exist.

Back before all of this.

It's as easy as imagining his face. His eyes and the

faint creases in his cheeks appear before me, and I see every possible detail about him. As much as the brain of a child can remember, at least.

I sense the change around me as my physical surroundings transform in my head. I can even feel him reaching out to me, beckoning me in the right direction.

That small speck of guidance is the only thing I need.

Within seconds, I open my eyes.

The concrete prison and metal chair are nowhere to be seen. Instead, I find myself standing in what appears to be a study. Ornate pictures and paintings decorate the walls, and a large stone mantelpiece frames a crackling fire. A wooden desk sits just beneath an impressive, round window.

My eyes scan the room, and a trembling breath escapes my lips when I take in the face of the man in front of me.

"Father . . ."

His aura pulls me forward. I take a cautious step as a strange feeling of terror catapults through my body. I can't explain it—this apprehension.

My gaze locks on his hunched figure. Leaning over the desk, he bows his head as his hand whips in furious repetition back and forth. I inch toward him, catching a glimpse of the book he's writing in before glancing at his face. He looks so young—so different from how he was the day he was taken from me all those years ago.

I study his expression, noticing the severe way he stares at the desk with his forehead scrunched into tiny wrinkles. A lump of uncertainty blocks my throat, but I swallow it back down.

Hesitantly, I peer over his shoulder.

February 28th, 2034

For so long, it was only rumors. First, it was a simple shift in policy. A change in the way the government was run. Then, it became something more. Whispers about assassinations and about an insurgency that had somehow risen up from the inside, taking down everything without having to resort to the more brutal methods of war. I'm not sure how they did it. Hell, I don't even know where they came from. No one does. All I know is that it was over before anyone knew it began. And now?

Now, the State is in power.

The strangest part is that there was never a catalyst. Never a single moment that indicated any of this was happening. They merely rose up like a phantom presence, weaving their intricate and controlling web through every facet of our society.

At first, people weren't concerned. They just saw it as nothing more than a newly elected government, but what they fail to grasp is that the State was never elected.

It wasn't long before they began to change us. Change the way we live and the way we function. Initially, it happened slowly. One minor adjustment at a time. Probably to avoid a panic more than anything else. Since then, things have happened more quickly. Our downfall is progressing at an alarming rate, and I'm worried no one notices that except for me.

Horrific acts plague everyday news, but they hide their crimes behind promises of peace and prosperity. How easily people are fooled. I, however, see them for what they truly are and for what they're trying to do. Rob everyone of their identity. Make every person the same in order to force them to conform. Frighten them until they obey. They've even introduced birth identification numbers and a sort of placement exam to help them achieve this end.

The numbers are to keep track of us, and the exam is to transform us into a more efficient society. Or so they claim. They say it will eliminate the waste and urge everyone to contribute. That it's in our best interest. Truthfully, it's just another means for them to assert their control. To make us follow their rules and live the way they want us to. A place for everyone, and everyone in their place.

He pauses, shifting his body a fraction of an inch as he laughs under his breath.

No one has a say anymore. We have to do what we're told or suffer the consequences—a trap that I'm concerned the majority will fall into. Something needs to be done before the people are too far gone to remember who they are. Before we're all brainwashed by the promises of the State. By fear. Before we lose ourselves completely. Rodrick agrees with me, and so our mission to find like-minded individuals *to join us and to battle this new evil begins. We already have the perfect starting point, so now all that's left is to turn our thoughts into action.*

We've even chosen a name for ourselves. What better way to describe our determination than to name our rebellion after a creature that can never die? Our resolve burns like fire, and so, we will become like the great winged bird from legend. PHOENIX. Together, we will rise up from the ashes of this once great nation and liberate our people from the tyranny that threatens to destroy us.

I glance up at him the moment his hand stops moving. When Nolan told me they were once friends, I didn't believe him. Seeing this makes it real.

My eyes glisten as I stare at my father in awe, feeling a newfound respect for the man in front of me. He leans back in the chair as I inspect his movements, only vaguely aware that the scene around me is changing.

The fire behind me cracks like a whip, grabbing my attention. Looking over my shoulder, I'm surprised to see the stone mantelpiece is no longer there, supplanted by a glass and steel box positioned within the wall like a transparent drawer. My eyes dance along the interior of the room, taking in the other not-so-subtle changes.

No paintings.

No pictures.

Just bare walls and muted colors. Gray, after gray, after gray.

Turning, I find my father standing in front of the rounded window. His eyes stare out beyond the spotless panes, but his expression is blank and distant. I notice the wooden desk is gone now too, replaced with one constructed of steel.

This representation of our cold society looms on the opposite side of the room like a warning. It no longer faces the window or the outside world. It no longer faces freedom. Instead, it faces a wall, perhaps to signify that there's nowhere to go. That there's nowhere to hide.

Perhaps to tell him he's trapped, just like the rest of us are in the future.

My body quakes as I walk over to my father, wishing he could see me. Wishing for some way to comfort his obvious distress.

Reaching out my hand, my fingers press against his arm, but he doesn't feel my touch. Ignoring the painful clenching of my heart, I peek up at his face. When I do, I immediately register how much older he appears to be. Aged from stress and fear, no doubt.

I watch as he takes a long, deep breath. A tremor runs over his fingers when he thumbs through the journal, searching for a blank page.

Once again, I read the words over his shoulder.

July 17th, 2036

The situation has become increasingly dire. We're struggling to get hold of the needed weapons and supplies. It's been difficult, nearly impossible, to find support, especially with the newly instated identification chips that are now mandated by law. They're tracking our every movement, hoping to flesh out anyone who might pose a threat to the utopia they're attempting to build.

Utopia.

This place is more like Hell.

Walls have been erected around the city, cutting off access to the outside world. Travel is strictly prohibited without special clearance, and the city has been separated into zones with the outlying areas now nothing more than one giant slum. A place for them to deposit the waste until they find a way to eradicate it completely.

For the time being, we're allowed to stay in our home, but it won't be long until they decide to move us too. Where we live will coincide with the jobs we're given, which will only lead to segregation and inevitably distance us from one another. Every move the State makes is intended to force us to conform—to disconnect us until the relationships we once shared no longer exist.

Families.

Friends.

I wouldn't be surprised if fear eliminates them altogether.

The State has broken off ties with our trade partners as well, but they've managed to calm the impending hysteria with promises of advancements in hydroponics and genetically grown meat. A daily cap has been put in place on almost everything, though. Food, medicine, and even water. It's all limited. Some products, like alcohol, are being phased out entirely. They claim it's only temporary, and with a little *time and effort, we'll be able to create everything we could possibly need for ourselves, right here inside these walls.*

At first, I thought this was just another way to prevent outside interference, but now I know it's meant to keep everyone in. At this rate, the next generation won't even know an outside world exists.

Placing his pen on the desk, he stops to rub his tired eyes. He looks exhausted and stares blankly at the page for at least a minute before continuing.

Another big shift concerns the State's supply of Enforcers. It's grown to an extraordinary level. Nearly tenfold compared to what it was less than a year ago. The "join us or die" mentality has taken over, and more are enlisting every day, eager to show their cooperation and loyalty to the tyrants who have overthrown us. Loyalists, as they're now called, are being rewarded while those who stand against this new rule are gradually weeded out and exterminated like bugs. Soon, there won't be any of us left. A curfew has also been put in place in an effort to keep illegal activities to a minimum, making our goals that much harder to attain.

Then there's the State's latest conquest. With the placement exam and the tracking chips, all that's left is to take away everything that makes us different from one another. Only by making us the same can they oppress us completely. They claim this is meant to make way for the advances of the future. A future they say we will build together.

More lies.

The State feels threatened by history and by anything that counterbalances the conformity they've been working so hard to put in place. Pyres light up the streets as Enforcers raid homes, burning any objects they consider to be in direct contradiction to their new, "improved" society. Their new world. They'll destroy the slightest reminder of what life was like before they arrived, even something as simple as a piece of furniture. Anything that suggests another way of life existed before they did.

People are feeding this ridiculous venture by accepting it, making the situation worse. I can see the extent of the State's reach in the things I hear said in passing on the streets. Individuals I've known my entire life are now preaching false truths that are inconsistent with the world we grew up in. It's as if they're in denial that society was ever different from what we know now. They've been brainwashed. There's no other way to put it.

I tear my gaze away from the journal, overwhelmed by the description coming to life inside my head. I'm able to imagine it with such clarity. The way the Enforcers barged into peoples' homes. How whole identities were ripped away as possessions were burned before their owners' eyes.

Memories.

Talents.

It was all taken away.

Make everyone the same, just as my father said.

For the first time, I truly appreciate what he showed me when I was a child. The books and instruments, as well as the piano he used to spend countless hours teaching me how to play. It never occurred to me how many people had to suffer for the privileges I took for granted.

How my father had to suffer.

I remember when we used to go on our "secret missions" as he called them. They often took us far away from home, and each time we traveled along a different route. A method, I now realize, meant to prevent me from being able to give the details of our excursions to anyone who might ask.

He always made me close my eyes when we got close, and I used to stumble along in the dark until he told me I could look. The only thing I can remember about that part of our journey is the smell. The musty odor and dampness clinging to the air around us. Father always made me change my clothes before going home. Probably to avoid Mother finding out what we were up to.

Thinking about it now, I can't help wondering if the place he used to take me to was one of PHOENIX's first hideaways. Where else could he have concealed something as large as a piano? Where else could he have taught me how to play it without fear of being caught?

Perhaps they used to gather such relics in the hopes that, one day, they might be put to use again.

In the hope that our history wouldn't totally be forgotten.

The scratching of his pen grabs my full attention, returning me to this moment. Locking my eyes back on the desk, I continue to digest my father's story.

The world as we know it, the old world, no longer exists. Truth be told, I'm beyond lucky that they haven't found this journal. I shudder to think what will happen if they do. Execution, no doubt. Or torture at the hands of the DSD. Another irony of the State. Atrocities hidden behind the guise of scientific research. It's no wonder so many people are falling into line and becoming nothing more than mindless sheep. Between the public executions and the very real likelihood of a stay at the DSD, everyone is frightened. It's impossible to know who to trust anymore, and the State is nurturing that paranoia each second of every day. Whoever is running this show has positioned their pieces nicely. The people are turning on each other without them having to lift a finger.

The world has gone to hell, and I'm not so sure how much more of this I can handle.

Pausing again, he licks his lips. When the pen touches back down on the paper, his hand shakes so violently that I'm unable to read what he wrote. Leaning forward, I narrow my eyes to decipher the scribbles.

My heart plummets into my feet when I make out

the words.

At least I still have Evandra.

My stomach drops when he mentions my mother, and the anger I've felt toward her re-emerges, burning me in a wildfire of hatred and rage. Her betrayal toward me. Her betrayal toward my father.

If only he'd known what she was like.

How did it happen? I wonder. *How did she find out his secret?*

Before I can determine an answer, the vision begins to shift, taking me forward to another point in time. As my surroundings settle, a sudden darkness veils the room. The only light now comes from the diminishing fire.

In a panic, I search for my father.

Turning in place, I find him sitting immobile in front of the steel desk. My heart pounds as I take my place by his side. Bending over to look at his face, I'm alarmed by what I find there. Prominent bags hang under his eyes, and his skin is sallow. His cheeks are sunken, and it appears he's tried, unsuccessfully, to hide them with facial hair.

My fingers tingle as I reach out for him, desperate to touch his shoulder.

They only find air.

I watch in horror as he pens a new entry.

March 7th, 2040

I always thought love was the greatest force in this world. That nothing and no one could ever come between us.

But I was wrong. Our damaged society has done the very thing I thought impossible. It has divided us.

I suspect she doesn't realize this. If she did, I would already be dead. After all, she has made it abundantly clear where her allegiance now lies. I'm not sure if it's fear or if she's simply been brainwashed by propaganda like so many others. Whatever the cause, Eva is no longer the woman I fell in love with.

It breaks my heart to write these words, but I must put my feelings and inhibitions aside. I must assume a new identity and pretend to be someone I'm not. I must abandon the progress I've made—all the work I've done in an attempt to right the wrongs committed by those who cast their menacing shadow over our lives.

For the sake of my unborn child, I must stay. Even if it goes against everything I believe in. Perhaps, one day, I will escape from this torment, but until then

He stops writing, leaving the sentence unfinished. Glancing down, I notice that his hands are shaking again. Mine tremble in response to the visible anguish tormenting him. Many seconds pass before he carries on writing.

This will be my last entry. With the world we live in now, even our thoughts are no longer safe. To those who were depending on me

I watch as a tear trails along his cheek and lands in the middle of the words written below.

I'm sorry.

With a careful movement, he closes the journal. Rising to his feet, his stride is steady but broken as he crosses the room. The glare from the burning embers casts an ominous glow across his face, and without a second of hesitation, he throws the book into the fire.

The vision ends as the pages burn.

SIXTEEN

MY LUNGS SEIZE, STRIPPING ME of oxygen as the comprehension of what I've seen wraps its vengeful hand around my throat. Tears burn my dry, cracked lips, and my heart falters, bowing under the strain of the tiny fissures forming along its edges. They work their way inwards, breaking me.

My knees buckle, and I'm aware of the concrete floor as it rises up to meet them. The room is distorted as if time has slowed, causing my suffering to be drawn out and amplified. As I collapse, my eyes stare blankly ahead, seeing only the ghost of my father's face.

I don't move. I couldn't even if I wanted to. My tear ducts are the sole functioning part of my body, tormenting me with physical reminders of my pain.

A pain that's now so much greater than it ever was before.

A soft whimper parts my lips as the hand that was suffocating me now squeezes my chest. For a moment, I wish for it to end my agony.

To end this. Once and for all.

Through the fog of despair shrouding my existence, I notice the sound of voices on the other side of the door. I can only just make out what one of them is saying.

"Something's not right."

A familiar voice.

Ezra's voice.

"Open the door," he pleads.

A pause. Then a reply, protesting his demand.

"I said open it!" he yells, refusing to back down.

Within a matter of seconds, the metallic slab is forced open. Retreating footsteps echo along the length of the hallway—more than likely belonging to whoever was guarding the door. I'm sure it won't be long until they return with reinforcements.

Although I don't turn to look at him, I can sense Ezra rushing toward me. I can feel his body heat as he squats beside me on the floor. I can hear his voice as he tries to coax me back from my inevitable descent into madness.

"Wynter."

His hand is warm on my shoulder, and his touch is gentle. Words form in my throat, but I can't find the means to speak. Running his hand along my back, he brings his face close to mine. His breath is warm as it tickles my lips.

"What is it?" he whispers.

His presence manages to seep through the impairing cloud, giving me the energy to lift my gaze. I stare at him, noticing the stunned concern in his eyes and wanting nothing more than to lose myself in their hazel depths. To swim in their warmth. To escape this pain.

Tears continue to slide down my cheeks.

"It's my fault," I breathe.

His eyes narrow, but I shift away from him before he has the chance to speak. Curling into the fetal position, I retreat into myself, unwilling to expose this feeling to anyone—especially to him. No one should ever feel this way.

Richter's face appears in my head in response to that thought.

No, I tell myself.

I wouldn't even wish this on the person I hate the most.

Ezra's hesitation expels from his body like a wave of heat. Still, after a few seconds, he rises to his feet and bending down in front of me, scoops me up into his arms. He holds me against his chest, and for the first time in a long time, I actually feel safe.

"Come on." His voice is a soft muttering breath in my ear. "We're getting out of here."

The feel of his arms is secure and reassuring—everything I'm only now realizing I need. I don't struggle. I don't fight against him in any way. Instead, I give in to everything he's been telling me, finding solace in the inescapable proximity of this moment.

His stride is steady as he carries me toward the door, but when he touches it, the scream of the metal might as well be an alarm. As if to reinforce this notion, Quinn appears in front of us, barring our exit and preventing us from taking a single step over the threshold.

Raising his gun, he points the barrel at me. His gaze and question, however, are both directed at Ezra.

"What the hell are you doing?"

Ezra's grip on me tightens. "Solitary confinement isn't doing her any good. She needs to be around familiar faces."

Quinn moves forward, sliding his body a few paces sideways to block our escape.

"How many times do I have to tell you she's dangerous?" he snaps.

"She will be if you keep her in here!" Ezra bites back.

Repositioning his hold on his weapon, Quinn's finger dances across the trigger. His jaw tenses as a vengeful growl climbs up his throat.

"Don't think I'll have any qualms about shooting you. Or her."

An unexpected click resounds in my ears, and looking up, I see Jenner standing behind Quinn, holding a gun to the back of his head. His eyes are hooded and full of an emotion I don't think I've seen from him before.

"I'd really rather you didn't do that," he murmurs.

As I watch him, standing there with his weapon upraised, I find myself remembering another moment in time. I see Jenner, flashing his typical carefree smile as he offers me one-on-one shooting lessons.

My fingers tingle as I recall the feel of my hand around a gun.

Quinn's anger is visible in the twitching of his cheeks, but he doesn't show any intention of moving. Another click pierces the silence as Ezra redistributes my weight, and I can just make out the sound of Quinn inhaling a sharp breath. I follow his gaze to see a second gun pressed against his abdomen.

His tongue curls up on the inside of his bottom lip, jutting it out. Muttering a string of indistinct curses, he reluctantly lowers his weapon. Jenner reaches around to take it from him, never once lowering his own.

Quinn casts a livid glare at each of us in turn before muttering, "Nolan will hear about this."

Ezra removes his gun from the ex-Enforcer's stomach, returning it to the holster on his belt.

"I'm sure he will," he says indifferently.

He takes full hold of me again as we exit the room. My body is weak, and I cling to him in a desperate need for support. It's strange. I can't remember the last time I felt this way after a vision. Ever since Dr. Richter installed the collar, it's been effortless. As easy as breathing even.

Not this time.

I can feel the ex-Enforcer's eyes following our every movement. As if goaded on by his expression, Ezra stalls beside him. Leaning in, his face lingers an inch or so away from Quinn's ear. I can only just hear the menacing words that breach his lips.

"Threaten her again, and I *will* kill you."

Jenner keeps his gun raised until Ezra and I have passed, maintaining his sight on Quinn until we round the nearest corner. The three of us then progress through the network of corridors, unfollowed, and even more surprising, undisturbed. I expect at least one of Nolan's lackeys to come after us, but so far, nothing.

After a few minutes, Ezra stops outside the entrance to another room. Unlocking the door, he files inside, signaling for Jenner to bolt it again behind us.

As we cross over the threshold, I'm alarmed by how much this space reminds me of my quarters at the DSD. A small cot is pushed against the far wall with a single chair tucked in the corner beside it. Other than that, the room is empty.

Ezra helps me over to the bed, only unhooking his grip on me once I'm positioned on top of the mattress. His touch is cautious—almost as if he's worried that the slightest caress might cause me pain. He tucks a pillow behind my back, and I immediately sink into it, resting my head against the wall.

I close my eyes, but I'm aware of the increasing distance between us as he lowers himself onto the chair. I hear Jenner plonk down on the floor beside the door.

Silence descends between us, but I'm not sure how long it lasts. Exhaustion creeps over me, drowning out my surroundings and making it difficult to focus on anything apart from the itchy clamminess of my skin. All I want to do is sleep, however, the strange tension flooding the room is like a blaring horn. I can't ignore it, no matter how much I try to.

My eyes peek open when Jenner's voice prompts the unavoidable conversation.

"What did you see?"

I notice Ezra flash an annoyed look in his direction, and I drop my eyes to the floor as I remember what I saw, too ashamed to meet either of their expectant gazes. Instead, I stare at a small thread coming off the blanket underneath me.

"I saw my father, back when he was still alive." Fresh tears burn my eyes, threatening to spill over. "He died because of *me*," I breathe. "He wanted to leave . . ." A lump swells in my throat, and for a few seconds, I struggle to speak. It takes my remaining strength to push out the final words. "But he stayed when he found out my mother was pregnant."

Once again, I find myself thinking of my mother and what I learned about her from my father's journal. How she put her loyalty to the State before her family—a loyalty which alienated the husband who once loved her. A loyalty which got him killed.

A loyalty which turned her daughter—her only child—into the equivalent of a walking corpse. Or grim reaper.

Or both.

The sound of Ezra's voice distracts me from my thoughts. His hand presses against mine, compelling me to meet his awaiting gaze.

"I'm sorry about what happened to him. I swear I didn't know of his involvement until recently. Still, I should've told you."

"No," I whisper, shaking my head. "It was something I needed to see for myself."

I stare at the far wall, although I don't really see it. The truth overwhelms me, followed by the memories.

"Besides," I grumble, swatting away the painful images, "for all you knew, I wouldn't have remembered him anyway."

"Does that mean you remember now?" Jenner asks. I can hear the hope behind his words.

Glancing at him, I ponder that question, turning it around countless times in my head.

Do I remember?

"Some things. I remember everything before I was initially taken to the DSD, and there are some things I remember since, like—"

"Rai," Ezra interrupts.

"And Wren Bilken," Jenner adds.

I nod, wondering why that is until I come to the only possible conclusion. Guilt. Having suppressed my responsibility for Rai's death for so long, it was only a matter of time before something would cause it to re-emerge. An unseen presence haunting me, now suddenly too real.

"What about us?"

My eyes lock with Ezra's, and I can't help feeling uncomfortable with this particular question. I don't want to keep hurting them.

The words tumble from my lips as I withdraw my hand from his.

"Everything is coming back slowly, in bits and pieces. But what I remember is usually in response to something, kind of like a reaction. I'm not sure there's anything I can do to speed it up."

For a while, no one speaks. Ezra and Jenner don't question me further, and as the minutes pass, we each become lost in our individual thoughts.

I may not fully remember them or what we went through together, but I remember enough—I *feel* enough—to want to keep them safe. The trouble is that I don't even know what we're supposed to be doing or how I can achieve that with everything going on.

Before, I only ever used this power to destroy. I never once thought of trying to protect someone with it.

What if I can't?

What if by trying to protect one, I inadvertently cause the death of the other?

I no longer find it surprising that I left them when I did. Notwithstanding the risk of what this power might do to them, it's become clear that Ezra and Jenner have no limits when it comes to me. I can understand it—they're afraid they'll lose me, just like they lost Rai—but that doesn't mean I accept it.

I can't just stand by and watch as they self-destruct.

"So, what's the plan?"

Ezra and Jenner exchange glances in response to my irate tone.

My eyebrows pull together as I let out a heavy, exasperated sigh. "You're both going to keep getting yourselves into trouble because of me."

"It doesn't matter. Everything's gone to hell anyway." Ezra's face and voice are oddly empty of emotion. "Besides, I don't think Nolan will bother you anytime soon."

"What makes you say that?" I ask.

He runs a hand along the back of his neck. "I think Bilken was a test. In fact, I'm sure of it. I think Nolan wanted to see how you'd respond under pressure. To see how you'd react."

A grimace twists my lips. "You mean, he wanted to see if I'd kill him."

I sensed it then, and now I know that my suspicions were right on target. What game is Nolan playing at? What does he hope to accomplish by using me?

Jenner leans forward, his expression darkening. "You heard what he said before. Bilken is only useful as an informant. Now that he's out of the State completely, it would be no big loss to anyone if, you know . . ." He drags a finger across his throat while making a nauseating sound with his mouth. "Plus if *you* did it, Nolan would have someone to blame to keep his own hands clean."

I choke out a breathy laugh. "All this from someone who claims to want peace." My head jerks back and forth in stunned disbelief.

Ezra repositions himself in the chair, drawing my attention to his rigid movements.

"Yeah, well, it wouldn't be the first time Nolan said something that didn't add up."

I give those words a moment to work through my brain. A sour expression distorts his features, making it clear that he's upset. Tilting my head, I examine his face, wondering what the problem is.

"Is this about my collar?" I whisper.

Ezra's eyes seem to flicker, but at first, he doesn't respond. When he finally meets my gaze, there's a sadness in his voice that I find unsettling.

"He knew, didn't he? What it's for?" He glances at my collar as if he can't physically speak the word. Straining his jaw, he looks away from it and me. "Just makes you think, if he lied to us about that, what else has he lied about?"

Once again, I'm reminded of how much Nolan seems to mirror Dr. Richter. The similarities between them are sinister, especially when I think back to that night in Zone 1. Particularly, the methods Richter used to trick us, and the way he killed Rai without hesitation or remorse.

So much of what happened that night rests on my shoulders. Yet, I still can't make sense of why I was there in the first place. I was never a member of PHOENIX. I had never held, let alone used, a gun. Hell, I couldn't even control my powers at that point.

What use was I going to be if things went wrong?

Which they did, a sarcastic voice sneers in the back of my head.

My eyes observe Ezra's face as I try to figure out how to approach this topic. I'm just beginning to warm up to him, and heading into this territory could very well destroy that.

Regardless, I have to know.

"Why did you bring me into Zone 1 with you that night?"

Ezra looks up at me, but his expression says nothing.

Narrowing my eyes, I charge forward with my verbal assault. "I had no weapons training, and let's be realistic here, I wasn't exactly in the best shape. I would've been a hindrance more than a help. So, why was I there?"

"I told you why," he says in a low voice. "Leaving you behind wasn't a bearable option."

It's easy to imagine myself in that original moment, reacting to those words. Even without my memories, I can see how I would've believed what he said—how I would've caved under the pressure of those hazel eyes staring back at me, just like they are now. After all, it was so foreign to me. So tempting.

So different from anything I'd ever experienced before.

But I'm not the same person anymore.

"Stop it," I breathe. "That might've worked back then, but it's not going to work now. I want to hear the truth."

His eyes widen as a soft gasp parts his lips. "That *is* the truth."

"Not all of it," I counter.

An unexpected darkness casts a shadow across his face, letting me know I've struck a nerve. Ezra breathes in before exchanging a glance with Jenner. When he turns back to face me, his expression is distant.

"It was better than the alternative," he admits.

"Which was?"

His fingers interlock as he leans forward in the chair, arms resting in a strained position on his knees.

"You have to realize how things were. People were frustrated and angry. Everything was reaching its breaking point, and we weren't sure how much longer we could sustain that way of life. Even the Heads of the different sects were fed up because we weren't any closer to achieving change than when PHOENIX first started . . . ." He lowers his eyes, concentrating on his fidgeting hands. "Then, we got the transmission from Bilken, and it seemed like an opportunity had finally fallen into our laps. The trouble was that it didn't go unnoticed that this opportunity only arose after you came to us for help."

His words trigger a memory lodged in the back of my mind, causing the events to re-enact in front of me as if I'm reliving them. I see the compound where I first got to know Ezra and the others. I see the people who lived there, remembering the fear in their gazes whenever they looked at me.

"I tried to appeal to everyone's sense of empathy to make them accept you, and at first, it seemed to work," he continues.

I remember his speech.

His charisma.

The way they all followed him—even the middle-aged man who stood amidst the crowd.

Nolan.

"But during that week you spent in a coma, we heard speculation linking you to the transmission from Bilken. How would it have looked if we left you there and then never came back? Our disappearance. Our presumed deaths. They would've been pinned on you. The people would've wanted someone to blame, and it would've been *you*." He pauses, taking in a single shaking breath. "Leaving you behind would've been the same as leaving a lamb in a lion's den. It wouldn't have ended well."

How blind I was then. How stupid.

How could I have ever believed that those people would accept me, especially considering what they knew? Or even more so, what they didn't.

Of course, they wouldn't have trusted me.

Of course, they would have suspected I was involved.

I think of Rai—of her death, and how they all probably blamed me for it.

A lump rises in my throat. "But what happened could've been prevented if I hadn't been there," I whisper.

"Or maybe you saved lives *by* being there," Jenner murmurs.

I peek over at where he sits by the door, feeling the full force of his gaze like a hand against my skin.

"Rai . . . that was unavoidable. She sought Richter out, so it would've happened either way. But there's no saying what would've become of the rest of us if *you* hadn't been there. Richter only called off the Enforcers because he needed you in one piece." The material of his shirt scrapes against the wall when he shrugs his shoulders. "You might not have stayed that way if we'd left you at the compound."

"You don't know if that's true." My voice is weak, the words barely audible.

"No," Ezra admits. "We don't. But what we do know is that we preferred the idea of bringing you with us and knowing you'd stay alive over the thought of leaving you behind and potentially coming back to a corpse. At least then, even if the Enforcers *had* killed us, you would've made it out. To me, that was worth sacrificing the success of a thousand missions, let alone one."

Those final words ring in my ears, deafening me to all other sound and once again reaffirming that he's telling me the truth.

For the first time since arriving here, I truly begin to feel like I can trust him and Jenner. They wouldn't have gone to such lengths to keep me safe if I couldn't. They wouldn't have compromised their safety for the sake of my own.

When I think of it like that, it's no wonder I was willing to follow them blindly into danger.

Still, what Ezra just said feels unfamiliar to me, and I find myself speculating why that is. Try as I might, I can't locate any memory of it in what little I remember.

"Why do I get the feeling this is the first time I've heard this?"

Ezra avoids my gaze when he speaks. "Because it is. I was trying to get you to stay with us. Can you honestly say you would have if I'd told you this back then?"

No, I silently answer.

I was determined to keep them safe. To keep them alive. If I had known the risks they were embracing, I would've never let them do it. I would've stopped them.

I would've left sooner.

Running a hand through my hair, I let out a deep breath, leaning farther back into the pillow as I peek up at the ceiling. A few hairline cracks run through the concrete, spreading out like a spider's web. It reminds me of what this power can do, in turn bringing out the memory of what it used to do to me.

The coma Ezra spoke of—I remember the vision that caused it as abruptly as if I'm seeing it again now.

Destruction and pain tear through my head, followed by a paralyzing aftershock of guilt.

A soft gasp seeps through my lips as it assaults me again, placing its heavy burden back onto my shoulders and stirring up the reason behind why I left them in the first place.

My hand trembles as my fingertips press against the collar. I never thought I would see the day when I'd feel relieved to have this reminder of Dr. Richter, but now that I know why I have it at all, I realize how important it is that I never take it off.

This is the only way they'll be safe. Even if it turns out Richter *can* manipulate me, this is the one way Ezra and Jenner will stay alive.

This is the only way everyone will stay alive.

So long as I have this collar, the world won't come to an end.

A shudder runs up my spine. My eyes lower, locking on Ezra and arousing one final question in my head.

"What if I hadn't woken up from that coma? What would you have done then?" I ask him.

His eyes meet mine for a split second before turning away again.

"I try not to think about it. But that's why I delayed the mission for as long as I could. I knew the risks of leaving you, and I wasn't prepared to take them. Luckily, you woke up before I had to."

An unnerving silence crowds the room, making it feel smaller than it actually is. I look between Ezra and Jenner who both seem intent on avoiding my gaze, unsure what else to say.

"So, what do we do now?" I wonder.

If Bilken was a test, then what's the next step Nolan is planning to take? He wants the Heart to be attacked, that much I know, but I have a feeling there's a bigger picture that we just aren't seeing.

The worst is far from over. I can feel it.

A huff of air bursts from Jenner's lungs as he folds his arms across his chest. His black hair falls in a dark curtain across his eyes, and in a begrudging breath, he grumbles the one answer we're all thinking.

"Now, we wait."

SEVENTEEN

I SEE MY FATHER, BACK during a time when I remember him being happy. Well, when I *thought* he was happy. He smiles at me, and I can feel the love in his gaze enveloping me in its warm embrace.

At least I had that.

At least that was real.

Suddenly, the image changes. Now I see him the way that I always see him—bloodied, beaten, and reaching for me. Always reaching for me. His lips breathe my name, although I hear what he's really trying to say hiding behind it.

The farewell he's too afraid to whisper.

A gunshot goes off. My father disappears, and instead, I see Rai standing in front of me. A smile pulls at the corners of her mouth, and this time, I'm the one reaching out—desperate to undo what never should've been done.

She vanishes almost as soon as she appears, leaving behind nothing but a splash of red. This brutal reminder of her death.

It's the only thing I see.

"Wynter."

I spin on my heel, drawn to the sound of the voice calling my name. Jenner stares back at me. His face is drawn and washed out. Pale to the point he already looks dead.

Our eyes lock, and my feet stumble forward until I notice the stain spreading over his clothes. With a stunned expression, he follows my gaze to his chest where the blood trickles outward, overtaking him like a flesh-eating disease. It consumes him before either one of us can stop it.

A swell of pressure pushes at the inside of my body, and I know without a shred of doubt that I'm the one doing this.

I'm the one killing him.

My eyes squeeze shut as my hands slam over my ears. Crouching to the ground, I beg myself to wake up.

"Wynter . . . ."

A ragged breath escapes my lips when I hear his voice. My eyes shoot open, and I look up to see Ezra looming over me.

"I'm sorry," he breathes.

A single tear spills down his cheek, and the sight of it freezes me—holding me in place as he disintegrates into dust.

I wake with a start, and a loud gasp bursts from my lungs as I bolt upright. Sweat beads along every inch of my body, pooling inside my clothes and causing the material to cling to me like a second skin. Breathing in, I count backward from ten to steady my racing heart.

I remember it so clearly—the vision that's plagued my life from the moment this condition first took over. I remember the destruction. I remember the nothingness.

Above all, I remember Ezra. At least, in that moment.

I cast a hesitant glance at the chair beside the bed, and a surge of relief rushes through me when I see him sleeping there. He's here. He's alive. Yet, that knowledge is overwhelmed by what I saw in my dream. By what's destined to happen to this world. To him.

I run a shaking hand through my hair, but the damp, knotted roots trap my fingers. Pulling my legs against my chest, I curl into a ball, resting my forehead on top of my knees.

What does this mean? Why am I seeing this vision again now?

Aren't we safe?

Isn't the collar preventing that future?

I jump, startled by the sound of Ezra's voice.

"What is it?" he asks.

Concern glows in his eyes, but I can't ignore how much it reminds me of my dream. The way he looked at me.

The way he *will* look at me.

Turning away from him, I grumble, "Nothing. I'm fine."

"Wynter."

He stands up, and I feel the mattress shift beneath me as he settles himself on the bed. We're sitting close enough together that the heat from his body radiates against my skin. It reaches out to me, but he keeps his distance—preventing us from touching.

"I know that look."

When I peek up at him, a smile forms on his lips.

"Please," he whispers.

I swallow, nearly choking on the hard lump forming in my throat. How do I explain to him what this feels like? How do I make it clear that everything in my life right now is similar to water being poured into a cracked glass? I'm unable to hold onto what I love because it will always leave me.

It all slips through my fingers before I can even touch it.

Exhaling through my nose, I shake my head. "It was only a dream."

My memory replays the terrible images as if it's punishing me for lying to Ezra. Then it hits me. Was this why I left before? Was this why I went back to the DSD? To Dr. Richter?

The answer stares back at me with hazel eyes.

The cure.

My participation in the State's war and my willing submission.

I went back to try to change things. To save Ezra.

Can the future even be changed? I ask myself. *Or did my actions bring about the very future I wished to avoid?*

Perhaps it was always doomed to happen either way.

The twisting in my gut tells me I already know what the outcome will be, and it brings one daunting understanding along with it. Regardless of the visions—regardless of the multiple choices that seem to stand in front of me—the only certain path for me in this life is death.

So long as I'm alive . . . Ezra will never truly be safe.

"What time is it?" I ask, desperate to forget that thought. I can't bring myself to look up at him.

"Not sure," he answers, shrugging his shoulders. "It's late, though."

Day and night seem lost in this place, held hostage by the unrelenting fluorescent lights hanging overhead. We're trapped in a strange cycle of timelessness, with each day melting into the next.

Letting out a heavy breath, I stretch out my limbs, and for the first time since waking, I realize we're alone.

I jerk my head toward the door. "Where's Jenner?"

"He went to do some damage control. I think he was worried about what would happen if we didn't try. He left once you were asleep."

The tone of his voice unnerves me.

"You were right," he adds. "We do need to be more careful."

"I guess that explains why Nolan hasn't come after me yet," I murmur.

He runs his hand across the back of his neck—something I notice he keeps doing around me.

"Like I said, I'm pretty sure Bilken was a test. By now, Nolan's more than likely convinced you aren't a threat to anyone here. At least enough to leave you alone for the time being."

Based on the look on his face, I get the distinct impression that he doesn't fully believe this sentiment. Not that I blame him. After all, something tells me that my part in this is far from over.

I prepare to press the matter, but Ezra deters me before I can speak.

"Are you hungry?"

Thinking of the few meals I've pretty much been spoon-fed during my time here, I suppose I should be hungrier than I actually am. The truth is, with everything going on, I find it hard to have much of an appetite.

"More than anything, I just want a shower," I moan.

Ezra grins at me. "I think we can manage that."

Offering me his hand, he rises from the bed, pulling me to my feet the instant our skin touches. I trail behind him as we approach the door, and I watch as he pokes his head out into the corridor—no doubt checking for any unwanted company. After a moment, he nods over his shoulder and leads us into the hallway. A soft gasp rushes from my lips when his arm snakes around my waist, bringing me close to him.

As we walk, I peek up at him out of the corner of my eye. Conflicting emotions tumble through my body—a strange blend of embarrassment and comfort. The familiarity I find in his company is overwhelming, and my heart races in response to it as if begging me to remember.

Once again, I meet the frustration of my amnesia head on.

Why can't I remember? For someone who can see the future at will, this should be easy.

So, why isn't it? Did I choose to forget? Or did my time at the DSD wipe away my humanity to the point where my memories vanished along with it?

Regardless, all that matters is that the memories are at least somewhat intact. They're still in there somewhere—fragments that are being pulled out of me, piece by piece. I have to believe I'm capable of remembering everything. Of remembering Ezra and Jenner.

I just need to find a way to unbury those lost memories.

Ezra's hand tugs at my waist, yanking me out of my thoughts and through a nearby doorway. Glancing up, I notice we're standing in the compound's washroom.

A shudder runs up my spine when he whispers in my ear.

"Wait here." Unlatching his arm, he takes a few steps away from me and flits around the room like a buzzing fly as he checks each individual shower and stall. Less than two minutes pass before he's back by my side.

"We're in the clear," he announces, flashing a gentle grin. "It's all yours."

Meeting his gaze, I nod in acknowledgement. I wasn't particularly concerned with other people being here, but then again, I can understand why he would take such a precaution—especially after what he told me before.

If PHOENIX already wanted to kill me once, then what's stopping them from wanting that again?

"I'll be waiting just outside if you need me."

I nod again but remain silent.

He lingers for a second before turning toward the door, and I watch his retreating footsteps until he disappears from view. Taking a deep breath, my eyes trail across the room until they land on the showers in the far left corner. I walk over to the nearest cubicle and turn the handle a few times. Water springs in an energetic burst from the nozzle.

Steam fills the air, forming a foggy layer on the concrete walls and steel barriers separating this shower from the next. The warmth is inviting, so I begin to remove my clothes. The dried sweat on my skin causes the black bodysuit to stick to me, making it feel like I'm pulling at one long, caked on bandage. Once it's off, I let it fall to the floor with a thud.

Breathing in, I stick my hand beneath the piping hot water. My eyes follow the drops as they slide across my fingers, and I find myself thinking back on everything I've learned since arriving at this place. About Bilken. About my father. About PHOENIX.

My role as a pawn, torn between two sides.

Rai.

Jenner.

Ezra.

The memory of what I saw in my dream. The very thought of that future becoming a reality.

It's enough to cause the air to catch in my lungs, suffocating me as heart palpitations cripple my body. Sharp, shooting pains spread throughout my chest, making it feel as if I'm being stabbed.

"Why bring me back if you know what I'm capable of?" I asked him.

Ezra's voice echoes in my ears, bringing everything full circle. *"For the same reason you keep seeing me in your head,"* he answered.

The bits and pieces I've seen of him re-emerge in this moment. I remember the feel of his mouth on mine. The taste of his warm breath as he whispered against my lips.

How could I love someone but not remember them? How could I not remember and still know it's the truth when they say I love them?

Why else would I have stayed with Dr. Richter for so long? I knew I was protecting something, even if I couldn't remember what it was. What other explanation is there for why I became a willing submissive to the State's demands unless I was still harboring those feelings in some way?

I loved him.

I love him.

But I can't remember him.

I can't . . . but I *want* to.

The tap squeals with a loud shriek as I shut off the water. Leaving my clothes abandoned on the shower floor, I head toward a row of mirrors hanging over an equal number of sinks on the side of the room near the door we came in by. Wet footsteps trail behind me as I stop in front of the nearest one. I fix my eyes on the glass surface, staring at my reflection.

The person gazing back at me looks like me, but all I find there is a stranger. As if in response to my thoughts, an image ignites in my head, showing me another version of myself. However, this one is different from what I see in front of me.

Suddenly, I know what I have to do.

Locking my eyes on the next closest mirror, I concentrate hard until it shatters into pieces. The shards scatter across the sinks and floor, sprinkling across their surfaces like a downpour of hail. Turning in place, I glimpse a large, solitary fragment by my feet.

As I bend down to pluck it up, my fingers graze along the sharp knifelike edges.

"Wynter?" Ezra's voice calls from behind me.

In a sluggish movement, I glance over my shoulder. His eyes are wide as he stares back at me. I can see the worry in their depths, but even more, I see the confusion as his gaze trails across my naked body.

My hand is steady as I raise the shard, balancing the tip in dangerous proximity to my throat. Ezra reaches out his hands, and his mouth parts as if to scream for me to stop.

A smile of acceptance forms on my lips.

"I want to remember."

EIGHTEEN

"WAIT!"

I ignore the sound of Ezra's panic-filled voice and sweep the shard within an inch of my shoulder. My free hand takes hold of my hair at the same moment, holding it in place while I tighten my grip on the broken fragment. The glass slices through the waterlogged strands with ease.

A relieved breath trickles through my lips as I feel a heavy weight lift off my soul. My reflection behind me calls out in response to it, beckoning me to face her. As I do, my fingers slacken, dropping the large chunk of unwanted hair to the floor.

My eyes flash to my shortened locks, the ends now sitting just below the metal collar. The difference is drastic, but it's also familiar.

I study my features. My hair. My different colored eyes. Many long moments pass before I notice that the room behind me has changed. Spinning on my heel, I find myself staring at a set of steel doors. Elevator doors.

The elevator at W. P. Headquarters.

Reaching out, my fingertips touch the face of my distorted reflection. Upon contact, ripples flow across the metal in a fluid-like motion until they engulf my surroundings, drowning everything.

Within seconds, the vision transforms, bringing me to my quarters at the DSD—back when I was first taken by them. My eyes blink, and when they reopen, I'm in the underground compound where I met Jenner and Rai.

I blink again. Hundreds of glass fragments surround me, tiled along the walls in the side room of Bilken's office. I see my face reflected in each one.

Face, after face, after face.

A swelling sensation overwhelms my body, twisting my stomach until I can't hold it at bay any longer. I try to fight against it, but I'm unable to contain this power, and the pressure rushes out of my pores in a single wave of release. When it leaves me, I hear the abrupt shattering of glass.

I see the monster—I see myself—in the millions of glass shards that fall around me like rain.

Face . . . after face . . . after face . . .

A sharp breath catches in my throat, and suddenly, I realize that I'm back in the washroom. Goosebumps rise across my naked body. My dark tresses lay forgotten on the floor by my feet. My reflection stares back at me from the mirror above the sink, waiting for my reaction.

At first, I don't move. Instead, I look at the woman in front of me, recognizing that she isn't a stranger any longer.

Now, we're finally one and the same.

A slight movement in the mirror attracts my

attention, and a soft gasp rushes from my lungs as I turn in place. My heart begins to race when I lock eyes with the person standing there.

"Ezra," I breathe.

I hesitate, keeping my distance as I take in his face. A strained disbelief distorts his features, but in spite of that, I see the flicker of hope in his gaze.

A lump blocks my throat as I choke back a cry. Tears spill down my cheeks, burning my skin and lips. The urge to run to him rips through my body, taking control of my every movement. All I can hear is the sound of my feet slapping against the floor.

I feel his delicious heat before I even get the chance to touch him. His eyes widen when I collapse into his arms, and although I embrace him, he doesn't hug me back. I can't help wondering if it's because he's afraid to believe what my physical actions are implying. If he's afraid to believe I've come back to him when so many factors suggested that I wouldn't.

His body shifts, and his hands wrap around my back in a slow, cautious movement.

"Do you . . . remember?"

His words are a mere tremor in my ear, but I can hear the apprehension that lingers there, ringing through my head.

I reposition my arms around his neck. Snaking my fingers through his hair, I hug his face to my breast.

"Yes," I exhale in a breathless voice.

His body is still, but I can feel his heart pounding in the very surface of his skin. Each beat coincides with the erratic tempo of my own.

"I remember everything."

His grip on me tightens as a faint sigh of relief parts his lips. I cling to him in response, holding him to me and breathing him in. For a long while, we remain this way, encased in each other's arms.

Tears continue to flood my eyes. Tears of happiness, for the most part, although I can't escape the cruel reality hiding behind this moment. Eventually, the weight of what I'm feeling becomes too much for me to bear.

"I'm sorry," I whisper.

I repeat this several times, unable to abandon the guilt of everything I've put him through.

What he must've felt when I left him and later, when he saw what the State had turned me into.

What he must've felt when I came back and didn't remember who he was.

If only I could muster the words to tell him why his suffering was necessary.

For the past few months, I've questioned my amnesia and deliberated over Richter's potential role in causing it. What I didn't grasp then, and what I'm only remembering now, is that forgetting my past was entirely my own doing.

I chose to abandon those memories—not only because of the longing they stirred in my chest, but because I was afraid that Ezra and Jenner would be in danger if I didn't. With how I was treated at the DSD, sucked of intel on a daily basis, I couldn't hide anything from Dr. Richter. If either of them ever became a target of the State, I would be helpless to protect them. Shutting out my past was the only way to guarantee their safety and to cope with the guilt I felt over leaving them.

Plus, Dr. Richter messed with my brain so often that it got to a point where blocking out certain things, like emotions and memories, became easy. The one positive to come out of the experimentation and torture I was subjected to.

Still, no matter how much I try to justify it, no matter how many times I tell myself I did it to protect him, I can't escape the impact of my actions. I've hurt him, and I'll never be able to forgive myself for it.

"I'm sorry . . ." I whisper again.

Ezra pulls away from me, and his hands slide up my arms, coming to rest against my cheeks. Cupping my face, he lifts my chin, tempting me to look at him. With a shake of his head, he leans his forehead against mine.

I choke back another cry as I push myself even closer to him, and for this moment, I allow myself to revel in his touch. In turn, I reacquaint myself with feeling him beneath my fingertips.

It's just as it was the first time. The influx of emotions I was never permitted to show rush through my body with rapid intensity. They ingrain themselves in every fiber of my being until, just like the monster, they take control—manipulating my actions as if they're an alternate personality.

A blush reddens my cheeks as I remember the details of that night. Of our one true moment together.

The way he kissed me. The way it felt to be that close to him.

I'm overcome with the urge to experience that again.

"Kiss me," I gasp.

His lips slam into mine with a ravenous hunger as his hands move along my naked body, caressing every inch. The way he touches me causes my nerve endings to spring back to life, igniting me with a fire that blazes through my veins and finally settles in the pit of my belly. After being numb for so long, I can barely handle the extreme sensations. Regardless, I need to feel more.

I need to be reminded of what I was before.

Pulling him against me, I back toward the showers, one step at a time. I keep his lips fixed on mine, refusing to release him. Luckily, he doesn't seem to want me to.

My feet brush against the black bodysuit that lay abandoned on the floor, collecting moisture. Kicking it aside, my fingers fumble for the metal handle on the wall. With one quick jerk, the water sprays down on both of us.

Ezra reels back, startled. My hands reach up and take hold of his face, forcing him to look at me.

"I need to feel human."

He gapes at me as the drops run across my exposed torso. The wetness soaks his shirt, but he doesn't move.

I bring my face close to his until my breath touches his lips. "Please," I beg.

With that single word, he's back in my arms. His mouth finds mine as my hands remove his clothes, desperate to feel his body.

Desperate to relive that moment.

He trails kisses along my neck, and I can feel his teeth as he hums against my skin. Three beautiful words rise up to meet my ear.

"I've missed you."

Our eyes meet, and without saying anything more, we allow the water to overtake us.

NINETEEN

EZRA'S HAND GRAZES MY SPINE as he zips me back into the black bodysuit. I breathe in when the damp material suctions against my skin, wishing I could just discard the damn thing altogether. Unfortunately, there aren't any other alternatives when it comes to clothing right now.

His breath is warm on my neck as he plants a kiss behind my ear. Heat flushes my cheeks until I'm once again consumed by the memory of our entangled bodies. I don't think I've ever felt more human than I have the two times we've been together—wrapped around each other and baring ourselves completely.

If only we could remain that way forever.

His fingers touch my shoulders once the zipper is in place. They linger there for a moment, squeezing the top of my arms before trailing along my torso in a gentle caress. I peek up as he shifts me around to face him, smiling as he brushes a loose strand of hair from my lips.

"Promise me, you won't run away this time."

I laugh under my breath before quickly stopping

myself. The air catches in my lungs as I'm reminded of the reason I left him in the first place.

I remember my vision. The impending end of the world.

I remember seeing everyone die.

I remember seeing *him* die.

All trace of humor rushes out of me, leaving me feeling empty and cold. I know I can't abandon him again, but I also know I can't allow that future to happen.

So, what can I do? It seems like our proximity to one another is what keeps triggering that vision, and it makes me wary of being near him. Then again, I have the collar now. I'm in control, which means that path is no longer our set future.

Right . . . ?

"Wynter."

I glance up to see Ezra staring at me. His face is drawn, and I can tell by his expression that he's alarmed by my silence. There's a subtle question in his voice, and through it, I can hear what he's really asking.

Clearing my throat, I whisper, "I promise."

I cocoon myself in his arms, avoiding his gaze. As he holds me close, I listen to the way his heart beats with a strange urgency. Pressing my ear against his chest, I try to discern the reason for his unease, and a part of me wonders if it's because he doesn't believe me. Not that I can blame him.

I don't believe me either.

After a moment, he takes a step back. His fingers brush my arm before taking hold of my hand.

"We'd better go," he murmurs.

I nod despite the overwhelming reluctance I feel.

Following his lead, I allow him to pull me from the room. Our hands remain interlocked, but I can't ignore the feeling that he seems worried about something. At first, I think his reaction is a result of our brief exchange a moment earlier, but then I realize it has nothing to do with me. At least not directly.

The instant we open the door, I see what's bothering him.

I meet it, face-to-face.

Half a dozen men wait in formation around the entryway, blocking our exit. We stop short when they raise their weapons, but it doesn't take long for me to grasp why they're here.

Throwing out his arm, Ezra pushes me behind him.

Scanning the small group, I'm not the least bit surprised to see Quinn standing among them. When our eyes meet, a vicious scowl forms on his face.

"Nolan wants to see you," he says.

Ezra and I exchange nervous glances, and it's as if we can tell what the other is thinking. Considering the circumstances, we're both well aware that we have no other choice except to comply. Still, the expression on Ezra's face makes me question what he's so afraid of.

We're escorted through the corridors. No one utters a single word, and the atmosphere is charged with an eerie tension, bearing down on each of us. Especially me.

My eyes dart between the men, and I'm unnerved by the difference that stares me in the face. These people are the polar opposite of the PHOENIX I knew just two years ago. In fact, if I wasn't aware of who was responsible for bringing me here, I wouldn't even recognize them.

What changed? I wonder.

Although I already know the answer.

The futility of their cause.

The isolation and loneliness.

Committing heinous actions that they once claimed to stand against.

I suppose this was always inevitable. If one path doesn't work, it's human nature to strive for another, more logical option. That's exactly what PHOENIX has done, all for the chance of a better future.

Or so Nolan says.

I peer up at Ezra, but he doesn't look back at me. His face is drawn, and his eyebrows are pulled together as if he's lost deep in thought. For a moment, I find myself second-guessing if he knew how PHOENIX was planning to use me. If he knew this was going to happen.

Quinn leads the way, soon halting beside a set of large double doors—made of metal, just like the others. Curling his hand into a fist, he pounds it twice against the steel. Within seconds, the doors open.

The barrel of a gun digs into my back, pushing hard against my spine and forcing me into the room. My heart falters as I stumble over the threshold, and I'm both relieved and terrified to know Ezra is here with me. Lifting my gaze, I see Nolan and a few of his lackeys standing before us.

He acknowledges us with a nod of his head, and his eyes linger on mine for an excessive length of time. He looks intrigued—as if he's only just seen something he didn't notice before.

"You look different," he comments. "More like your old self." A smile peels at the corners of his lips.

"I feel like my old self, too," I mutter, not bothering to hide the snide tone of my voice.

Rodrick Nolan. I remember who he is now, and I can't deny that I'm surprised by this turn of events. He came across as such a gentle man before. Humble even.

I visualize the last time I saw him—back when Ezra made his speech to the people of PHOENIX, assuring them that I wasn't their enemy. Nolan had been that face in the crowd. The one they all looked to for guidance and acceptance. The silent leader who I now realize was simply biding his time, playing his twisted games from the shadows.

I remember who he is . . . and his expression tells me that he's well aware of it.

"Good," he says. "That will make this easier."

Time seems to slow as a feeling of dread clutches my chest. Before I can move to stop it from happening, two of Nolan's men grab Ezra while Quinn places a gun to the back of his head. A sick grimace of pleasure crosses the ex-Enforcer's face when he kicks the back of Ezra's legs, bringing him to his knees.

A scream of panic tears from my throat. "What are you doing?"

I begin to move forward, but Nolan's voice stops me in my tracks.

"Don't even think about it."

Quinn clicks off the safety on his gun as if to echo that warning.

A crippling feeling of helplessness overwhelms my entire being. Even though I could easily kill every person in this room, I doubt myself now that I have someone to protect. What if I'm not fast enough?

What if Quinn shoots him before I can intervene?

My eyes drift to where Ezra struggles on the floor. As I watch him—as I see the threat of imminent death hanging over his head—I realize that I will do whatever Nolan tells me without question. As sick as the thought of being a puppet again makes me, I will do whatever it takes to keep Ezra safe. I refuse to let anything happen to him because of me.

I refuse to let him die.

A lump swells in my throat as I try to swallow my anger, using every ounce of willpower I have to shove it back to a place where it won't put us in further danger. My hands ball into fists as I struggle to maintain control.

My eyes shift back toward Nolan when he speaks.

"Now, Wynter. I have something I wish to discuss with you."

Shaking my head, I whisper, "Why are you doing this?"

His sinister expression remains unchanged, for the most part. The one difference is in his eyes, which stare back at me with a mocking innocence, suggesting I've left him no other choice in the matter.

Suggesting this is my fault.

"So that you will cooperate," he answers. "Now that you have your memories back, you know what's at risk."

I twitch, baffled into temporary silence. Why didn't I see any of this coming? With everything Nolan's told me, I've always known I couldn't trust him, so the depths of his depravity should come as no surprise. Still, I've been so preoccupied with attempting to make sense of my broken memory and so determined not to use my powers under duress that I never took the time to consider using them to protect myself.

How could I have been so foolish? How could I have allowed things to get to this point?

Nolan moves forward, pacing in front of me. Each step is confident, intimidating even, as if he knows he's about to get exactly what he wants.

"I need you to tell me when the first attack will happen." When I don't respond, he clarifies. "On the Heart."

I can't stop myself from laughing. After all, I should've known. Plus, there's the irony of the situation and the reality that I might have seen this sooner if I had bothered to look into their plans.

One last humorless chuckle flees the confines of my lips. "I thought you weren't going to use me," I breathe.

"I don't want to use you. I want to show you the importance of helping our cause. Of preserving mankind."

My eyes narrow in disbelief. I reel back, amazed by his ignorance. "Preserve? Thousands of people will die."

If he can't realize the error of his ways, then maybe he can hear them. Although, I don't truly believe that he will.

As if to prove me right, my plea falls on deaf ears.

"More will die if we do nothing," he murmurs.

A feeling of nausea grips my stomach, weakening my resolve. Nolan's voice once again assaults my senses, making the queasy feeling overwhelming me even worse.

"You'd be doing the people a service."

My eyes widen as I'm brought back to my initial time at the DSD. I remember my first proper meeting with Dr. Richter and the similar words he said to me then.

"You'd be providing a great service, not only to science,

but to the State as well."

If only Nolan could see the similarities that I do.

"You know, Richter said the same thing to me once. Before he tortured me. Before he accelerated this disease. Before he imprisoned me for two years and turned me into a weapon." My teeth are clenched together by the time I finish speaking.

"I'm not asking you to fight," Nolan counters. "I'm asking you to save lives."

For a moment—a brief moment—I almost believe him.

Instead, I thrust my finger toward Ezra. "By threatening one of your own?" As the words rise from my throat, something in my head seems to click into place. I didn't understand it before, but now I do.

Ezra's and Jenner's disobedience.

The guards and soldier types I've encountered here.

The lack of normal civilians.

"That's why you worked from the shadows before, isn't it?" The realization springs out of me in a quiet, stunned voice. "That's why you let Ezra play leader. You knew they wouldn't follow you if they saw how you really are. If they knew what you really wanted."

The calm façade vanishes from his face—the mask sliding away and revealing the true nature hiding underneath. At the same moment, I notice Ezra hang his head. Glancing at him out of the corner of my eye, I realize he must've known about Nolan. Or, at the very least, suspected it. That's why he hasn't been involved with what's going on here. That's why he's been rebelling.

All at once, I'm hit with the truth. A truth I've been ignoring.

Ezra and Jenner are only here for *me*. They came here

to get me back the only way they knew how. Even if it meant betraying their morals. Even if it meant going against everything they believe in.

I stare at Ezra with an odd combination of remorse and gratitude. I'm tempted to say something to him—anything to show that I know what he's done for me.

Before I get the chance, Nolan's voice cuts me off.

"Ezra was a mere figurehead. He never had any real power. I was the acting Head of that sect, and I made every decision, every move. Besides, the people do not need a charismatic leader. They need a strong one. Someone who will rise up from the ashes of the ruined State and rule them."

"Rule?" I splutter in an incoherent whisper. "What happened to freedom?"

Nolan looks at me now with a dark intent in his eyes. As I stare back at him, I come to grips with the foreboding notion that this man is truly dangerous. Maybe even more so than Dr. Richter.

In an ominous breath, he says, "Even free people need someone to keep them in check."

What happened to not wanting to lead through fear? I'm tempted to ask him.

Maybe he doesn't think that he would be. Maybe he's convinced that he can rule while still maintaining some semblance of free will. Even if he could, it doesn't mean they would be any better than the State.

Silence descends upon the room like a veil of darkness. Time seems to freeze, and for a long while, no one even moves. When it feels as if the last speck of sanity will abandon me, Nolan asks the all-important question that's been balancing on the tip of his tongue.

"Now then," he says, clapping his hands together. "Will you do as I've asked?"

My eyes dart around the room as I consider what he's requesting of me. In an absentminded movement, my fingers rise to my neck and caress the metal collar.

My breath hitches as a sudden thought takes hold of me.

Can the DSD still access my collar? I wonder.

Can they obtain data or see the information it's collected from my visions? If they can, it means they'll be able to discover Nolan's plan. Or, at the very least, see enough to stop what's going to happen.

I purse my lips as I shake my head. If they *could* do that, they certainly would've put two and two together by now. The collar collects so much more than just the information on what I see. It collects my whereabouts—or it did before PHOENIX disabled the tracking chip.

A heavy feeling in my gut tells me the collar is useless in this respect. The only thing it's good for at this point is keeping me in control. If Dr. Richter had the means to access it, he would've found me by now. I'm sure of it.

My heart clenches as I stare at Ezra, still on his knees with a gun pointed at his head. If I do this for Nolan, people will die. If I don't, people will still die. Except in that scenario, Ezra and Jenner will be included among the casualties.

No, I tell myself. *Regardless of the alternative, I can't allow that to happen. I can't lose them, too.*

Exhaling a deep breath, I meet Nolan's gaze and nod my head once in unwilling agreement. It's all I can do to buy myself some time until I can figure out a better course of action. If there is one.

Oddly, in this moment, I find myself wishing for the one thing I never thought I would ever want.

I find myself hoping Dr. Richter will find me.

TWENTY

I TAKE IN MULTIPLE DEEP breaths, inhaling through my nose until my lungs are so full they can't hold any more air. Clearing my mind, I focus every thought on a specific moment in the future.

On the one moment Nolan wants me to see.

Closing my eyes, I embrace my inner darkness. The sights and sounds around me fall into the backdrop, but through the fog that veils my consciousness, I can still feel every person in the room watching me. Their anticipation mirrors my own.

It happens almost at once. I sense the change in my surroundings as the future comes to meet me, welcoming my existence like a long-lost friend. Swallowing my apprehension, I open my eyes.

As to be expected, I'm back in the Heart.

Back in Zone 1.

My feet stumble forward as my lips part in shock, stunned into silence by the horror I see around me. The city I knew is gone, and what stands before me now can only be described as complete and utter destruction. How reminiscent it is to the first vision I ever experienced makes this entire scenario even more daunting.

I remember it. The end of the world.

Yes. I shudder. *This is exactly what it looked like.*

My eyes trail across the ground and along the mangled bodies scattered among the dirt and debris. I take it all in, suppressing the nausea and heartache rising in my throat. Behind them, I can feel a scream there. A pure, hysterical cry of terror.

Once again, I think back to my original vision, remembering the endless blanket of death that I alone will be responsible for. What I see before me now replicates that image so closely that I can be forgiven for confusing the two. However, I didn't cause this death, this destruction.

This is someone else's doing.

So, what does this mean? I'm in control now, so that vision I saw when my condition first developed— back in the classroom at W. P. Headquarters—will no longer come from me.

But then what about my dream?

Unless, this is only a precursor. Unless the end of the world is fated to happen, regardless of the role I play in its destruction.

I'm hit with a sudden, foreboding thought. *What if the universe wants it to happen?*

What if Mother Nature has a backup plan— an alternative in case I fail to deliver the mass extermination it has in store for us?

What if the apocalypse will happen anyway? No longer because of me, but because of war?

Project W. A. R., a voice whispers in the back of my head.

A shiver runs up my spine when I make the connection. This attack will only happen because of me. Because of what I am.

Maybe I will be the cause of it, after all.

The rubble crunches beneath my feet as I take a hesitant step forward. As if in response to the movement, my surroundings begin to change. Everything vibrates, pulsating like a beating heart until it reverts to how it was before—moving backward to the point in time when the attack first began.

I see the explosions.

I see life return to the broken corpses around me.

I see the buildings and monuments repair themselves as the cloud of dust hanging in the air melts away into nonexistence.

A clock chimes, echoing through the reconstructed plaza. Glancing over my shoulder, I notice the large tower overlooking Zone 1. Narrowing my eyes, I make a mental note of the time before peering at the outer rim where the date encircles the clock's face.

"Two days."

Breathing in, I open my eyes, and suddenly, I find myself back in the compound. Nolan stands in front of me, wearing an eager but stern expression.

"Two days," I repeat through a heavy breath. "It'll happen in two days."

He assesses me for a moment, squinting his eyes as he searches my face—presumably trying to determine if I'm lying. I remain still under his leering gaze, refusing to give him any reason to doubt me.

"Very good," he finally says. "Thank you for your cooperation."

He waves his hand, signaling to Quinn and the other men, who lower their weapons in response.

I risk a glance out of the corner of my eye, and an intense relief courses through my body when Quinn retracts the gun placed against the back of Ezra's head. His chest rises and falls as he takes a deep breath, but he doesn't move otherwise.

Content with Ezra's safety for the time being, I fix my unblinking gaze back on Nolan. He crosses the room to a desk positioned in the far corner and drags his hands across the glass surface. The desktop purrs to life in response, revealing the computer hidden within. His fingers tap the screen, but I can't see what he's doing.

A flare of irritation consumes me, triggered by his dismissive attitude even after what I've done for him. Unable to stop myself, my body reacts. Two guards attempt to detain me when I begin to storm forward.

"Their blood will be on your hands!" I scream.

Strong arms wrap around me, but I don't struggle against them. I don't want to be like Nolan. I despise the idea of being responsible for any more unnecessary deaths, especially when I'm well aware of how many I've already caused.

Nolan looks up at me but says nothing. Focusing his attention back on the screen, he waves us away with a flick of his wrist.

My feet scrape against the floor as I'm escorted from the room—his lackeys dragging me away with no regard for my well-being. Yet again, it alarms me how similar they are to the people at the DSD. If Nolan is the spitting image of Richter, then these people are his orderlies.

Letting out a breath, my body goes limp as I succumb to what's beginning to feel like the natural progression of my life. This place is nothing more than a mirror image of everything I went through before.

The two men gripping my arms tug me toward the door, but they hesitate when Nolan's voice projects across the room.

"Oh, Wynter," he calls.

My heart pounds with violent intensity as his sinister footsteps echo off the concrete, resounding in my ears. Keeping his hands clasped behind his back, he glares down at me with a sickening expression of superiority.

"I've summoned the Heads of the other sects. When they arrive, you will be required to meet with them. They will wish to hear what you've seen for themselves." Turning away from me, he mutters under his breath, "That is not a request."

With another wave of his hand, the guards continue their onward march, hauling me off to who knows where with Quinn leading the charge. I look behind me to see Ezra receiving the same treatment, and it only now hits me what he's gotten himself into. He'll be viewed the same as me from here on out. A danger. A menace.

A *threat*.

A part of me wonders if he understands what that means. Although I suppose, in the long run, it doesn't matter. What's done is done. One way or another, it's clear that the short-lived freedom we enjoyed before is now over.

Within a matter of minutes, we find ourselves back outside the door to my personal prison. The handle squeals as Quinn yanks it open.

"What the hell is this?" I hear Ezra growl.

A vague hint of a smile plays on Quinn's lips, becoming more apparent when the guards shift position.

A muffled cry of protest forms in my throat as I watch them take turns kneeing Ezra in the stomach. The only thing stopping me from intervening is the gun aimed at the back of his head. Once they're finished, they push him to the floor and kick his injured body to the other side of the doorway. My heart seizes as he crumples into a helpless, wounded ball.

My eyes lock with Quinn's, but no words can convey what I'm feeling right now.

Smirking, he purrs in a taunting voice, "Payback's a bitch."

Ezra grunts as he gasps for air, and as soon as the guards release their hold on my arms, I rush to his side. The door clangs shut behind me.

I cast an angry glance over my shoulder before turning my full attention to Ezra. In a careful motion, I brush my hand against his forehead while the other gently touches his shoulder. The whole time, a feeling of guilt rushes through me.

I've done this.

He's here because of *me*.

My lips quiver with an emotion that threatens to choke me. A soft groan coming from the corner distracts me from it for a brief instant, but when I look up, that feeling of guilt returns—weighing me down as it doubles on top of me.

"Jenner," I gasp.

Even though he's pressed against the wall, I can still see the blood and bruises covering his face. His entire body shakes when he releases another breath.

Without a second thought, I dart across the room. Crouching to the floor, I try to be mindful of his personal space—especially considering his current condition. However, I can't resist the urge to reach out and touch him. He flinches when I place my hands on his cheeks.

"What happened?" I breathe.

An unexpected smile crosses his face, and I reel back in shock when he croaks out a laugh.

"I don't think he appreciated me putting a gun to his head."

He coughs a few times but quickly covers his mouth. A feeling of alarm takes hold of me when I glimpse the spray of blood coating his fingers.

My jaw tenses as my teeth grit together. Staring at Jenner's face, I make a silent promise to myself. I vow that, if the opportunity presents itself, Quinn will pay for what he's done.

A grunt of pain alerts me to Ezra's presence, and I glance up to see him standing beside us, holding an arm across his midsection. Leaning against the wall for support, his lips curl into a grimace as he slides to the floor.

"How long have you been here?" he asks Jenner once he's settled.

Jenner shrugs his shoulders as much as he's able to. "Pretty much since I left your quarters last night."

My eyes widen as a fresh wave of guilt washes over me. When I was with Ezra, Jenner was here. In pain.

Alone.

A shiver runs across my skin at the thought, and in spite of the control it gives me, I find myself resenting the collar around my neck. If only I didn't always have to be on the lookout. If only I could just see the important things when I need to.

I stop myself. This isn't the collar's fault. This is *my* fault. If only I had been more aware. If only I had been more concerned with anyone other than myself. My mind was preoccupied with everything Ezra, and there was no room for Jenner in my head at that moment.

I'm startled out of my thoughts by the sensation of a finger poking my left cheek. I look up to see Jenner staring at me. His hand drops to the floor as he smiles.

"You're you again . . . aren't you?"

My eyes begin to burn, and I sniff, holding back the tears—all too aware they'll do nothing to help us. To help him.

"How did you know?" I wonder.

Once again, he pokes my cheek, grinning at my expression. "That," he whispers. "That's how I know. It gives you away. It always gives you away." He pauses to take a long, deep breath. "I'm glad you're back."

"I'm sorry it took me so long."

The way he looks at me is unbearable, so I reposition myself on the floor between them and turn my eyes so I'm facing the steel door. It would be easy for me to open it. Too easy, even. I just don't have that same level of confidence when it comes to keeping Ezra and Jenner alive. Anything could happen beyond these walls, and without absolute certainty, it's just not worth the risk. Not yet, at least.

Not without knowing more about our current situation.

Ezra unleashes a loud howl of exasperation and slams his fist once against the wall. A tremor runs over my hand as I rub it across my forehead, feeling my own frustration taking hold.

Letting out a sigh, I mutter, "Everything is so different now. I don't understand it."

At first, neither one of them responds. A strange unease clouds the room, although I can't pinpoint the direct cause of it. Finally, Ezra's voice breaks the silence.

"We saw the first changes shortly after you left."

A feeling of dread sits like a lead weight in my gut, forcing me to accept his impending confession.

He knew.

"There were more meetings. Intel became highly secretive, and before we were even aware of it, Nolan had come out of the woodwork. He had somehow convinced the other Heads to elect him as our leader. I'm sure it wasn't too difficult, considering the part he played in establishing PHOENIX in the first place. After the chips fell into place, his demeanor changed. It became clear that his motives weren't to simply dissolve the State, but to rule in place of it . . ."

Seeming to sense his vacillating emotions, Jenner carries on in his place. "What's even worse is that the other Heads supported it," he grumbles. "I think they got tired of nothing happening."

My eyes dart between them, but I'm not sure what to say. Jenner's comment makes sense. I even remember him telling me once that he wouldn't be surprised if PHOENIX wound up negotiating with the State at some point. Still, there's so much I don't quite grasp beyond that.

"At first, we were on board. I mean, *anything* had to be better than the State, right? But we were blind." Lowering his eyes, Jenner shakes his head. "We knew Nolan's ultimate endgame but had no idea how he planned to get there, and he did a damn good job of getting what he wanted without having to do any of the dirty work himself. He made it seem like your extraction was our idea and that we'd be responsible if things went wrong."

"A burden we were willing to bear," Ezra whispers.

When I meet his gaze, he looks away as if embarrassed.

"We were only ever here for you," he admits. "We knew it was the one chance we'd have to get you back, and Nolan was aware of that every step of the way. When you told me about your collar, I began to suspect what was going on, and our little get together with Nolan just now confirmed it. He would've gone through with the extraction regardless of us because he needs you to execute his plan. He only kept us around as bait to get you to cooperate and deliver what he wants. Actually, thinking of it like that, we've probably unknowingly been prisoners this entire time. I doubt we would've ever been allowed to leave." An expression of disgust crosses his face when he looks up at me. "We've been used . . . just like they're planning to use you."

"That explains why Nolan didn't just kill me right off the bat."

I didn't understand it before, but now his motives make sense. He needed my power to determine when the State would be at its weakest. Aware that I wouldn't cooperate, he also knew he would need something to ensure my compliance. So, he used the only advantage he had by forcing me to regain my memories and then threatening the only two people I care about.

Just as I've felt many times in the past, I can't ignore the fact that I'm always playing a part and being used as a pawn in someone else's war.

A predestined role which I can't seem to escape.

"It won't be long now."

I cock an eyebrow at Jenner in fearful confusion, alarmed by his cryptic words.

"When I went to try to pacify the situation, I overheard Nolan say they won't have any further need for you once everything is *in place*." He bends his fingers in the air to emphasize the end of this statement. Sneering, he adds in a quiet voice, "Or us."

My heart drops.

"It's all my fault," I breathe. "I should've never come to you for help in the first place."

I can't escape the feeling that everything that's happened since I first met PHOENIX is because of me. Rai's death. Ezra's and Jenner's imprisonment. It's all because of me.

The people I love always get hurt.

"Hey." Ezra reaches out his hand and grabs hold of mine, forcing me to look at him. "Don't say that. We'll find a way out of this. We always do."

Pulling away from him, I hang my head, and my hands tighten into fists as my helplessness looms over me. For someone who has experienced such terrifying power, it's maddening how limited I am by it.

Is there nothing I can do to stop this? I ask myself.

I did what Nolan wanted me to do, exhausting my usefulness in the process, and it doesn't surprise me at all to hear they no longer need me alive. Even if they did, they would just continue to use Ezra and Jenner as leverage, which is the exact reason Nolan wanted me to regain my memory.

Why else bring Bilken into it? Why else allow me time with Ezra? Without them, I was nothing more than a mindless drone. A killing machine created by the State with no reason to turn against it.

Trepidation moves through me as I grasp Jenner's words.

If I'm no longer needed, they won't be either.

I can't let that happen.

I can't let anyone else I care about die.

A peculiar feeling of déjà vu swallows me whole. It points out the irony of my thoughts—how the very idea that made me leave them before is now the one thing holding me here and pressuring me to do nothing.

To let the pieces fall where they may.

Once again, Ezra groans in frustration. Leaning forward, he glances between me and Jenner. "So, what now?"

I stare off into the nothingness of the room, aware that we only have one option.

Mimicking Jenner's statement from yesterday, I mutter, "Now, we wait."

TWENTY-ONE

MY EYES DART UP WHEN the door swings open. The metal screams, shrieking with agony as it seems to reach out to grab us where we sit huddled in the corner. Ezra and Jenner stumble to their feet, and I follow suit, sliding my hand along the concrete wall to guide me up.

Quinn steps over the threshold with his fingers wrapped around his gun. "It's time."

Ezra takes hold of my hand, and I feel Jenner touch my shoulder. We move forward together as one cohesive unit.

As we walk, I'm unnerved by Quinn's blank expression and stillness. The entire time, I wait for the inevitable drawback.

I discover what it is as soon as we reach the doorway.

Extending his arm to block the entrance, he growls, "Only her."

Ezra's arm tenses, and his hold on me tightens until the grip of his hand is painful. Leaning forward, he brings his face within an inch of the ex-Enforcer's.

"If you think there's any way in hell—"

Remembering what happened the last time he pissed off Quinn, I shove my body between them, eager to defuse the situation.

"It's okay," I mutter.

In truth, I'm apprehensive about going through this alone, but I can't allow Ezra to get into any more trouble because of me. At the rate he's going, I'm surprised he hasn't already gotten himself killed.

His hazel eyes meet mine, incredulity and anger burning within them. My fingers squeeze his in an attempt to calm those raging emotions.

"I'll be fine," I reassure him.

He doesn't respond, but he also doesn't try to restrain me when my hand slides away from his.

Turning away before I can change my mind, I follow Quinn through the open door—never once looking back as the metal clangs shut behind us.

Trailing after him, I trace his every footstep through the corridors in silence, following like a shadow. Although I'm unfamiliar with the route he takes, I'm well aware what awaits me at the end of it.

The meeting Nolan spoke of with the other Heads of PHOENIX.

I try to visualize their faces, wondering if they're as twisted and manipulative as their leader, but all I can imagine is a sea of masks. Identical, emotionless, and hiding their true intent.

A grimace twists my lips as pins and needles attack my skin, and a ball of anxiety forms in my stomach, making me feel sick and even more unsettled than I did only moments earlier.

Why not look? I ask myself.

I consider that option for a few steps. Even if I did look, it wouldn't do any good. I can't change what's going to happen, no matter what I see.

Plus, there's the added issue of Quinn. I know how he feels about me. After all, he's made no secret of his contempt for my existence. With that in mind, it's a very real possibility he may view any attempt to use my power as a personal threat against him. I could handle him with ease, but the truth is, I don't want to. At the end of the day, he's an innocent in this. I may not like him, but that doesn't mean he deserves to die.

Glancing up, I pass a few minutes studying the back of his head. I'm overcome with a genuine feeling of curiosity, and so I quicken my pace until I'm walking beside him. The rigidity of his stride becomes more apparent when he casts a suspicious look at me out of the corner of his eye.

Now or never.

"What's your problem with them?" I ask. "With Ezra and Jenner?"

A small mocking laugh rises up from his lungs, and for a brief instant, I'm amazed that he's going to answer.

"They don't respect authority or the rules," he grumbles.

"Spoken like a true Enforcer," I note. I ignore the scalding look he flashes in my direction.

Silence fills the corridor as I ready myself for what I'm about to do. It's risky, but it's the only option we have.

"You abandoned the State because you don't agree with their methods."

He looks startled by my statement but manages to maintain his composure. After a few seconds, he clears his throat—immediately firing back, "It's *you* I don't agree with. What I've seen you do. No one deserves that."

A rush of anger overtakes me. Throwing myself in front of him, I block his path. He reels back as every part of his body freezes in place, except the hand clutching his gun.

"And I deserve what the DSD did to me? I never asked for any of this."

Inhaling a deep breath, I calm myself down and refocus on the task at hand. I can only hope what I'm saying will eventually get through to him.

"Do you honestly think I would've killed those people if I had another choice?" I whisper.

His expression is vacant, although his lips are pursed together. With the unresponsive way he's reacting, they may as well be sewn shut.

My hands squeeze into fists as the anger returns. "You say it's me you don't agree with. If that's the case, why did you leave the State just to join an organization that intends to use me as well?" I meet his cold gaze with a fiery glare of disgust. "Where's your conscience now?" I spit.

My words seem to hit a nerve because his expression transitions into a resentful scowl. His sharp tone bites back at me. "My conscience is clear."

I cock an eyebrow in doubt. "Will it still be clear when thousands of your countrymen lay slaughtered in the streets?"

His upper lip twitches. Instead of responding, he raises his gun and shoves the front of the barrel into my ribs with a rough jab. "Keep walking."

His threat doesn't faze me. That weapon is nothing more than a mere toy I could rip away and turn back on him without even having to lift a finger. I only refrain from doing so because of Ezra and Jenner. Like

I've told myself before, I can't allow them to pay for my actions.

We continue our onward trek in silence. The sound of our footsteps echoes throughout the corridor like the gentle ticking of a clock, counting down to the fateful moment that ultimately awaits me. Quinn stops beside yet another metal door, bringing that moment closer.

I linger behind him as he bangs the side of his fist against the steel. When it creaks open an instant later, he takes a reflexive step back.

My expression remains unchanged when he turns around to face me. For a split second, our eyes meet, but he looks away as he elevates his chin and presses his back against the wall. Lifting his arms, he signals toward the door with the end of his gun. When I don't budge, he jerks his head to reiterate the action.

Sweat breaks out across my palms as my hands ball even tighter, and breathing in, I take a reluctant step forward. I can feel Quinn's eyes following my movements as my body crosses the threshold, but I'm far more concerned with what stands in front of me.

My first reaction is alarm. Figures surround me on all sides, and I would have been astounded by the number of people present in the room if I hadn't expected it based on what Nolan said earlier. This would be an important meeting. Paramount to the future of PHOENIX.

Armed guards line the walls—at least six for each of the Heads sitting along the rounded edge of a table that spans the entire length of the room. A large half-moon construction made of steel, it's the only piece of furniture in the otherwise barren space. With the exception, of course, of the single chair facing it.

The chair meant for me.

A hum of chatter settles around me like a cloud of smoke. It only dies away when, one by one, the people acknowledge my presence. The legs of a metal chair scratch across the floor, drawing my attention to Nolan, who now stands to welcome me.

"Ah, Wynter," he says in a pleasant, surprised voice.

Ironic considering he's the one who called me here.

He waves his hand in a dramatic gesture, ushering me to the solitary chair positioned across from him. My every step is confident and steady as I march toward it.

Nolan returns to his seat once I've lowered into mine. He then claps his hands together before spreading them out in front of his chest, indicating the others sitting beside him.

"Allow me to introduce you to the Heads of PHOENIX."

He rattles off a string of names, but I don't hear a word he says. Instead, I focus on their faces.

Six men of varying ages sit across from me, accompanied by one woman who looks to be in her late forties.

Probably around the same age as Mother, I muse.

I rest my gaze on her, trying to determine if she's someone we could look to for aid or if she's all that more terrifying because of her ability to infiltrate this world of men. A faint modicum of respect for her swells in my chest, but it disintegrates the second I remember why she's here, and even more so when I remember that she supports Nolan's plan.

His voice pulls me back to the reason for this meeting.

"We were just discussing what you told me before,

but why not let them hear it from you? While you're at it, perhaps you can enlighten us on the details."

I suck in a sharp breath. My jaw tenses, preventing me from speaking. After what feels like an eternity of silence, I reposition myself and clear my throat.

"I've already told you when it'll happen. What more do you want to know?"

Nolan holds out his hand to stop me, causing my apprehension to grow. My stomach twists with a sensation similar to the one I often felt around Dr. Richter.

In a casual tone, he suggests, "Why don't you start by telling us what sort of attack we should expect? What will the fallout be?"

It takes everything I have to suppress my anger. These are people we're talking about. People are going to die because of his planned inaction, and here he is, acting as if they aren't important. Mere pawns to be used.

As if they're the same as me.

Bile rises in my throat as my stomach flips. Nolan's attitude toward the impending death toll is so far beyond appalling that I can't even think of a proper word to describe it. All I know is, for the first time in my life, I'm grateful that my father is dead. Thankful that he isn't alive to see this—to witness what PHOENIX has turned into.

Biting the inside of my lower lip, I fight back the tears.

This isn't the sort of world he wanted.

Swallowing the nausea, I straighten my back, trying to remain as calm as possible. "The attack will be isolated to the Heart, but it will be devastating," I answer. "Thousands will die."

I've said these exact words to him once before. I suppose on some level, a part of me hopes he'll finally hear what I've been saying while another part of me—a far more sensible part—knows that he won't. That he can't.

Or maybe he just doesn't care.

"And the State's response?" he asks, proving the sensible part of me right. "What of the aftermath?"

My lips begin to move, but before I can speak, one of the other Heads joins in on the conversation.

"Martial law, no doubt."

My eyes shift to the woman.

"The attack will result in chaos," adds the man sitting at the far left side of the table.

I jump when the elderly man beside Nolan slams his hand down hard on the steel surface. "That makes it the perfect time to attack!" he barks.

Muttering their agreement, the other Heads second his statement.

All except for Nolan.

"Or a dangerous time," he says.

He taps his fingers against the whiskers on his chin and stares off into the room behind me as if lost deep in thought. With the future of PHOENIX and our entire country standing before him, I don't blame him for taking a moment to consider his options—assuming he hasn't already made up his mind.

"Wynter," he breathes suddenly. "What are your thoughts?"

I gape at him in shock, taken aback by his unnecessary need to include me in a debate I'd rather avoid at all costs. The fact that he's forcing me to participate makes my disdain toward him that much more potent.

Why ask for my advice when he'll only do the opposite? Why offer my opinion when I know he won't listen to it?

"The entire Heart will be crippled. Isn't that what you want?" I whisper.

I wince when his lips pull up into a smile. Either he finds my attitude toward him amusing, or he really is as sick and twisted as I fear.

In a graceful, fluid movement, he rises from his chair.

"It's decided then. We'll move out after the first strikes and penetrate the Heart before the State has the opportunity to respond. We'll utilize the tunnel system to remain clear of the bombings, then go from there." He claps his hands together while grunting, "That concludes this meeting."

Noting the dismissal in his tone, the other Heads begin to stand. As the meeting adjourns and the sound of shuffling feet thunders throughout the room, Nolan makes one final announcement.

"Rest now while there's still time."

As he says this, his eyes land on mine. There's a hint of knowing in his gaze that unsettles me beyond reason. I'm not quite sure what it is that I see there, but I can say with certainty that, for once, I've met someone even worse than me.

Someone with more blood on their hands than the very person responsible for causing this damn war.

TWENTY-TWO

I REMAIN IN MY SEAT, staring at the spot where Nolan stood only seconds ago. The way he looked at me. The way he spoke those final words.

I could sense the warning hidden there.

The threat.

Breathing in, my lungs constrict when I hear the sound of heavy footsteps. They reflect off the floor, resounding around me and growing louder until they stop altogether, lingering like a shadow just behind my seat.

A slight stench wafts toward me, accompanied by a wave of heat that radiates with such intensity from the person's body that I can feel it like a hand pressing against my back. I tense, awaiting the confrontation about to descend on me at any moment.

"You must be relieved. Your part to play in all of this is coming to an end."

Looking over my shoulder, I see Wren Bilken standing behind me. With a quick glance around the room, I realize we're the only two still here.

His large frame blocks out the fluorescent light hanging above us. His stance is intimidating, but I remind myself that he's human. He's no different than the bodies that have piled up at my feet.

Still, I'd be lying if I said his words didn't affect me. After all, there's only one possible end for someone like me, especially now that I'm no longer needed. I'm too dangerous to keep alive, and despite the fact that I'm cooperating with PHOENIX and doing what Nolan wants, he's undoubtedly aware that he can't rein me in forever. Dr. Richter tried and look at how well that turned out for him.

There will always be someone else out there. Someone stronger who can take me away and turn me back on the person I belonged to.

The charade can't go on for much longer.

My eyes narrow as I stare at Bilken, and a long moment passes before my voice breaks the silence.

"And what about your part?" I ask. "It seems your services are no longer needed here either."

His eyes are dark as he stares at me, and in many ways, it reminds me of the first time I met him—back when I was being interviewed for my work placement exam. Back when my life still held some semblance of normality. The terrorizing fear he struck within me still lingers in the back of my brain, despite everything I've been through since that moment.

"I have many talents and qualities that will be indispensable when we build the new world." His lips pinch into a tight, menacing grin. "There's still use for me yet."

"I thought the State *was* the new world," I sneer.

He shrugs, keeping his tone indifferent. "There's always room for improvement."

An irritating expression crosses his face, and I'm overcome with an uncontrollable urge to hit him. It takes everything I have to smother that feeling. To remind myself of Ezra and Jenner locked away in that cell and how their very lives depend on the actions I take now.

Inhaling a deep breath, I redirect my anger into a simple question. "Why abandon what you worked so hard for? It must be exhausting to keep starting over."

Although we're alone in the room, I'm aware that others are bound to be lingering nearby. Quinn, in particular. As if in response to this thought, I notice him hovering by the doorway.

Bilken turns away from me, and his heavy footsteps resume as he begins to pace the length of the floor behind my chair.

"The world is always changing," he says. "The ones who survive are the ones who know which side to choose when the time comes."

I gawk at him in genuine bewilderment, following his every movement.

Shaking my head, I whisper, "You couldn't have anticipated this. You couldn't have known it would get to this point."

His footsteps abruptly cease. "Couldn't I? The signs were all there."

He carries on with his pacing, and I notice the distance between us shrink as he moves closer to the table. I watch him, never once allowing myself to miss even a single breath.

"Perhaps you don't know this . . ." He hesitates, seeming to rethink his words. "Or maybe you do, and you simply don't wish to accept it. The State was once no different than PHOENIX. They were a group who desired change and saw the opportunity to rise up and make their mark. Unfortunately, not every organization has good intentions."

Disbelief floods my system, spreading throughout my body like venom rushing through my veins. *"The State was once no different than PHOENIX."* I roll those words over in my head, trying to determine their validity.

Is it true?

Could it be true?

I recall my own epiphany when I first noticed the similarities between PHOENIX and the State. How I had compared them to two sides of the same coin.

Is it true? I ask myself once more.

Of course, it is, a small voice in the back of my head answers.

"Like many radical regimes of the past, the very thing the State wanted would be the thing to destroy it." He pauses for effect, lowering his voice as he breathes that single all-important word. "Power. They wanted too much too quickly, and it was always inevitable that it would lead to their destruction."

I scowl. The hatred I feel intensifies in this moment, consuming my body like a sickness. With each passing second, the feeling grows, feeding that loathing until it's the only emotion left within me.

"What next, then?" I ask. "PHOENIX takes over and ten or twenty years down the line, they're heading in the same direction. Do you abandon them, too?"

His jaw tenses, and I notice a hint of a human emotion seep through his otherwise inhuman shell.

He takes a step forward, and similar to a menacing storm cloud, his broad figure looms over me. I don't rise from my seat, but I don't look away either. Unlike the frightened girl he met all those years ago, I refuse to turn away from him now. To be intimidated.

Out of the corner of my eye, I notice his hands ball into fists.

"Do not confuse ambition with loyalty," he growls. "Men like me get into positions of power because we do what must be done to survive and get ahead."

Labored breaths escape his lips, and in a strange way, he reminds me of W. P. Headquarters—the very organization he once represented. The day I went to take my placement exam, the building towered over me—much like he does now. He's a terrifying and even somewhat threatening entity, but in reality, he's nothing more than an obstacle that must be overcome.

A smile curves along my lips as I picture him as the small, pathetic man he really is. The trouble is, as he said himself, men like him do whatever they have to. They step over people and destroy anyone blocking their path to success.

My eyes widen as his voice cuts through the air like a knife. Each syllable drives the blade deeper into my chest, opening my heart and slicing it in two.

"Your father chose loyalty over ambition. Look where that got him. Maybe if he'd been smart, he'd still be alive."

His words engulf my very existence, wrapping around my body and turning me into ice. I can't speak, move, or think. All I'm able to do in this moment is feel.

And what I feel right now is anger.

The rage bubbles through my veins, coursing through my body like an unruly fire. The heat of it melts through the ice within seconds—freeing me of its hold.

Without thinking of the consequences, I leap out of my seat. The metal clangs to the floor as I push against it, pouncing like a wild cat. The last of my humanity falls along with the chair—discarded in this flash of madness.

Bilken stumbles back when I land on his chest. His heavy frame crashes to the concrete floor, sending a tremor throughout the room. I'm light and quick compared to him, and I pin him down in spite of the fact that, if the roles were reversed, he could overpower me with ease. My legs straddle his torso as my hands reach for his neck.

I consider using my powers on him, but it would be far too easy—too unsatisfying. No, in this moment, I want him to feel *me*—to feel my hands extinguish the miserable life he has betrayed so many others to cling to.

His large body struggles beneath me, and I know with one wrong move, he could throw me off. I'm small compared to him. Minuscule even. But what he didn't anticipate—and still doesn't seem to understand—is my ferocity. The animal caged within me is finally freed, clawing in savage hunger at his throat.

Unfortunately, my fight only lasts for about thirty seconds.

A pair of strong arms wrap around my waist, tearing me away from Bilken before I can do any real damage. A sharp pain rushes through my hip as I'm thrown onto the floor.

I look up, ready to pounce again, only to find myself at the end of a gun. Reeling back, my eyes land on the person standing behind it.

On Quinn.

"Enough," he hisses through clenched teeth.

When I make no attempt to move, Quinn holsters his weapon and reaches down to lift me up. His grasp is firm around my arm, and his fingers tighten further once I'm back on my feet.

He holds me in place as Bilken steadies himself. I watch as my victim pushes himself off the floor and straightens his clothes with a few aggressive strokes of his hands. Without another word, he storms toward the doorway, only pausing to give me one last heated glare.

"Loyalty will be your downfall as well. Like father like daughter. At least your mother had the sense to know which side to choose."

His words are sharp, plunging the figurative knife even deeper into my chest.

"What?" I gasp.

He ignores me as he crosses the threshold, taking any answers with him.

A fog of confusion muddles my brain, disorienting everything around me. What does he know about my mother or about her loyalties?

"Wait, *what* did you just say?" I scream after him.

Quinn steps in front of me, barring me from moving. Instead, my eyes follow Bilken until he disappears from view. The entire time, every fiber of my being focuses on one emotion and one emotion only.

Hatred.

I never hated anyone or anything before all of this happened. It wasn't a natural part of life as dictated by the State, and as such, it was an unfamiliar feeling to me. When I met Dr. Richter, I thought I understood what it felt like, but now I realize I was wrong.

I will never despise anyone as much as I despise Wren Bilken. With one exception, of course.

Me.

When it really comes down to it, what Bilken said is the truth, and it makes me hate myself even more than I hate him. Because loyalty *did* kill my father. Not loyalty to his country or loyalty to PHOENIX. Not even loyalty to my mother, his wife.

It was his loyalty to me that caused his death.

Closing my eyes, I take a deep breath. All the while, I register Quinn's grip on my arm. Without meeting his gaze, I nod my head, allowing him to lead me from the room in silence.

TWENTY-THREE

MY FEET DRAG IN A repetitive, slow trudge through the corridors, trailing behind Quinn as we retrace our steps back to the room where Ezra and Jenner remain imprisoned. The extreme rage that took hold of me only moments before has dissipated, leaving me feeling deflated and weak.

My thoughts revolve around Bilken. I could've killed him for his callous remark about my father, but how would I have felt afterward when I know what he said is true?

My father.

My father . . .

I knew his loyalty had killed him from the moment I read his journal. One more burden of guilt I now carry on my shoulders. Bilken believes the same thing will happen to me, but the only future I'm aware of is the one I first saw at my work placement exam.

The thought of it haunts me, and once again, I'm reminded of what will happen in the Heart when the State is attacked.

Which future awaits us? One of them?

Both of them?

What's stopping me from finding out? I wonder.

After everything I've done, after everything I've seen, maybe I just can't stomach the idea of any more death. I've witnessed enough destruction to last me at least four lifetimes, and quite frankly, I've had enough of it. At this point, I would rather carry on blind than experience another vision.

Perhaps, I simply don't want to face the harsh truth that made me leave Ezra and Jenner before. The reality that would make me leave them again in a heartbeat.

The cruel and tragic irony that *I* will be the one to kill them.

I'm not clear on what the future holds for us anymore, but from the unsettled feeling clawing and twisting my gut, I can say with near certainty it's not one I want. That comprehension makes thoughts of my death more appealing. If my death means Ezra and Jenner will be safe, if it means they'll stay alive, then I'll do what has to be done.

One way or another.

Quinn comes to a sudden halt, and glancing up, I see that we've arrived at the room. I take a step forward, ready to be reunited with Ezra and Jenner, and to face whatever future stands in front of us together. At least, until I can find the right time to end things.

Seconds pass, but Quinn doesn't move to open the door. A cloud of suspicion muddles my thoughts when he spins on his heel to face me.

"Why didn't you use your powers back there?" His voice is hushed, and a rare reluctance shows in his expression.

The last time I saw it, he was still an Enforcer.

I furrow my brow, bewildered by his question until I realize he's referring to the altercation with Bilken. With my bloodstained track record, I don't blame him for feeling confused.

A heavy sigh escapes my lungs as I drop my eyes. "I remember who I was before. That inhuman puppet you met a few months ago? That's not who I really am."

I lift my gaze. The look on Quinn's face tells me that he's considering my words and trying to determine if I actually mean them. A smile pulls at one corner of my mouth.

Of course, I mean them.

Just not in regards to Bilken.

"Or maybe I wanted to know how it would feel to choke the life out of him with my own two hands." The savage words breach my lips before I can stop myself from saying them.

Quinn steps away from me as his face contorts with an unmistakable revulsion. Without uttering another word, he pulls open the metal door.

I'm not the least bit surprised when it slams shut behind me.

Ezra and Jenner leap off the floor despite their injuries and close the distance between us before I can even take a breath.

"Wynter!" Ezra's fingers clutch my face as his eyes search my body to ascertain if I've been hurt.

I pat the back of his hands, assuring him countless times that I'm fine.

Exhaling a deep breath, I brush between them, nudging the tops of their arms with my shoulders. I can feel their eyes watching me as I plod across the room, but I say nothing as I slump to the floor in a tired heap.

Once again, they're beside me within seconds. They both crouch so they're on my level, bringing their bodies in a close huddle toward mine. Although I don't look up at them, I can sense their concern.

"What happened?" Jenner asks in a quiet voice.

My hands shake as I press them against my chest. Just thinking about what I know makes my stomach churn, threatening to bring up every last shred of self-respect I still possess. Leaning forward, I hang my head between my knees, hoping the feeling will pass.

When I finally speak, the sound of my voice reverberates off the floor and reflects back in my ears as if to mock me.

"The other Heads support Nolan's plan," I whisper. Glancing up, I watch as they exchange solemn glances.

Ezra runs a hand across the back of his neck. "I thought they might."

The exasperation I've felt so many times in the last few weeks returns to swallow me whole. It runs through my body, infecting me until the madness has all but taken over.

"This is so messed up," I breathe in a bid to maintain my sanity.

Curling into a ball, I look up at Ezra and Jenner, thinking of the differences between now and where we were just two short years ago.

"Isn't there anything we can do to stop this?" Shaking my head, I put forward the one question I've been too afraid to raise before now. "Where's everyone else? Where are Duke and the others who were living in the compound? I haven't seen any of them here."

Nolan was probably well aware of where their

allegiances would lie, should he try to take over. Although the people looked to him, they looked to Ezra even more, and I'm willing to bet he knew that. Still, the nature of this place is nothing like the PHOENIX I once knew. Or at least *thought* I knew. These people are far more like Enforcers than refugees, and that worries me to no sensible end. The thought of where our potential allies might be troubles me even more, especially considering they may be the only ones who can help us.

"When we relocated Outside, the majority were redistributed to the other sects," Ezra reveals. "We assumed it was because this base is smaller and meant to be operational more than anything else. But it quickly became clear that this was always intended to be a haven for the more radicalized members. The ones who truly matter to PHOENIX."

Well, that explains the militarized feel of this place, I muse.

"Yeah, and now that we know what Nolan was up to, it's obvious he did it to stop a rift from forming. Avoid any chance of mutiny by keeping us apart," Jenner adds.

So, as far as we know, they're alive. Hopefully, we can use that to our advantage, should it ever come to that.

"You know I really do wonder sometimes." Ezra licks his lips as he turns his eyes to the floor. "I wonder if we really are any better than the State."

His comment resonates with me, and I find myself remembering what Bilken said about the State and PHOENIX. A part of me is tempted to tell them, and yet, I don't feel like it'll do either of them any good to hear it. It certainly won't boost anyone's morale in this situation.

I breathe in, fighting back a scream. It wasn't supposed to be this way. PHOENIX was supposed to be *good*. They were meant to rise up and save our ruined country.

Not make it worse.

A faint whisper tickles my ear as Rai's voice comes to life in the back of my brain. She said those very words to me about PHOENIX being the good guys. Would she still believe it if she could see them now? Would she insist they're doing what is necessary for the common good? That their actions are warranted?

Rai sacrificed love.

Ezra abandoned his family.

Jenner carried on in spite of his pain.

My father gave up his life because he dreamed of a better world.

However, this isn't what any of them wanted.

A part of me wonders what Nolan was like before he became the cold, calculating monster he is now. Did he have a family? Did he actually want the better world that PHOENIX was created to fight for, or was he like those organizations Bilken spoke of? The ones like the State who didn't have well-meaning intentions for our world.

The sound of Jenner's voice diminishes my distress as his words pierce through the futile doubt and indecision we all seem to be feeling.

"Did you see it?" He clears his throat before looking away from me. "PHOENIX. Did you ever see a single thing that suggested it was good?"

My eyes widen in response to his question, and my chest aches as my heart falters, working to accept what I've failed to grasp this entire time.

Growing up, we always heard about everything the State blamed on PHOENIX. The terrorist attacks. The fear that surrounded our everyday lives. I know they were never responsible for those crimes because Jenner told me as much, and even Dr. Richter admitted it.

Still, what more do I know about them?

I've been blind. Fooled by the friendships and love I found within their ranks. I know the people I met in that compound two years ago. I know they were good people—*are* good people. However, I'm beginning to realize that, while they found refuge with PHOENIX, they were never truly a part of it. Not really. Not when there are people like Nolan running the show, deciding and dictating their every move.

This whole time, they were the real victims. Instruments to be used for someone else's gain.

Just like me.

I suppose, on some level, I always knew this was a possibility. It would've been naïve of me to think that power can't corrupt even a worthwhile cause, especially after everything I've been through and seen. I just never questioned PHOENIX's motives because there were people like Ezra, Jenner, and Rai serving as the face of it and assuring me their actions were morally guided.

"No," I finally answer, shaking my head.

Jenner slams his fist hard against the floor, and I'm taken aback by his unexpected show of anger.

In a trembling voice, he growls, "Everyone who died . . . it's all been for nothing."

As I stare at him, it occurs to me that he must be thinking of his family, who died because of his affiliation with PHOENIX.

Reaching out my hand, I clasp my fingers around

his. When he looks up at me, I squeeze once, letting him know I'm here. A small smile tugs at his lips, but in spite of it, he looks sad.

"Before, we had a reason to fight," he murmurs. "But now? Now, we don't even know which side to fight on."

"Neither," Ezra snaps. "Neither choice will bring justice to anyone."

I'm surprised by the defeated tone of his voice, but at the same time, I don't blame him for feeling this way.

The State.

PHOENIX.

How do you pick a side when neither one is willing to do what's right? When neither one gives a damn about helping the people who need it most? Maybe this isn't about picking sides. Maybe this is about taking action rather than waiting for the worst to happen.

"You still have friends," I point out. "You don't need to support either side, but the fight isn't over. Those people you defended, the ones who looked to you for guidance, *deserve* a chance at freedom. You have to decide for yourselves which is the lesser of two evils and live with it for their sake. For the sake of the future."

As the last word rushes from my mouth, an image flashes through my thoughts. My eyes glaze over as my pulse quickens, and I'm reminded of the fear that I can never escape.

In spite of what I've said, I'm unable to ignore the voice echoing in my head.

If there's still a future to fight for, it says.

TWENTY-FOUR

MY TOES TAP AGAINST THE floor as my body rocks back and forth. Each passing second ticks by, counting down to the grim future that awaits us any second now. I count each one as I focus my mind, anticipating the moment that will inevitably change everything.

A sharp breath catches in my lungs, and Ezra and Jenner turn toward me in response.

"It's happening," I whisper.

Out of my peripheral vision, I notice the meaningful look they exchange. Neither one of them moves, but I ignore their blatant unease, keeping my eyes locked ahead.

An instant later, the first impact sends a tremor through the compound. The room quakes, causing a blanket of dust to come down on us like snow. We all cast a nervous glance at the walls and ceiling, sharing the same visible relief when they remain intact.

Without thinking, I jump to my feet. A budding hysteria clutches my throat as I recall the images I saw in my head, depicting this moment. As I remember the scene of destruction that felt far too real.

The scene of destruction that *is* real now.

Ezra grips my hand as if to hold me back. "Wynter—"

"I need to see it," I gasp, cutting him off.

He and Jenner stare at me, wide-eyed and unsure. I can sense their apprehension, even if they choose not to voice it.

An exasperated sigh trickles from my lips. If only they could know what I'm feeling right now. If only they could understand what this is like.

Fixing my gaze on Ezra, I mutter in an anxious breath, "For once, I need to see it with my own two eyes."

The expression on his face gives off the distinct impression that he wants to argue against this idea, but for whatever reason, he maintains his silence.

Jenner clears his throat and brushes a thick layer of dust off his shoulder. "It's time we figure out what we're going to do anyway. We can't very well stay here."

"Okay," Ezra agrees. Nodding at me, he adds, "Lead the way."

They flank me on each side as we move toward the steel barrier blocking our path. I stare at it for a brief moment before shooting a warning glare over my shoulder.

"Stand back."

I turn toward the door as a surge of power bubbles within me. Breathing in, I allow it to expand until the pressure is strong enough to do what's needed. Leaning forward, I push it out of my body, watching as the metal caves, snapping off its hinges with a sudden blow and falling to the floor with a heavy thud. Ezra and Jenner jump back when it slams against the concrete.

My feet shift into an attack position, preparing for the interference I suspect stands on the other side. But when I peer through the entryway, I'm surprised to find the corridor empty, with the exception of the unconscious figure lying motionless beneath the door. A small trickle of blood seeps out from under the metal.

Jenner steps around the steel and lets out a long, drawn-out whistle. Crouching to the floor, he checks the body for a pulse. Peering up at me, he attempts to hide his true emotions behind a smile.

"There are worse ways to go," he murmurs.

I swallow. I didn't want to cause any more needless deaths, but I knew the risks involved with doing things this way.

Taking a deep breath, I shake it off. "We should move before others come to investigate."

Ezra appears beside me, and I watch him as he glances down both lengths of the hallway.

"Assuming anyone even heard that," he says. "They're probably all up top, watching the show."

Jenner shrugs his shoulders. "Well, we know which way to avoid then."

A soft gasp escapes my lungs when Ezra's fingers wrap around mine. Lowering my eyes, I peek at our linked hands. This one gesture is enough to tell me that he'll be at my side every step of the way.

No matter what.

"Let's go," I breathe.

My feet take off in a hurry, following Ezra and Jenner as they lead me through the maze-like structure with ease. With each turn, I expect to meet resistance or to find someone who isn't aware we've escaped. However, each corridor is just as empty as the last, making it appear as if the entire place has been abandoned.

Every few minutes, another tremor rocks the compound. The very thought of it unnerves me, making me wonder about the weapons being unleashed on the Heart. We're Outside—far enough away that we shouldn't feel such shockwaves.

Yet, we do.

Once again, I think back on that fateful meeting with Nolan and being forced to recount the attack we're about to witness first-hand. The image of mangled corpses and debris fills my head, causing overwhelming nausea to radiate through my body. The power behind it is crippling.

Shaking away the memory, I concentrate on our hurried trek through the compound. The hallways become narrower as Ezra steers us deeper into what's beginning to feel like the belly of the beast. Finally, we come across a staircase leading up to a metal door. In contrast to the cellar pathway that took us into the farmhouse, this entrance is more like the hatch doors littered throughout the tunnels under the city.

We skip the steps two at a time, racing to the top. Jenner throws himself forward, expelling a loud grunt as his hands grip the metal wheel affixed to the door. A cold rush of air hits my cheeks as it gradually squeaks open, and I breathe in, embracing this fresh lifeline.

Jenner climbs out first, followed by Ezra, who turns to help me over the threshold. I stumble, blinded by the glare of the late afternoon sun, which is just now making its descent over the horizon.

As my eyes adjust to the brightness of the outside world, I take a long moment to assess my unusual surroundings. Glancing at our feet, I see the hatch door embedded within the dirt, nestled on the outskirts of the same field encircling the farmhouse. The house itself stands a couple hundred yards in front of us. Hopefully, at a safe enough distance that no one will notice we're here. Unless, of course, Nolan discovers we've escaped and decides to send a patrol to find us.

I try not to think about that. Instead, I focus on the silhouette of the city in the distance.

My *home*.

Explosions dot the skyline around it. The fire erupting from each impact is visible, even from where we stand, miles away from the devastation. A shudder runs up my back, causing goosebumps of fear to pop up along my skin.

This destruction and brutal slaughter.

This is my fault.

It's retaliation for what I am. For what I've done.

I imagine the innocent people caught up in this war. A war they never wanted or asked for. One they were oblivious to, despite the fact that it was brewing right beneath their noses. Now, they'll pay the ultimate price.

This . . .

This is my fault.

My entire body trembles as those words play through my head on a loop. Taunting me. Blaming me. Through it all, the only thing in this world that holds me to my wavering sanity is the feel of Ezra's hand around mine. His grip tightens, but I don't turn to look at him. Feeling him beside me is more than enough.

Tears prick my eyes as the attack continues. With each blast, I try to remind myself that I never had a choice. I did what I had to do to protect the people I love. I'm not the only person who would've caved under such pressure, and I'm certainly not the only one to blame for all of this. Besides, at least my actions were quick. If Richter had been in control of me, like he threatened so many times, I can't say that he would've shown such mercy.

My thoughts cease mid-sentence, coinciding with the abrupt silence. A soft breeze brings a rain of ash with it, which settles on top of the overgrown fields. Other than that, the world seems to freeze as if time has stopped altogether.

The only movement in the whole universe comes from the single word running in a rampant spiral through my brain. Without hesitation, it spills from my lips.

"Richter."

Ezra looks at me, and I can feel his body stiffen at the mention of his brother. I turn to meet his startled gaze, hoping he'll understand.

"I need to know. I need to see if he's still alive." Shifting my body until I'm standing in front of him, I lift my hands to take hold of his face. Leaning forward, I touch my lips against his. "I need to know if I'm finally free of him."

He considers me but says nothing. Dropping his eyes, he nods his head.

Reaching for his hand again, I squeeze it once before taking a step away, putting distance between us. Focusing on the Heart, I ready my mind, searching for Dr. Richter amidst the chaos and ruin. Although a part of me hoped for his interference with Nolan, the inhuman part would rather find him among the corpses. Regardless of Nolan's plans, nothing would give me greater pleasure than to see Richter dead.

I breathe in. Looking for something so precise and particular is like searching for an object in complete and utter darkness. I envision each of the places I might expect to find him, but none so much as the DSD. When I pinpoint his position, it's as if someone has suddenly turned on a light. The vision hits me at once.

I see him standing in front of me, alive and well. However, this vision is strange—so unlike anything I've ever experienced. Usually, I'm like a ghost, haunting the boundary between two worlds without being able to affect either. But here, it's as if I'm a complete and vital part of it.

As if he knew that I would seek him out, he hisses in a serpent-like voice, "Hello, Wynter."

I reel back, wondering if he can see me. But when he continues to speak, I realize this is more like a recorded message—a broadcast he's prepared for the pre-emptive moment I would play right back into his hands.

"I knew you wouldn't be able to resist looking for me. While I appreciate your concern, I know that's not the real reason you're here."

He folds his hands across the glass surface of a desk in one of the exam rooms at the DSD. Other than that, he doesn't move or blink.

"How does it feel to watch your city burn?" he asks me. "To see men, women, and children die . . . all because of what you are."

An audible, sharp breath seethes through my teeth, creating a low whistle as my jaw clenches. The hatred and anger boiling within me are all-consuming. If I was actually in this room, I would shove those vile sentiments back down his throat.

"Make no mistake," he says. "This is as much your fault as it is the State's."

His every syllable feeds my rage until his expression abruptly changes. I'm jolted by the silent plea burning in his gaze.

"That's why you have to come back. Together, we can salvage what's left and protect our country. We can shelter our beloved Heart and rebuild." Lowering his eyes, he shrugs his shoulders. When he looks back up at me, the fleeting emotion in his eyes is gone. "Or, you can leave me here to die and watch everyone else depart this world with me. Perhaps that's what you want. To see me die."

I narrow my eyes when he rises from his seat. His footsteps reflect off the tiled floor as his tall frame crosses the room in a lithe but unhurried movement. I shift position along with him, now nothing more than his unwilling shadow.

"But you wouldn't wish that on an innocent, would you? You're not willing to let everyone die, to watch the people you *love* die . . . . Are you?"

The tone of his voice is foreboding, and I'm not sure I like where this one-sided conversation is heading.

A fresh apprehension takes hold of me when he halts beside a construction of opaque screens positioned in the middle of the room. I watch his hand as it dances along the control panel beside it.

His eyes glow, and for a moment, I swear he can see me.

"You're not willing to let *her* die . . . ."

His long finger pushes a button. A second later, the screens vanish into thin air, lowering their outer shields to reveal what's hidden behind them.

My eyes widen when I register the bed, and when I take in the sight of the beautiful woman laying upon it. The sound of her beating heart projects from a monitor, resounding like small claps of thunder throughout the exam room.

"Rai . . . ." I gasp.

"Are you?" his voice croons in my ear.

Everything seems to double as an overwhelming feeling of trepidation strangles me. All I can comprehend is Richter and his lips, which curl into a smile as the vision around me crumbles. As the last of the image shatters, I hear his voice hover over me, repeating the very statement he used to manipulate me two years ago.

"Think about it, Wynter. You know where to find me."

"It can't . . ." I breathe.

A gust of wind hits my face, forcing me to suck in a lungful of air. It feels as if I've been trapped underwater and have only just now clawed my way to the surface. My heart and lungs throb as if to exacerbate that feeling.

My feet stumble forward, and my arms extend— reaching for Rai in manic desperation. Ezra's hand grips my shoulder, ripping me away from the delusion. Overcome with weakness, I lose my balance. My knees buckle as I collapse to the ground, but he catches me before I can fall.

"Wynter! Wynter, what is it? What did you see?"

A terrible pain clutches my heart as I lift my gaze. A fearful reluctance chokes me into silence.

"Rai. She . . . she's alive," I finally manage.

Ezra's hold on me slackens, but he doesn't respond. His eyes glaze over, and Jenner rushes forward to support my weight, grabbing me when Ezra's hands pull away.

"Wait. *What* did you just say?" he stammers.

I swallow the lump pressing on my windpipe and clear my throat as I take a step back.

Ezra doesn't look at me, and Jenner doesn't seem to know what to make of my admission.

"Richter has her."

I don't elaborate, choosing to gauge their individual reactions instead. Ezra appears to have gone into a state of shock, and I'm afraid further information may be the catalyst that will tip him over the edge. Jenner, on the other hand, takes the news surprisingly well.

"How is that possible?"

I shake my head as a rush of panic takes hold of my body. "It doesn't matter how it's possible. We have to go back."

"Are you sure?"

Jenner and I turn at the same instant, taken aback by the unexpected sound of Ezra's voice after so many moments lost in the quiet depths of his own despair. I cock an eyebrow, confused by his question.

"Did you actually see her . . . ?" he asks.

I glance away as I'm overcome by the memory of her laying there, unconscious but *alive*. Without uttering a single word, I nod my head in response.

"All right," he says.

Throwing back his head, Jenner huffs out a strained breath. "Let me guess, we have to go to the DSD," he grumbles.

I'm stunned by how calm and collected he is. Until I remember the strength he's shown so many times before. The strength we'll need if we're going to make it through this.

My lips part to speak, but the sound of a husky voice behind us interrupts me.

"I'm afraid I can't allow that."

We turn to see Nolan staring back at us, surrounded by the entourage of soldiers he's collected. I notice Quinn standing among them, his wrathful gaze fixed solely on me.

I tense in preparation for the unavoidable fight before us. I could destroy each one of them before they could even make a move to stop me. Or, at least, I could have before I retrieved my memories, back when I was still a cold, unfeeling monster.

What about now? I don't want to be that monster, but could I be if the situation called for it? On the other hand, what about Ezra and Jenner?

What if, by acting, I risk their safety?

Nolan steps forward, causing my body to go still. I don't move a muscle—too afraid of what might happen to the only remaining people I care about if I do.

His eyes dart between us. "You have each been invaluable in getting PHOENIX to this stage, but you have become a nuisance that we can no longer afford."

As he says this, the soldiers behind him begin to scatter like ants, circling around us.

"Our infiltration and subsequent overthrow of the State are reliant on secrecy and cooperation, neither of which you are able to give us." Clicking his tongue, he adds, "And I can't very well leave you to run rampant through the Heart."

He positions himself in front of Ezra, and in a paternal gesture, places a hand on his shoulder. "It's nothing personal," he says.

A sad smile twists his lips—a fake expression of

sympathy that I don't buy for a single second.

With no other sentiments to shove in our faces, he retreats toward the farmhouse, taking the majority of his trained dogs along with him. The remaining soldiers train their guns on Ezra and Jenner, ensuring my cooperation.

As the distance between us increases, Nolan stops once to look back over his shoulder. Our eyes meet as his final words to me carry through the air.

"Wynter . . . say hello to your father for me."

Turning away, he waves his hand, and my heart drops when the order I've been dreading finally arrives. The sound of it is like a gunshot in the silence.

"Kill them," he growls.

TWENTY-FIVE

A GUTTURAL GRUNT RESONATES IN my throat as the hard toe of a boot comes into contact with the back of my legs. My knees buckle, and I collapse into the dirt, now in the vulnerable position they want me in. Pinning my arms behind my back, rough hands clasp my wrists together.

Gritting my teeth, I come to terms with my weakness. My eyes burn as the same two questions consume my every thought.

How could I have allowed us to wind up like this?

Why the hell did I just sit by and watch things get to this point?

Shaking my head, I shift my hands, feeling my fingers rub together as I work to loosen the fresh restraints binding my wrists. Every attempt ends in failure—a reminder of the consequences of my inaction.

My lips tremble as I take a deep breath. There's only one way out of this. Only one way to undo the mistakes that got us here in the first place. *My* mistakes.

However, unleashing my power could lead to the

exact outcome I've been hoping to avoid. After all, I know what will happen if I try to fight back—if I try to get out of this.

My eyes dart between Ezra and Jenner.

All it takes is one wrong move and they'll both be dead.

I watch as they're also forced onto their knees, just far enough away from me that I don't feel close to them. Too far away for me to reach out one last time. To touch their faces.

To apologize.

I consider my options in the minimal time we have left. Heavy footsteps plod along the overgrown earth behind me. Three sets echo back in my ears. One armed guard per hostage.

It feels as if Nolan left hours ago. I'm surprised he didn't stick around to see us executed. To make sure the deed is done. I suppose it doesn't matter because, either way, he's getting what he wants. A country in the palm of his hand and the one person hindering him forced out of the picture.

My eyes stare ahead as I revert to the detached persona of the monster living inside of me, doing whatever is necessary to avoid fear, especially when its grasp could crush me at any second.

I glance at the ground before turning my gaze to the exterior of the farmhouse. In these final moments, this will be the image that sticks with me.

A feeling of rebellion forms a bubble in my chest. This can't be it. I've *seen* the future. I know what awaits—assuming that path still stands in front of me.

This can't be it.

Can't it? a voice in the back of my head asks me. *Can't the future be changed?*

I've wondered that question more times than I can count. If I believed that it couldn't, I wouldn't have gone to the lengths I did to keep myself away from the people I care about. If I didn't think the future could be changed, I would've spent what remaining time I had left with the two people in this world who mean everything to me.

Every step that I've taken has been to alter the grim fate that belongs not only to me but to the entire world. Still, a shadow of doubt forces me to recognize the apprehension that's plagued me since I first began to regain my memories.

What if the future can't be changed? Even worse, what if by taking an altered path to avoid what I've seen, I have inadvertently caused the very future I wished to avoid?

I'm not sure I'll ever know the answer to that. So for now, there's only one question I have to ask myself.

Will our lives end here?

I focus on where Ezra and Jenner kneel beside me. Although I don't look at their faces, I can feel their fear—just as I can feel the strength they're both attempting to build up around it. To act brave in the face of death, even though they don't have to.

My jaw tenses as my teeth grind together. A resolution forms in my brain as I finally come to a decision, and the helplessness I felt before washes away—lifting off my shoulders once I reconcile myself with what must be done.

No more inaction.

No more waiting.

No more allowing anyone else to decide my future.

Regardless of what awaits, I refuse to let them do this to us. I will *not* let Ezra and Jenner die because of me.

In spite of remembering who I was before, I'd be lying if I said I'm not different as a result of everything I was forced to do. I've changed. Monster or not, I accept it because that change will be what saves us now.

My ears prick up at the sound of a muffled conversation between our would-be executioners. Readying myself, I listen to every word, searching for the perfect moment to strike.

If this is going to work, I need to be sure of where they are.

"Which one do you want?" The voice of the man who speaks is deep and unfamiliar to me.

My body goes rigid when I sense one of the guards. His footsteps reverberate through the ground like the faint ripple of an earthquake. The aftershock ceases when he stops less than a foot away from me.

"I'll take the girl," he answers.

A strangled breath catches in my throat.

Quinn.

Considering why he left the State, I'm surprised that he volunteered for this. Then again, a part of me can understand why he'd jump at the chance to do it.

"Fine," the first man barks. "I'll take care of this one."

My heart catches in my chest when the guard chooses his target. Out of the corner of my eye, I see him bring his face close to Ezra's ear. His rumbling voice whispers a string of venomous words, which carry along the breeze in a gentle croon, allowing me to hear them.

"You and your girlfriend can go out together."

Ezra's hands ball into fists as his entire body shakes

with rage and fear. Something tells me he would kill that man if he was able to.

His eyes meet mine, and for the first time since we met, I see true terror in his gaze. A loud breath rises from his lungs, and I can sense the apology that lingers on his tongue. The worry that he's let me down.

I jerk my head in a slight gesture of disagreement.

"Don't be afraid," I breathe. My words are nearly silent.

Inhaling, I close my eyes, prepared to do what has to be done.

Three soft clicks resound in my ears as the safety is turned off on the guns aimed at each of our heads. My heart races as I call up every ounce of power I have, focusing the building pressure on the guards positioned behind us. Uncertainty twists my gut, but I force it away, determined to fight—determined to be the monster how ever many times it takes to keep us safe. Hope blossoms behind any remaining doubt.

Hope that we'll walk away from this alive.

I breathe in once again. However, just as I'm about to unleash hell on our captors, an unexpected scenario flashes through my thoughts. Having concentrated my attention on the guards for the past few moments, I'm able to see it with perfect clarity.

A smile pulls at my lips.

A sudden, deafening gunshot causes an unbearable ringing in my right ear. My eyes snap open and dart toward Ezra before turning to the body on the ground just behind him.

The man guarding Jenner releases a confused, stuttering breath. "What—"

Another shot. I only look at his body long enough to see the blood dribbling from the hole in his forehead.

Ezra, Jenner, and I turn at the same instant, fixing each of our unblinking gazes on Quinn. He doesn't return our questioning stares or offer any explanation.

Instead, he leans down to unbind my hands.

"I still don't like you," he mutters under his breath.

A quiet laugh escapes my lungs as a rush of relief soaks into every muscle of my body. I had hoped for this. I even tried to instigate it by pointing out the flaws in his argument for helping PHOENIX.

Never once did I actually think he would take the bait.

As soon as my hands are free, I stumble over to Ezra. Falling to my knees behind him, I quickly work to liberate his wrists.

"Are you okay?" I whisper.

As I reposition myself in front of him, my fingers grip his face, searching for any lasting damage in the depths of his hazel eyes. He looks back at me and nods, no longer shaken by our near death experience.

Quinn releases Jenner, and soon, we're all on our feet. We stand in an awkward group, ignoring the two dead bodies beside us and wondering where to go from here.

The confusion is more apparent on Jenner's face than anyone else's.

"Am I missing something here?" The marks from his restraints are red and raw, and he takes turns gingerly rubbing each wrist as he speaks.

Ezra takes a protective step in front of me, fixing the full force of his stare on Quinn. "Why help us?" he asks him.

The ex-Enforcer looks at the ground as if ashamed. "She was right," he says, allowing his eyes to drift to mine. "I can't live with it."

Ezra and Jenner exchange bewildered glances, but neither push the subject any further. At this point, they're probably just glad to have someone on our side. An unexpected ally to be sure but an effective one at least.

The four of us huddle together, trying to decide on a course of action.

"What now?" Ezra wonders, looking to me for guidance.

"First, we have to go back for Rai. We can't just leave her there, especially not with Richter."

He and Jenner both nod their heads in agreement.

"We need to get to the tunnels, then," Jenner chimes in. "It's the quickest way to Zone 1."

"That's impossible."

We all glance at Quinn as a cloud of tension descends around us. If he's going to reject our ideas, he damn well better offer up an alternative.

His brow wrinkles as a hint of annoyance casts a shadow across his eyes. "Nolan has them monitored. He plans to move citizens underground until peace can be established, and with the chaos happening up top, everyone in PHOENIX is being utilized. There won't be a single unmanned route we can use."

"If peace *can* be established," Jenner grumbles. "The State has pissed off a lot of people." He casts an apologetic look at me before adding, "No offense."

"None taken," I mutter back.

Ezra lets out an irritable growl. "Okay, so how do we get in?"

Once again, we all turn to Quinn. As an ex-Enforcer, he'll know the Heart better than any of us—even better than Ezra and Jenner, who spent so much of their time traversing the tunnels.

"There is one way, but it'll be heavily guarded and will require a bit of . . ." He hesitates for a moment before meeting my gaze. "Force."

"*Now* you want me to use my powers?"

"Kill a few to save many. I don't like it, but it's the only way in. Maybe once we're there, we can find a way to stop this."

No one argues with that. Besides, it's not as if we have any other choice right now. If we're going to save Rai and put a stop to what's happening, then we're going to have to get into the Heart, one way or another.

Ezra takes hold of my hand as if seeking my permission since so much of this depends on my abilities. The look on his face tells me that if I say I'm on board with it, he'll be right there with me, standing by my side.

I glance at Jenner, who smiles back.

"We're with you," he says.

Nodding my head, I focus on Quinn. Embracing my part in this, I say the only words I can.

"Show us the way."

Grunting in acknowledgment, he holsters his gun and bends to retrieve the weapons from the two bodies beside us. Tossing them to Ezra and Jenner, he signals for us to move.

"We'll have to make our way there as quickly as possible since we have no other option except to go on foot. Stay close and follow me."

We keep low to the ground as we progress through the fields. The occasional gunshot can be heard in the distance, and we have to take cover multiple times, fearing we've been spotted by one enemy or the other.

The State.

PHOENIX.

They're both the same to us now.

By the time we reach the outskirts of the Heart, it's nightfall. The black walls of the city stand a short distance away with a massive gated entrance in full view of where we're hidden.

I've never seen it up-close before. Prior to being taken by the DSD, I never even ventured any farther than Zone 2. Looking at it now and knowing what I know, I'm surprised there's even a gate here at all.

Why construct a way out if no one is ever allowed to leave?

My eyes scan the obstacle ahead. Barbed wire lines the top of the wall, and high towers stand on each side of the reinforced steel doors. The entire operation is heavily manned, but it's nothing I haven't dealt with before.

Quinn waves his hand, gesturing for us to follow him. Crouching to the ground, he leads us to a new position behind an armored convoy truck a few feet away. We press our bodies against the large tires to stay out of view of the blinding spotlight passing by every thirty seconds or so. Leaning in close, he provides a detailed breakdown of what we're up against.

"Lookouts are positioned in the turrets," he whispers. "See those small protrusions?" Reaching across my chest, he points to the window-like holes within the walls. "Snipers."

"It doesn't matter," I breathe. "I'll be able to sense them."

Quinn looks at me, but I don't return his gaze.

I shift my body to move out from behind the truck. However, before I can stand, a strong hand grips my arm, holding me back. Glancing over my shoulder, I see Ezra staring up at me.

"Be careful," he begs.

One corner of my mouth twitches into a slight, reassuring smile. Then, without another word, I step out into the open.

TWENTY-SIX

THE NOISES AROUND ME ARE faint and indistinct. Even though I'm aware of yelling voices, the only sound I can make out is my own steady breathing. Each inhalation drums in my ears as if I'm submerged underwater. In many ways, I might as well be.

The dirt crunches beneath my feet as my body inches forward. The spotlight never relents, shining down on me like some physical force intent on trapping me in its grasp. Unafraid, I stare up into its glow, for once wanting the world to see me for what I am.

"Freeze!" a voice calls.

I take a step, ignoring it. I'm almost there now. The gates will be within my reach at any moment.

"Stop!"

I keep moving, never once allowing myself to look away from the light.

"I said stop!" the voice shouts again.

A bullet grazes the dirt roughly an inch from my right foot. In a sluggish daze, I fix my eyes on the ground. It calls to mind something similar that occurred back when I was still fully consumed by the monster. That incident seems like it happened years ago now, and yet, the monster is still here.

Now, we have molded together into one complete being.

Taking a deep breath, I turn my attention to the wall in front of me. I glance between the turrets positioned on each side of the gates before locking my gaze on the small openings Quinn warned me about.

Snipers, I remind myself.

My tongue trails across my lower lip as I resume my march forward. Another side of me creeps to the surface, taking over, but I don't fight against it.

This is the only way.

Bullets hail down around my body like rain, and seconds later, drop into the dirt with a thousand dull clunks. Dozens of panicked voices tear through the otherwise silent night as the Enforcers blocking our way attempt whatever they believe it will take to stop me.

They know who I am. I can tell by the genuine fear on their faces.

Regardless, I don't hold back.

My body barely exhausts even a fraction of my power. Although I'm sorry for what I'm doing, I'm aware that I'm no better than Nolan—killing my own countrymen to achieve my own end. I have to keep telling myself, it's just as Quinn said.

Kill a few to save many.

As much as I don't like it, this is necessary. If we don't make it past here, then we'll never be able to stop the further slaughter that awaits.

If we don't move past these gates, we'll never be able to save Rai.

The shouting grows louder as I focus every last bit of energy on the Enforcers guarding the wall. Each snapping neck reverberates in my ears, stabbing me with regret over the innocent lives I'm responsible for ending.

"Kill a few to save many," I whisper to myself.

Thinking only of what has to be done, I push my self-condemnation aside, forcing it deep into a dark abyss along with the other guilt I've accumulated over the years. It lumps together, weighing like a tumor in the base of my heart.

Silence descends like a blanket, covering everything. Streams of residual gunfire smoke billow in an ominous wave through the air, casting a thick haze across the bodies littering the ground. The gleam of the lingering spotlight only emphasizes this aura of death, making it clear that no one has survived.

Shifting my feet, I widen my stance, latching my eyes onto the reinforced steel gate. A surge of pressure swells up inside of me, pushing against my insides as it fills every inch of my body. With a loud grunt, I urge it out in a wave of power—targeting the large doors.

The screaming metal pierces the hush as it's ripped from its hinges. Landing at my feet in a crumpled heap, it kicks up a veil of dust, causing the particles to graze against my skin like flakes of snow.

I turn my head when I sense the others approaching. Ezra and Jenner stare at me, and I can feel the heat from their combined gazes burning into the back of my head. I keep my eyes trained ahead, refusing to look at them—not wanting to witness their unavoidable horror.

"Let's go," I bark before either of them can speak.

Pressing forward, my feet step around the twisted

hunk of metal.

We pass through the entrance into the Heart, and in a strange way, it's as if we've entered another world. Empty of human life, the decrepit scenery of Zone 7 surrounds us with the insignia marking our location dotted at the corner of every building and street. It looms around me like a visual echo, bringing everything that's happened over the last three years full circle.

Upon entering the city, I turn to face Quinn. "What's the fastest way to Zone 1 from here?"

He peers into the shadows as if searching for an answer. "I'm not sure. It's hard to say without knowing what sort of response we may be up against. With the attack, the surviving Enforcer units will be on high alert."

"We may have to use the tunnels, after all," Ezra says.

Quinn lifts his hand in protest. "I told you, it's too risky. Besides, once Nolan catches wind that you've escaped, he'll have people out looking for us. Our chances are better up top since the State isn't actively hunting us down."

The image of dead Enforcers takes shape inside my head.

"Not yet," I grumble.

We stand in a silent huddle, contemplating our lack of a plan. We were so focused on getting back into the city that we never stopped to consider what we'd do once we got here.

"What about the trains?" Jenner proposes.

Ezra shakes his head. "All likely to be shut down to keep everyone in their respective zones. Maybe even destroyed depending on which parts of the Heart were hit."

A smile crosses my face. Of course, the obvious option is always the last to be considered.

"No." I laugh, grinning at Jenner. "No, they're not. It's brilliant."

I see the train system in my head, along with each of the empty stations. The perfect pathway to Zone 1.

To Rai.

"Even if they aren't operational, we can walk along the tracks and have a straight shot back to Zone 1," I explain. Glancing around the immediate area, I push the idea even further. "Where's the nearest station?"

"The eastern perimeter," Quinn grunts. "Follow me."

He maneuvers us through the abandoned streets, and as we jog through the darkness, I'm surprised to see that Zone 7 appears untouched—apart from some pre-existing damage. It's as if whoever dropped those bombs chose to bypass this place on purpose.

A feeling of apprehension claws its way up my throat, but I swallow it back down. Bowing my head, I tail Quinn's steps.

Minutes pass, piling one on top of another until we've been running for a full hour. Ragged breaths spill from my lips as the exertion forces me to recognize the sheer magnitude of the Heart. This city is my home, and yet, I failed to notice something as obvious as its size because of the simple fact that it was never vital for me to know.

There was so much I never realized until it was spelled out in front of me. So many limitations that were put in place, not only to discourage unnecessary contact between zones but between people in general. Our cold, detached nature . . .

The State made us this way on purpose.

My thoughts go in circles, working around everything I've learned about the State and PHOENIX. Even with my visions, I'm not sure which side is right. The State brought destruction upon themselves by waging their needless war, but as Richter said, the blame rests on my shoulders too. Then there's PHOENIX—advocates for change who have succumbed to their own impatience and are now willing to sacrifice the lives they once vowed to fight for.

Who's right? Who's wrong?

How do we change what's doomed to happen?

How do we end this war before the future I saw becomes our *only* future?

The farther we progress into Zone 7, the more I notice that it reeks of abandonment. Maybe Nolan already evacuated this part of the Heart, but I feel like we'd be aware of that by now if he had made such a move. Besides, I doubt he could work that quickly.

I push that fleeting worry to the back of my mind, focusing on our primary motive for this moment.

Get back to Zone 1.

Find Rai.

Those two thoughts keep me going when my lungs threaten to fail.

Another thirty minutes pass before we reach the station at the eastern perimeter. Upon arriving, we find it just as deserted as the streets, and as we hurry down the stairs, I notice the concrete flooring is coated in refuse—no doubt a result of the panic that ensued after the attack.

Our steps reflect through the expansive lobby, chasing behind our movements like a shadow of sound. The chorus of noise beats back in our ears, accompanying our labored breaths. We only slow our advance when we reach the barricade of turnstiles. Quinn and Jenner leap over them with ease while Ezra hangs back to help me. I ignore his outstretched hand and catapult my body over the barrier.

It's a strange sensation. After so many years of playing by the rules, it's a rush to break them now with this small act of rebellion. Even though I've done far worse over the years, this moment somehow feels more significant to me. Symbolic, I suppose, of the complete break from my life before.

We run past each platform, searching for the train that will take us to Zone 1. Every corridor of the station is abandoned, leading me to assume the residents must be taking shelter or hiding in their homes until the worst is over.

Or they're dead.

I try to discard that thought.

Rounding the final corner, we spot a train already stationed at the platform we've been looking for. A wave of relief washes over me, and the feeling becomes more prominent when I notice the string of doors standing open as if to welcome us. As if to encourage what we're trying to do.

We board the train without hesitation or delay and proceed to the control cabin at the front of the first car. When we get there, we discover that the door is locked tight.

Quinn steps in front of us and unholsters his gun. In an aggressive forward movement, he slams the end of his weapon against the door, hitting the glass window with violent thrust after violent thrust. But nothing happens. Not even a hairline crack or a chip.

I allow him to attempt this for a full minute before

my patience runs dry.

"Move," I growl, pushing him aside.

In less than ten seconds, I make short work of the door, and within another ten seconds, we're all crammed in the tiny room. Taking a step forward, I approach the control panel, allowing my eyes to scan the complex array of buttons.

After a moment, I glance at Ezra and Jenner.

"Either of you know how to use this thing?" I ask.

Ezra rubs his hand against the back of his neck. "Well, the trains are fully automated. Once we turn it on, the computer will do the rest."

"Yeah, easier said than done." Jenner rolls his eyes, mimicking my exact thoughts.

We take turns fussing with the buttons, searching for a way to operate the train while Quinn stands just outside the ruined doorway, keeping watch for any potential interference. An air of frustration clouds the room, overwhelming us.

Ezra lets out a heavy sigh, and I can tell that we're all thinking exactly the same thing.

If only Rai were here.

We continue working in silence, attempting sequence after sequence to no avail. The only hint that our efforts are even making any headway is the faint glow of the console, indicating that the train hasn't entirely lost power. Still, annoyed with the lack of progression, I take a step back to consider our options. Each passing second counts down to the uncertain and minimal time we have left, and every minute we waste here only makes me more anxious. If we don't get this moving soon, we'll have to go by foot.

I wince when Jenner kicks the side of the console, but the sound of it assaults me with a sudden idea.

Closing my eyes, I retreat into my mind and channel my thoughts back to the last time this train was used. I see the operator enter the cabin. I watch his hands move across the panel, bringing the train to life.

My eyes open at once.

"Stop," I gasp.

Ezra and Jenner freeze, and I can sense Quinn glancing over his shoulder at me. Without paying attention to any of them, I position myself in front of the control panel and wave my hands in a silent request to give me space. My gaze trails along the console as my fingers dance over the buttons.

A green hologram shines up across the glass windshield a moment later. The light from it reflects into the tunnel ahead of us, casting a dull shine onto the metal tracks.

An automated voice echoes through the cabin. *"Authorization code required."*

Leaning forward, I input the string of numbers I saw in my head. As my fingers enter the last one, a chiming sound rings above us. Another green glow illuminates the console as the lights in the ceiling flicker on, engulfing our bodies in a blinding glare. Once my eyes adjust, I exchange glances with Ezra and Jenner. No one dares to speak until the automated voice returns.

"Welcome," it announces with cheerful acceptance.

The train jerks forward, picking up speed as it races toward Zone 1.

Jenner claps his hands in sarcastic celebration. "Well, that was easy."

Ignoring him, I trudge back into the passenger compartment of the car, feeling a sudden need to sit down. Collapsing into the nearest seat, I rest my head against the window.

Time passes in a daze as the constant whir of the train lulls me into a strange semi-conscious state. I only rouse from my inattention when a warm arm grazes my shoulder. Peeking up, I see Jenner staring at me.

"Are you all right?"

My fingers fidget in my lap as I mull over his question. I lower my eyes, looking at the paneled floor instead.

"For two years, she was right under my nose, and Richter, he . . ." A hard lump blocks my throat as a familiar sensation of self-loathing takes hold of me, resurfacing from the darkest depths of my mind. "I should've known," I whisper.

Rai. In so many ways, I feel like I've let her down. I let her down the night we thought she died, and then again by not realizing she's been alive this whole time.

My heart contracts in my chest, making me wince. Once more, I'm forced to face the crushing weight of my inescapable guilt.

Jenner grabs my hand. Our fingers interlace, squeezing together, and his touch brings me a sense of comfort I desperately need in this moment. If anything, it tells me how much I've missed him.

When I meet his gaze, he flashes an understanding smile. "The price of full control," he breathes.

Those words sit at the very core of my body, making me nauseous.

I think back to that conversation we had following my extraction. I think of how distant I was. How cold and unfeeling.

The guilt resurfaces to consume me yet again.

His free hand touches my shoulder, consoling me, even though I don't deserve it.

"As far as you were concerned, as far as we were *all* concerned, Rai was dead. You had no reason to look for her." He tightens his grip around my fingers. "You couldn't have known."

He's right. I know that. Nevertheless, I can't help feeling at fault for everything that's happened. For everything that always happens to the people I care about.

Jenner leans back in his seat, pulling away from my grasp and turning his darkening gaze to the black tunnel beyond the windows.

"Did I ever tell you how I joined PHOENIX?" he asks.

I cock an eyebrow, taken aback by this unexpected turn in the conversation. A sad smile forms on his lips when I shake my head.

"I was eighteen," he says. "I was pretty stupid at that age. Hard to believe, I know," he adds with a laugh. "I don't know why, arrogance maybe, but I always thought I was a cut above the law. I tested what I could get away with on a daily basis but with no regard as to how it might affect anyone else.

"Anyway, one night, I was out past curfew. I saw a girl about the same age as me. She was lying on the side of the road, and two Enforcers were kneeling over her. At first, I thought they were trying to help. I thought maybe she was injured or had fainted or something. But then I heard her screams . . . and I saw one of them cover her mouth as the other . . ."

My eyes widen as I grasp what he's saying. Despite not having seen it myself, I can imagine the girl he speaks of. I hear her smothered cries in my head just as clearly as I visualize the Enforcers that took advantage of her.

"I couldn't see her face," he murmurs, "but something about her reminded me of my sister, Adley. You probably don't know this, but I'm a twin. I *was* . . . a twin." His lips tremble at those final words.

My eyes search his face. He never spoke of his family in any detail before, and because of his past, I never wanted to pry. Still, this information shocks me.

Biting his lower lip, he balls his hands into fists. When I look down, I notice them shaking.

"For all I knew, that could've been her," he says. "Maybe not at that exact moment, but what was preventing them from doing that again to someone else? To her? If they weren't stopped, there would be a next time, a time after that, and a time after that." His fingers clench tighter as he relives the memory.

The pain he's experiencing is heartbreaking to witness, and I'm tempted to reach out to comfort him. I ignore that urge, afraid that I would somehow be invading those feelings. Unsure if such a gesture would even be welcome.

Shaking his head, he releases a low, humorless laugh. "I couldn't bear the thought, so I tried to do something about it. One scrawny eighteen-year-old kid up against two fully armed Enforcers? I didn't stand a chance. Luckily, Ezra and Rai intervened. They were out searching for new recruits and curfew-breakers were the ideal candidates. Willingness to disobey and all that."

He runs a hand through his black hair and lets out a disheartened breath. "They were able to stop my stupid ass from getting killed, but not before one of those bastards shot that poor girl in the head. In the end, I couldn't save her. Who knows," he adds, shrugging his shoulders, "maybe she would've survived if I had just left it alone."

I recall the moment I met Jenner, and every memory of him since plays after it in a loop. I could always tell there was a deeper, more complicated layer underneath his carefree, positive attitude.

Now, I finally understand what it is.

"They got what was coming to them, but it's pretty hard to hide one body, let alone two, especially when there are cameras everywhere. I knew they'd seen my face, and I panicked. I should've turned myself in, but I ran like a coward instead." His voice is soft, and I can hear the shame behind every word.

"My parents. My sister. Whereas most families nowadays only exist because of the State's mandated need for procreation, we were unusual in that we genuinely cared for each other. And how did I return their love?" he asks. "I let them pay for my crimes. My sister, who I loved more than anything and anyone, who came into this world with me, and who I thought I was somehow protecting . . . *I'm* the reason she's dead."

A single tear trails down his cheek, but he quickly wipes it away.

"Jenner . . ." I breathe.

His voice cuts me off. "I guess what I'm trying to say is . . . that's why you mean so much to me."

I hesitate. "Because I remind you of your sister? Or because I remind you of that girl . . . ?" Both scenarios ignite a horrible sadness in my heart.

An inexplicable smile pulls at his lips as he turns to meet my bewildered gaze. "Because you remind me that, until something changes, there will be nothing I can do to save the people I love." Taking a deep breath, he adds, "*That's* my reason. *That's* why I fight."

When I first met Rai, she told me that everyone in PHOENIX had lost someone or something and that those losses were their reason for fighting for a better world. It's no different for Jenner, except similar to me, his regret is what drives him more than anything else.

Understanding our similarities makes me see him in a different light, and for once, it feels like I can truly relate to someone. Like there's another person in this world who can see me in a way no one else ever could.

Once again, my guilt resurfaces. After all, how have I repaid him for everything he's done for me? For being my friend and defending me. For rescuing me from Richter.

I forgot who he was.

I failed to protect him when he needed me most.

Above all, I broke his heart.

The words escape my lips in a rush. "Jenner. About when I left—"

He holds up a hand to stop me. "It's fine. Do you think I care if you choose me or him? We have so many bigger things to worry about right now." Reaching forward, he tucks a loose strand of hair behind my ear. "All I care about is your survival. I just want you to live, Wynter. How you decide to do that really doesn't matter."

Everyone is silent for the remainder of the journey. Jenner and I sit together, and his warmth brings me the comfort and calm I need to counterbalance the anxiety raging within me. Ezra sits across from us, contemplating unspoken thoughts while Quinn stands beside the nearest door, looking out into the darkness of the tunnel—possibly questioning his own part in this.

Just like with the mission to meet Bilken two years

ago, I can't escape the feeling that we're walking into a trap. I consider using my power to discover what awaits, but the truth is, I'm too afraid to. If I were to see something I would want to change, would I still have the strength to do what needs to be done?

This disease. This power. No human should have to suffer through such a curse. The future is meant to be uncertain so that we can live every moment in the here and now. So that we can walk through life unhindered and unafraid—not spend it running from a future that's impossible to avoid.

I make a silent promise to live that way from now on. As much as I'm able to, at least.

Taking a deep breath, I ready myself for whatever lies ahead. The future.

Our future.

It begins now.

TWENTY-SEVEN

THE STATION IN ZONE 1 is dark and eerie. The lights overhead flicker in sporadic bursts with the buzz of the dying bulbs adding a terrifying feel to an already sinister quest. Our footsteps are deafening in spite of our attempts to remain quiet, and we pause multiple times, afraid of the uncertain sounds reflecting back at us in the darkness.

When we make it to the exit, we separate into two groups—ducking to either side of the stairway leading up into the city. Quinn and Jenner stand to the left while Ezra and I huddle together to the right.

Quinn peers around the corner but slinks back behind the wall a second later. Glancing over my shoulder, I notice the flash of a spotlight as it beams across the opening above us. I turn to meet his gaze.

He jerks his chin toward the stairs and mouths the words, "How many are up there?"

My back presses against the concrete behind me. Breathing in, I close my eyes and concentrate only on the area above us. After a moment, I peek over at

Quinn.

"Two by the entrance," I whisper, "and three more patrolling the square."

Repositioning his gun, he cocks the slide in preparation. "Got it."

Without another word, he dashes up the steps. Jenner flashes a surprised look at us before chasing after him, and Ezra and I follow—sprinting up the stairwell with no idea what's about to happen.

A surprised gasp breaches my lips when Quinn hits one of the Enforcers standing by the entrance on the head, using the end of his gun to knock him out. Rushing forward, Jenner grabs the soldier on the other side, putting him in a chokehold. The man fights back at first, gripping at the arm locked tightly around his neck and squirming right up to the moment his body goes still. Jenner drops him to the ground in an unconscious heap.

Ezra helps them hide the bodies while I stand watch. They tuck them away in a dark corner of the station lobby—somewhere out of sight where no one will stumble across them by accident. By the time they regain consciousness, we'll be long gone from here anyway.

When we return to the surface, Quinn gathers the Enforcers' weapons and unloads the ammunition clips, which he then tosses to Ezra and Jenner. I observe his every movement, amazed by the immense difference between the man standing before me and the trembling boy I encountered on the helicopter. I have trouble believing it's even the same person, making me wonder what happened to him to inspire this drastic change.

Whatever the cause, I'm glad for it.

I linger by the station entrance, using the time to assess our surroundings. My eyes scan the square ahead, and a shiver runs up my spine when the vision I saw before arises in my thoughts. The attack that transpired here comes to life right in front of me with only one alteration between what I see now and what I witnessed in my head. The darkness of night hides the damage well, however, the memory of the destruction is seared into my brain, scarring me forever.

I shake my head to rid myself of the image, fixing my gaze on the distant forms of the three Enforcers in the area ahead. Another shudder hurls through my body when the beams from their flashlights bounce off the bodies covering the ground.

Bile rises in my throat. My hand slaps over my mouth to hold it back, but the nausea is overwhelming. It takes all of my strength not to spew on the pavement in front of me.

A faint whistle grabs my attention, and turning, I glimpse Quinn and Jenner bent low to the ground, darting through the shadows. Ezra moves to follow them but stops in his tracks when I lag behind.

Sprinting back over to me, he whispers in a hurried voice, "We can't stay here." His hand takes hold of mine, forcing me to look at him.

In a weary daze, I lift my head. Meeting his gaze, I swallow and nod, trying my best to ignore the blanket of death laid out in front of us. Choking back the feelings of repulsion and remorse, I allow him to lead me after the others.

We stick to the densest patches of darkness, crouching to avoid detection. The piles of rubble littering the streets act as our hiding place whenever Enforcers come within an uncomfortable distance of our position. Quinn guides our every step since he's the most familiar with the layout of the Heart. Despite our rocky past and his unresolved feelings toward Ezra and Jenner, I'm grateful that he's here, helping us regardless of the danger it's put him in. More than anything, we needed an ally.

At this moment, I couldn't have asked for a better one.

As we progress through the city, I'm forced to recognize the atrocity of the recent attack. Still, it occurs to me that, without it, we wouldn't have this freedom of movement. The uncharacteristic darkness that surrounds us reinforces my suspicion that the bombings knocked out security cameras, surveillance lights, and every other piece of technology that would alert authorities to our presence. The only reason we managed to operate the train was because there was a functional source channeling power into the station. If it weren't for that, we would still be back in Zone 7.

Although I feel responsible for what's happened here in the Heart, I try to find solace in the fact that, if the attack hadn't occurred, we might've never known about Rai. With all the horror and sadness that's been unleashed upon this day, at least there's that one trace of hope shining through it.

Quinn comes to a sudden halt, and in a panicked gesture, motions for us to hide. Ezra drags me behind a ruined wall, which lies in disjointed pieces across the ground. We bow behind the remains while Quinn and Jenner stoop behind similar chunks of debris about twenty feet away. Fear prickles my skin as my eyes dart between their faces.

I stare at Jenner, wary of the distance separating us.

My heart races in wild bursts as we wait. Ezra

clutches me against him, and we hold our breath as much as we're able to—doing everything possible to remain undetected. His grip on me tightens when we register the thrumming approach of a vehicle.

The tires tread across the wreckage before coming to a complete stop just next to our hiding place. I peer at Quinn who casts an uneasy glance over his shoulder.

Following his gaze, I watch the patrol of Enforcers as they descend from the armored truck. Their heavy boots pound against the pavement, kicking up clouds of dust with each step. Their voices echo even more loudly.

"Start over there. This zone is to be cleared by morning."

I hear the sound of clashing rocks as they uncover the wounded trapped beneath the rubble. For the briefest of moments, I find myself hoping they might be here to rescue them.

But just like in Jenner's story, these Enforcers are not good people.

My eyes widen in shock as they throw the mangled corpses into the back of the truck. Body, after body, after body, with no care for how they handle them. They don't even bother to check to see if any of them are alive. Until—

"Hey! We have a live one here!"

I can just make out the strangled voice of a woman. Her bloodied hand sticks out from where the rest of her body is buried, thrashing in desperation for someone to see her. Two Enforcers react, but neither one offers any help.

Her cries continue. Out of the corner of my eye, I notice the senior Enforcer turn in place, releasing a grunt of annoyance. A grimace distorts his face, and after a moment, he walks over to join the other two men.

"Well, what are you waiting for?" he asks. When the men exchange glances, he elaborates with a sigh, "She's crippled. This one's nothing but a burden now." His eyes fix on her broken body as his hand moves to his belt. Without hesitation, he pulls out his gun and puts a bullet in the top of her head.

Rage blossoms in the core of my body, forming an immense build-up of pressure. My hands ball into fists in an effort to contain it, but I can feel the anger seeping from my pores in a hungry search for revenge. The broken wall behind us begins to crack, taking the brunt of my wrath.

Ezra grips me tighter, holding me against him to calm my distress. Leaning into his chest, I try to get my emotions under control. I might have the power to protect us, but invisibility is still our best shot at getting out of this alive.

Thankfully, no one seems to have noticed my minor relapse, and after another few minutes of searching the area, the Enforcers finally proceed down the street. A breath of relief trickles from my lips when they pass out of view.

Once we're sure they're gone, we continue our trek through Zone 1. We manage another few kilometers before we come across another unit.

Unlike the last, this contingent is much larger.

We group together in one place this time, observing at least two dozen armored trucks lining the pavement. They unload wave after wave of Enforcers—each one armed and suited as if in preparation for battle. A single commanding officer paces in front of the converging company, barking out orders.

At the distant end of the road, a handful of soldiers erect a blockade. Just beyond that, I glimpse an eerie bright light. A humming noise resounds through the immediate area as the immense television screen positioned in the square farther ahead—typically used for the news and important State-mandated announcements—blinks back to life after a few static-filled attempts. We shrink back to remain hidden as a booming voice carries through the night.

> *"Attention, citizens. For the next forty-eight hours, you are under house-arrest. Following that, the nationwide curfew will be moved forward from 18:00 to 16:00. Please understand, this is for your own safety. We ask that you remain calm in this time of crisis and that you obey your local Enforcer units as they work to return our city to normal."*

The screen flickers once, then goes black, hurling the surrounding area back into darkness.

An unsettled feeling twists in my gut when I grasp that this means our time is running out. The State is getting everything back into working order, and we have no way of knowing how long we have before that happens. Before the cameras turn back on.

Scanning the crowd of Enforcers, I debate what to do.

"The Heads were right." We all turn to face Quinn, but no one says anything. Letting out a deep breath, he adds, "They're beginning the first phase of enacting martial law."

"What does that mean exactly?"

He meets my gaze, and my heart drops when I register the grim look on his face.

"It means things are going to get a whole lot worse before they get better. *If* they get better."

"Well, let's hope Nolan can appease whoever's attacking us before that happens," Ezra says. "Or before a civil war breaks out when the people realize the State can no longer protect them."

No one speaks following this statement, far too aware of the very real likelihood that a lot of people are going to die. And soon.

"Would that happen?" I whisper. "Everyone has been subdued for so long . . ."

Jenner tilts his head, cocking an eyebrow. "It didn't take much to turn you around," he points out.

"It was the same with us," Ezra murmurs, his voice so hushed I barely hear it.

Once, he and Jenner were no different than me. I have to keep reminding myself of that—of the fact that they're victims of our society too. Looking at them now, it's hard to imagine them as oppressive servants of the State. Doing what they're told. Following blindly. I suppose the opposite could be said of Quinn. He was the perfect example of what we were intended to become, and yet, here he is—sacrificing all of it because of the simple fact that it's wrong.

"A little doubt can go a long way," he muses.

Those words echo in my ears. As much as I want to believe them, I worry that we won't have the chance to see such a concept in action.

"I think the State is far more likely to just kill everyone," I grumble.

Quinn repositions his gun as he pulls himself up.

"We have to move. If we stay here any longer, someone will find us." He jerks his chin, indicating a narrow street to our right. "The DSD is that way."

Keeping a close eye on the nearby patrol, we follow behind Quinn. He takes us along a route that moves us away from the Enforcers, and as we chase him through the back alleys and streets, I notice the familiar features of the area—recognizing them from the last time I returned to the DSD.

I remember that moment with perfect clarity. The moment I let Richter fool me with the promise of a cure.

A growing weight presses down on me the closer we get to the facility, but I try to ignore the feeling.

Focus only on Rai and whatever we have to do to save her.

I concentrate on that thought as we round the corner that will take us to the front entrance of the building. Apprehension stirs in the pit of my stomach, taking hold as we're knocked back by the unexpected destruction awaiting us. My eyes trail along the shattered remains as I step across shards of metal and glass.

My body spasms as I feel the DSD beneath my feet.

I shake my head in disbelief. "It's as if they knew where to hit."

Quinn raises his gun, keeping his voice low as he scans the perimeter. "PHOENIX has always had inside help. How else do you explain their cache of weapons and food?"

"What does that have to do with anything?" Jenner asks. He holds his own gun close to his body as he positions himself beside me.

Quinn glares over his shoulder at us, and the look on his face suggests that the answer is obvious.

"What's to say that whoever did this didn't have someone on the inside?"

"What, you think the attackers have a spy within the

State?" The skepticism in Ezra's voice passes over into his lingering sneer.

"Anything's possible," Quinn points out. "I'm here helping *you*, aren't I?"

Jenner leans forward, and his hot breath tickles my ear. "And aren't we just lucky to have him," he murmurs.

I suppress the grin working its way onto my lips. Clearing my throat, I take one last look at the demolished entrance.

There's no way we'll be able to get in through here.

With only one option left, I make my way toward the side of the building. I can feel Ezra, Jenner, and Quinn watching me in confusion.

"There's a back door," I call over my shoulder.

I don't know which surprises me more, the lack of Enforcers patrolling the area or the fact that the back entrance to the DSD—which required more security than the rest of the building combined—is deserted and hanging off its hinges. The light on the keypad affixed to the adjoining wall blinks red.

As I stare at it, I get the impression that it's trying to warn me.

Quinn enters first, followed by me and Ezra with Jenner bringing up the rear. The lights in the first corridor shudder to life only to extinguish and cast us in pitch blackness again seconds later. We stick close together, uncertain what we'll find here.

"Where is everyone?" Jenner's words carry through the hallway, haunting our every movement. "This place is deserted."

My eyes dart from side to side, searching for the slightest hint of life. After a few paces, Quinn freezes in place. Using the barrel of his gun, he pushes open the nearest door.

"Is it?" he breathes.

All the air catches in my lungs when I glimpse the blood covering the floor. It expands out in a massive puddle from beneath the collapsed ceiling.

The only visible part of the body is an arm.

My feet stumble back as the guilt and rage rise to consume me. Once again, I'm forced to accept my fault in this needless death and destruction.

Ezra's hands wrap around my arms. "It's okay," he says. "Just keep walking."

Parts of the facility lay in ruin while other parts appear untouched. The anxiety running through my body forms a tight ball in my stomach, making the entirety of my nervous system a jumbled mess. I'm not sure if it should relieve or concern me that my uneasiness is shared by the others.

Ezra shakes his head. "This doesn't feel right."

I follow his gaze as he casts a suspicious glance along the corridor.

"Do you reckon it's a trap?" Jenner asks him.

A trap. Just like the one we walked into with Bilken.

"It wouldn't be the first time," I mumble under my breath.

When I lift my eyes, my feet stumble beneath me, freezing in place. My heart begins to race, climbing up my throat as if intent on choking me.

I feel Ezra's chest against my back as he presses his body against mine. Concern floods his voice as he releases a muted gasp in my ear.

"What is it?"

I don't look at him. Instead, my eyes lock on the door at the end of the hall—the entrance to Exam Room B.

The irony is like a slap in the face. Of course, this is

where he'd be waiting for us.

"In there." I signal toward the door with a shaking finger. "That's where I saw him."

Quinn and Jenner glance down the corridor, but Ezra never looks away from me. Shifting so that we're standing face-to-face, he clamps one hand around mine as the other cradles my cheek.

"Hey. I'll be with you the whole time," he promises.

I meet his gaze, and reluctantly—fearfully—I nod my head.

Taking a step forward, I embrace this moment. As I do, I try to imagine what awaits us on the other side of that door.

TWENTY-EIGHT

THE HANDLE OF THE DOOR is cold against my skin, sending an icy shudder through every inch of my body. Unsteady breaths spill from my lungs when the latch clicks, echoing in sinister repetitions down the length of the corridor. As I take a cautious step over the threshold, the darkness of the room swallows me in a single mouthful.

My eyes lock on Dr. Richter. Turning at the sound of our entrance, his gaze meets mine as that familiar, menacing smile pulls at the corners of his lips.

"I knew you'd come," he purrs.

The lighting in the room is dim—emergency fixtures from a backup generator. The glow they cast around him is terrifying, making him even more threatening than I've ever known him to be before.

Quinn and Jenner both raise their guns. My unease about this mission and the very real possibility that we've walked into a trap resurfaces, making me wonder if we made the right choice by coming here. Ezra doesn't seem to feel that same fear.

Or if he does, he fails to show it.

The anger he's been suppressing takes full control, shining through his eyes and burning everything in its path with the intensity of fire.

He fixes that energy on his older brother as the rage claws its way out from the depths of his soul. It finds freedom through his voice, reflecting across the room in a turbulent wave of sound.

"Where is she?" he yells.

That ominous smile remains intact as silence overtakes us. We all watch Richter, waiting for him to say something—to make a move that will reaffirm my concerns about being here.

Taking a step to the side, he reveals the control panel I saw in my vision. His long fingers swipe against its surface, causing the opaque screens behind him to dissolve into nothingness. In less than five seconds, they lower their clouded defenses.

We see Rai on the other side. Her body lies unmoving on the oversized bed, and she's naked apart from the small square of white paper protecting her modesty. Machines surround her while tubes protrude out of her arms. A heart rate monitor is positioned near her head, beeping at least once every other second.

I can sense the others' shock, and in truth, I share the same emotions despite having already seen her like this. Perhaps that's because I never really believed she'd be here.

With how much Richter's lied to me over the years that I've known him, I assumed this was just another one of his games. A sick ploy to get me back. Nothing more.

Just like usual, I've underestimated him.

Ezra staggers toward the bed. His movements are weak and listless, but the expression on his face is even worse. I don't know which is stronger—the disbelief at seeing her here or the heartache of knowing we weren't able to prevent it.

Dr. Richter clicks his tongue and waves a finger in disapproval. "I wouldn't do that if I were you."

Ezra freezes, and I notice that the rage that took hold of him mere moments ago is gone, leaving him seeming deflated and helpless.

"Is she actually alive?" he whispers.

"Of course," Richter answers. "Did you honestly think I would kill her?"

A wave of relief rushes through my body, but I also can't ignore the apprehension that shadows over it.

Rai is alive . . .

So, why do I get the feeling that something isn't right?

"What did you do to her?" I blurt out before I can stop myself. "Why isn't she conscious?"

Dr. Richter steps away from us. Quinn and Jenner keep their sights aimed at his chest, but I know neither of them will shoot. Not yet, at least.

The reality is, it doesn't matter if we have him outnumbered, just like it doesn't matter how much I want to see him dead. The fact remains that we came here for Rai. Until we know what's wrong with her, Dr. Richter can't be touched. Not when he's the only person who's able to bring her back.

Positioning himself beside the bed, his lips twitch as he touches the side of her face. "I did what I had to do, but I was careful," he murmurs.

His thumb caresses her cheek, drawing my attention to the dark scar denting her forehead.

Bile rises in my throat as I'm brought back to the night we lost her. When that recent vision showed me that she might still be alive, I was riddled with doubt. I wasn't sure if I could believe it. Yet, the one thing that *made* me was the daunting realization that we never saw her die. The only proof of her demise was that soul destroying gunshot. That and the blood that stains my every waking thought.

For the past few moments, I began to think what he did to her was a clever ruse to fool us. A trick of the eye to damage our morale.

But now . . .

"You really did shoot her," I breathe.

I stare at Rai, grasping the reason behind her medically induced coma. Dr. Richter was right. She isn't dead.

However, I'm not sure she's completely alive, either.

All the air expels from my lungs, and it feels like the small speck of hope I had has abruptly disappeared, robbing me of its warmth. We fought our way here because we were sure we'd be reunited. Now, I see that was nothing more than a broken dream being dangled in front of us. More bait that I've once again been foolish enough to take.

Dr. Richter trails his hand along Rai's exposed body. Disgust and anger stream through my veins, making me cringe at the way he touches her. His violating sense of entitlement is far worse than anything he ever did to me. What I was put through was inhuman, but this is just wrong.

"I'm sure you're familiar with our story by now," he says to me. Looking at her, he adds, "I knew she would never come back to me willingly. Raina . . ." He pauses to smile at some unspoken memory. "She was always stubborn."

My eyes prick with tears. "So, you're keeping her

like this? Like a living doll you can just preserve behind glass?"

"She is *mine*," he snarls. "She always has been. I will do whatever it takes to keep it that way, even if that means I can only have her like this."

My head shakes in spastic jerks as I'm bombarded by the guilt that always threatens to suffocate me. Yet again, I'm shaken by the knowledge that, if I had only seen what was going to happen sooner, then maybe I could've prevented this from happening. Maybe then, Rai wouldn't be here, spending the rest of her life as a prisoner in her own body.

Regardless, I'm not the only one to blame for this. What Dr. Richter has done is inexcusable, and just as I've felt countless times before, I would love nothing more than to see him dead. Still, I'm held back by the confusion surrounding his motives.

"Why are you doing this?"

What are you getting out of it?

"Why does anyone do anything?" he asks. "The events of our past shape us into the people we will become. It determines who we will love, and who we will hate." His eyes flash to his brother as he says these last words.

Ezra's face contorts with anger. "*Why* do you hate me? What have I ever done to you? I never asked Rai to come with me!"

Dr. Richter's nostrils flare at the mention of Rai's abandonment. In an attempt to compose himself, he straightens his coat. A grim smile tugs at his lips.

"This goes back much farther than just her, little brother. So much farther." He drags a finger along the curve of his chin as he turns his ominous gaze back to me. "I wonder . . . How long did it take you to realize that *she* is the one Mother spoke of?"

Ezra's face drains of color. Dr. Richter takes advantage of the lingering silence, torturing us with his indecipherable agenda.

"You were always her favorite. After the visions started, she couldn't even bear to look at me. But you? She always looked for you."

His resentment toward Ezra is accompanied by a tinge of what I assume must be jealousy. It's unexpected. This whole time, I thought Richter's hatred of his brother revolved around one thing.

Rai's decision to join PHOENIX and the misguided assumption that Ezra had stolen her away.

I never would've guessed it had to do with their mother. After all, they were both witnessing a dying parent without any answer for what was happening. Neither one of them was at fault.

At the same time, it makes sense in a twisted way.

I can almost imagine their mother now, and it isn't difficult to guess what she saw.

"She probably knew what you'd become," I point out. "What you would do to people like her."

"Cause and effect," Richter counters. "An endless loop with no sure way to tell which was the cause and which was the effect. I'm sure you understand that better than anyone by now."

He's right. That very notion has played on my mind for the last two years, especially recently. With everything I've seen, it's only natural that I would wonder about the path that leads to those moments.

Are my visions set in stone? Will they happen no matter what I do? Or will they only occur *because* I've seen them? By bearing witness to the future, do I accidentally set the world on that course?

Am I the cause?

Or am I the effect?

His rambling interrupts my thoughts.

"Was I always destined to become like this? Or did I only turn into what I am because she cast me aside? Perhaps, if she had never shut me out, I wouldn't have become the very thing she hated."

"Or feared," I whisper.

His eyes dart to mine as if I've just uttered the most offensive words possible.

Shaking his head, he says, "My mother had nothing to fear from me. Even my father, who had her institutionalized and who I blamed every day for her death, even he had nothing to be afraid of. But you?" he growls, turning his gaze back on Ezra. "If it wasn't for you, if it wasn't for those visions, she would still be alive!"

The words Ezra once spoke to me resound in my head, bringing to light the possible reason he might be to blame for their mother's death.

"One green, one blue. Wynter. Look for Wynter."

He told me himself that their mother kept seeing me, but *why* she did is still a mystery to all of us. Whatever she saw, it must've been important enough to want her son to find me.

Unfortunately, her other son found me first.

One green. One blue.

Wynter.

Look for Wynter.

Did that repeated sentiment become ingrained in Richter's brain? Was that what led to his career selection—this need to decipher his mother's dying words? To find not only the meaning behind them but the reason for the visions that caused her death?

Did *I* make him this way?

A visible darkness covers his eyes like a veil, and he looks back at Rai before glancing at me.

"Those who appear innocent are always the ones we should fear the most. You are a fantastic example of that."

"How much of what you do is for the State and how much out of revenge?" Ezra asks him.

"The State is a mere tool," he admits. "A means to an end. Without them, I never would've had the resources to find someone like you, Wynter. Someone who would allow me to retrieve Raina and bring her home."

It doesn't make any sense. I knew of his personal reasons for using me, but I always figured his loyalty to the State was just as important. Why else would he continue utilizing my power if the only purpose he wanted me for was already achieved?

"Why continue the charade then?" I nod toward where Rai lay unconscious on the bed. "You got her back over two years ago. Why keep using me?"

At first, he doesn't answer. The seconds turn into minutes, which seem to turn into hours. Time reaches a sort of standstill, freezing me in a persistent state of dread.

A chill runs across my skin when that familiar smile forms on his lips.

"Because I wasn't done with you."

Ezra steps in front of me, forcing my body behind his with a shove of his hand.

"What the hell is *that* supposed to mean?" he barks.

Dr. Richter glances between us.

"I will admit a large facet of it was down to pride. When you work for so long on something, it's only natural to wish to see it used in the manner for which it was intended, even if that wasn't your initial reason for pursuing it." He clasps his hands behind his back as he takes a step forward, closing the distance between us before I can even think or react. "Once upon a time, I may have concerned myself with petty politics, but I have only worked to further the State's agenda because its interests aligned with my own. They wished to take over the world, and by doing so, I would have the opportunity to observe Project W. A. R. in action."

He stops less than three feet away from us. That smile stretches from ear to ear as his eyes pierce straight through to the core of my body.

"I have conflicting feelings toward you. After all, you were the focus of the visions that killed my mother. I should hate you, and yet, I find myself drawn to you in a way I've never felt with anyone else. Not even Raina. She is my heart, but you, Wynter . . . You are my *soul*."

A shockwave of disgust lashes out at my very being. His words stab me with the force of a blunt knife.

He laughs when he sees my expression. "Don't mistake me. You are nothing more than the physical embodiment of my life's work. But that work has become important to me. Almost as much as breathing. I couldn't pass up the chance to witness your rebirth."

My feet take a reflexive step back, and I notice Ezra go rigid where he stands in front of me.

"For nearly fifteen years," Dr. Richter continues, "I've been driven by one thought more than anything else. I've bided my time, waiting for the perfect moment to exact my revenge as you so graciously put it. What makes it all the more satisfying is that it'll affect you more than anyone, dear brother."

"You hate me because of your own deluded issues. As far as I'm concerned, you've more than made your point."

I flinch when Richter begins to laugh. The sound bounces off the walls, swarming around us in a vocal cloud.

Out of my peripheral vision, I notice Jenner and Quinn reposition themselves in preparation for the possibility that things are about to take a turn for the worse.

When his laughter ceases, a simple question takes its place.

"You still don't get it, do you?"

I push Ezra aside, bringing myself within a foot of those perceptive gray eyes. "What I don't get is why we're wasting time talking about this with everything going on out there." Casting a quick glance over my shoulder, I add in a lowered voice, "I came back. I'm here now. Whatever you want, I'll do it."

Fixing my eyes on Richter, I stop myself from looking back when I hear Ezra and Jenner begin to protest. After all, they react just as I expect them to. Just as I always knew they would if they had any idea what I was planning.

"That wasn't why we came here!" Jenner shouts.

In a pleading whisper, Ezra mutters my name.

Taking a deep breath, I confront the one outcome I've been avoiding this whole time. Ezra stares at me, and I can see the confusion and fear working its way across his face. His expression makes me think of that moment back in the compound when he made me swear that I wouldn't run away again.

If only he knew how much I wish I could keep that

promise.

Tears burn my eyes as I murmur the only two words I seem to know. "I'm sorry."

He screams for me to stop, but I've already begun concentrating on what needs to be done.

There's no other way.

My mind kicks into action, and in one easy movement, I rip the weapons from their hands. They clatter against the floor as a large bubble of pressure builds up in my chest. Tears roll down my cheeks, but I commit to this betrayal and focus my power on the only people I can trust.

Ezra chokes out my name again as I use my ability to lift him into the air. Breathing out, I pin his body to the wall and then do the same with Jenner and Quinn. In the back of my mind, I imagine the glass and steel desk on the opposite side of the room, and all it takes is a single thought to bend it to my will. Within seconds, it's twisted around the three of them in a vise-like restraint.

I exhale when the deed is done, ignoring Ezra's expression as I turn back toward Dr. Richter. A smug grin takes shape on his face, but I ignore that as well.

"We can stop what's happening. We can fix things together, just like you said. No one else has to die."

Leaning forward, he brushes his hand in a tender caress against my cheek. I resist the urge to shy away from him, but the glow in his eyes alarms me even more than his proximity.

"My precious angel of death." Bringing his face close to mine, his lips tickle my ear when he whispers, "Do you really believe that I wish to fix this?"

Bewilderment rips through me as an intense feeling of fear swells up inside my body. Reeling back, my eyes latch onto his, but words fail me when the cold hand of terror grips my throat.

"For years, my mother spoke of you," he says, "and I knew exactly who you were from the very moment we met. It was almost too perfect. Like killing two birds with one stone."

"What are you talking about?" I stammer.

"My perfect revenge and my greatest curiosity tied together in a single entity. The unanswerable question as to what my mother saw. The source of the repetitive visions that killed her. The one thing my brother would love more than anything else, and the very thing it would destroy him to lose."

Suddenly, it hits me.

How could I have been so stupid?

I've been playing into his hands this entire time. He wanted this.

He always wanted this.

"You sparked my curiosity, and I had to know more." His eyes trail across my face with an unwanted fondness. "I spent two years trying to create more of you, but every time the experiment failed. Don't you understand, Wynter? You are perfection. You are one of a kind, just like the beautiful blood that runs through your veins."

His hands glide through my hair, grabbing hold of my head and pulling me close to him.

"It was always meant to be you and me. We were meant to come together and see this through to the end."

My eyes widen as his true intentions finally come to light. They rise up like a wave and crash over my entire being, pulling me under the surface and holding me there.

Drowning me.

That terrible smile—the one that always took hold of his lips when he tortured me.

I see it again now.

"What you fail to understand is that I don't wish to save this world. I wish to see it burn. My greatest desire is to witness my mother's vision. *Your* vision." He glances past me as if I no longer exist. "And I wish for Ezra to watch it happen. To watch you die and not be able to lift a finger to prevent it, just like I was unable to stop him from poisoning Raina against me."

A raging hysteria twists my stomach, but I can't move. I can't breathe.

He continues, even though the voice in my head is screaming for him to stop.

"When I saw you together that night two years ago, I knew what I had to do. I knew to achieve the end I desired, I would have to cultivate those emotions. To make him love you even more, I tempted you away— all in the hope that it would torture him to know of the sacrifice you made to keep him safe. But it didn't take long for me to realize that, so long as you're in control, I would never see either of my wishes come to fruition. If I'm being honest, PHOENIX did me a favor by intervening. Only through losing you did I grasp what's necessary to reach my goal."

I hear Ezra make a muffled sound behind me, but I pay no attention to him—too consumed by the endless questions buzzing in my head. One stands out more than the rest.

As the words rush from my mouth, a terrible feeling weighs in my stomach.

"You knew where I was the entire time, didn't you?" The memory of the surveillance drones takes hold of my thoughts.

He cups his hand around the back of my neck and trails his thumbnail along the edge of my hairline.

"I've always been with you. Right here."

Vomit burns my throat as I visualize the hidden tracker implanted by my spine. Shaking my head, I force myself to focus on what he said before.

"But Rai—" I gasp, trying to make sense of it.

He presses a finger to my lips, silencing me.

"We will be together," he assures me. "Until the end, just like we were meant to be."

He leans in again to whisper in my ear, and my body shudders at the feel of his hot breath on my skin.

"Now show it to me. Show me the destruction you spoke of."

As his fingers graze my throat, everything around me becomes distorted, encompassing me in a solitary devastating sound. It thunders around me, reigniting my worst nightmare.

I hear it over and over again, pounding in my ears like a raging alarm. I hear the click of the lock as it pops open. I hear the sound of the metal as it collides with the ground.

The air kisses my newly exposed neck. My hand trembles as I touch my collar bone, and in a stunned daze, my eyes crawl to the floor.

All the while, my mind forms only one coherent thought. My knees buckle as it gravitates to the forefront of my brain, coming down on top of me as if carrying the weight of the world.

It crashes to my feet alongside my collar, taking my control with it.

END OF PART TWO

THE STORY CONTINUES IN
SUBJECT ZERO

COMING SUMMER 2018

DEAR READER,

Thank you for reading *Type X*! I hope you enjoyed the second part of Wynter's story and that you'll continue this journey with me in the third and final installment, *Subject Zero*.

To keep up with the latest news about my work, sign up for my newsletter at www.maphipps.com/newsletter. Subscribers will also receive *The Richter Files*, a Project W. A. R. companion serial told from the journalized perspective of Dr. Richter. My website also features an interactive version of the map found at the beginning of this book.

I love to hear from readers, so feel free to get in touch! You can contact me directly through my website or on any of my social media accounts.

Thanks again for reading *Type X*. I hope you'll continue to enjoy my work!

ACKNOWLEDGMENTS

This story wouldn't have been possible without the help and support of so many people. First, I would like to thank my editor, Catherine Stovall. I couldn't have done any of this without you. Thank you for your unwavering encouragement and guidance.

I would also like to extend my gratitude to Alisha Wood. We began as nothing more than an author and a reader, but we have quickly developed into so much more. Although we stand on opposite ends of the world, I am glad to call you a friend. You helped make this book what it is, so thank you from the bottom of my heart. P. S. Jenner sends his love.

A special thank you to Nathalia Suellen for your beautiful work on the cover. You are a master at taking my ideas and bringing them to life. Thank you for putting up with my nitpicking!

To Maranda Schoppert and Rebecca Gibson, my two original readers who always know how to push me—thank you for always listening to my incessant ramblings about story ideas and for brainstorming with me when I'm stuck.

I can't end these acknowledgements without thanking someone very special. To Martina McAtee, my publisher and sassy soul sister, I honestly don't know where I would be without you. There is no one else I would rather have on my side in this industry.

Lastly and most importantly, thank you to my husband, Daniel, for giving our family a wonderful life and for telling me every day how proud you are of me.

ABOUT M. A. PHIPPS

M. A. PHIPPS is an American author who resides near the ocean in picturesque Cornwall with her husband, daughter, and their Jack Russell, Milo. A lover of the written word, it has always been her dream to become a published author, and it is her hope to expand into multiple genres of fiction. *Type X* is her second novel.

Visit her online at **www.maphipps.com**.

OTHER BOOKS
BY
SEVEN SISTERS

In the small town of Belle Haven,
where the paranormal is normal, one girl
must embrace her true self . . .

Or die trying.

www.7sisterspublishing.com/martinamcatee

CPSIA information can be obtained
at www.ICGtesting.com
Printed in the USA
LVOW10s1443270218
568023LV00001BA/10/P